Accidents of Providence

Accidents

OF

Providence

Stacia M. Brown

Houghton Mifflin Harcourt
BOSTON • NEW YORK
2012

For information about permission to reproduce selections from this book,
write to Permissions, Houghton Mifflin Harcourt Publishing Company,
215 Park Avenue South, New York, New York 10003.

www.hmhbooks.com

Library of Congress-in-Publication Data
Brown, Stacia M. Accidents of providence / Stacia M. Brown.
p. cm.
ISBN 978-0-547-49080-9
1. Unmarried mothers—Fiction. 2. Trials (Murder)—England—Fiction.
3. Levellers—Fiction. 4. Great Britain—History—
Civil War, 1642–1649—Fiction. I. Title.
PS3602.R722885A67 2012
813'.6—dc22
2011015933

Book design by Brian Moore

Printed in the United States of America
DOC 10 9 8 7 6 5 4 3 2 1

Are not two sparrows sold for a farthing?
And one of them shall not fall on the ground without your Father.

—MATTHEW 10:29

An Act to Prevent
the Destroying and Murdering
of Bastard Children
(1624)

WHEREAS *many Lewd Women that have been delivered of Bastard Children, to avoid their shame and to escape punishment, do secretly bury or conceal the Death of their Children, and after, if the Child be found dead, the said Women do allege that the said Child was born dead, whereas it falleth out some times (although hardly it is to be probed,) that the said Child or Children were Murdered by the said Women their lewd Mothers, or by their assent or procurement.*

For the preventing therefore of this great mischief, Be it Enacted by the Authority of this present Parliament, that if any Women after one month next ensuring the end of this next Session of Parliament, be delivered of any Issue of her body, Male or Female, which being born alive, should by the Laws of this Realm be a bastard, and that she endeavor privately either by drowning or secret burying thereof, or any other way, either by her self or the procuring of others, so to conceal the death thereof, as that it may not come to light, whether it were born alive or not, but be concealed, In every such case, the said Mother so offending shall suffer Death, as in case of murder, except such Mother can make proof by one Witness at the least, that the Child (whose death by her so intended to be concealed) was born dead.

— **Corporation of London.** *Anno vicesimo primo Jacobi Regis, &c.*

(London: printed by Samuel Roycroft, Printer to this Honourable City, 1680) (21 Jac. I c. 27)

Prologue

MARY NEVER MEANT to be that kind of Huguenot. Since her husband's death she had worked hard to make herself invisible. For five years she had labored in London as a glovemaker, slowly building the smooth façade of a widow's anonymity. Over time, most customers had forgotten her French name, had forgotten she was a stranger. She kept her head low. She spoke flawless English. But on the night of November 2, Mary du Gard came out from the shadows.

She did so grudgingly. In the first place, the moon was glaring and leering at her; she could not sleep. In the second place, her assistant was up to no good. So Mary pulled on her boots, pinned up her hair, changed her sleeping robe for a jersey skirt, and became what she'd never wanted to be: someone who got involved. She followed her assistant out the back door of the glove shop onto Warwick Lane. She crept behind at a safe remove, watching as Rachel Lockyer carried a tightly wrapped bundle half a mile north to the Smithfield market, past the old slaughterhouse, and to the edge of a thicketed woods beyond. Mary looked on but did not follow her in. Though a Protestant of the truest sort, she retained the common superstition that those woods were haunted at night.

The next morning, at first light, Mary asked God what she

should do about what she had witnessed. And God said: You are My servant; you know what to do. Mary bowed her head and wrestled with herself. Then she returned to the slaughterhouse. In the security of the morning sun she entered the woods and scrabbled up the bundle Rachel had buried. She brushed the dirt out of its crevices and wrapped her shawl around it, so she would not touch what was left. For a moment she was tempted to leave things as they were, to return it to the earth, to let God be the judge. But a pang of duty stabbed her. She pushed the shawl partly aside. What she saw was enough. Gently Mary lifted the bundle. She clutched it to her chest and carried it back to Warwick Lane. What she held was a talisman. What she held was a rupture. All manner of lies and deceptions would fall to their knees as she passed. And though Mary had never been a mother, she understood, better than most, that the lives of children are more complicated than the lives of men. So she made her way back to the glove shop with a heavy heart, and she hunted down her assistant, who was in the back room snipping satin and old velvet. She shoved the burden at her all in a rush, because she needed to be rid of it, because she wished she were someone else; and she said to Rachel Lockyer, quite clear and cold-like, colder than she felt, "Is this yours? Is this what you have gone and done?"

That was when it started. It was 1649, the year everything happened, the year the wheels of providence rattled backward.

November 1649

One

ໆ

THOMAS BARTWAIN, CRIMINAL investigator commissioned by the Council of State, was standing outside the Sessions House in Old Bailey warming his bones under a weak London sun when he realized he was a quarter-hour late for his first deposition.

He coughed and checked his notes.

"Christ," he muttered, and wobbled back into the courthouse as fast as his thick, bowed legs would let him. He handed his papers to his secretary, a tall and jaundiced man named White who in recent months had begun refusing to doff his hat to persons of authority. When Bartwain questioned this practice, given the volatile and warring times in which they lived, his secretary growled, ornery as a drunk without a drop, that his hat-doffing was no one's business.

White glanced down at Bartwain's notes. "You want to see *how* many witnesses today?" His face wore a dour mien. "There is no way to interview all these people. You're running late as it is."

"Their summonses have been delivered," the investigator said. "They will be arriving throughout the day. Knock on my door just before each hour so I don't fall behind. You understand the severity of the accusations against this woman, this Leveler, this what's-her-name."

"Rachel Lockyer," the secretary said.

"Yes, that's it. I need all the information I can find."

White nodded reluctantly. "Shall I bring in your first witness? She's here."

"Yes. Send her into my chambers. And bring me something to eat while you're at it. I'm famished." The investigator coughed again. He was sixty-one years old and his lungs were not good. Ever since the Council of State had assigned him to investigate the discovery of a dead infant behind the Smithfield slaughterhouse, his wheezing had been worse than usual. He stepped into his chambers, squeezed his fleshy stomach behind the desk, and adjusted his powdered wig. Then he picked up his quill, which he wielded like a scepter in between writing sentences.

Rachel Lockyer's case had made its way to Bartwain's doorstep ten days before and so far he detested everything about it. After receiving the coroner's report, he had interviewed a handful of witnesses, most of whom volunteered neighborhood gossip as testimony. From them Bartwain learned that Rachel was a spinster who lived independent of her mother (her father was dead), that she was poor (a glover's assistant), and that she had spent time in the company of the Levelers (those political troublemakers), as had her younger brother, Robert, who'd recently been executed by firing squad for mutinying against his captain in the Parliamentary New Model Army. Only one witness, a gray-haired haberdasher named Katherine Chidley, had provided any information pertinent to the case at hand. Chidley recounted a series of examinations she had conducted of Rachel's physical person and insisted Rachel had tried to hide a pregnancy from those who knew her. "She is the mother of that infant Widow du Gard found," Chidley declared. "I have no doubt of it." And while Chidley confessed she did not know the identity of the father, another witness—a homeless boy named Thom with a shock of orange hair whom White had had to drag in by summons and who remained reluctant to talk until Bartwain bribed him with candied flowers, which the child gulped down whole—reported being asked to deliver a message from Rachel to one of the Leveler leaders, initials *W.W.*, who

4

at the time was incarcerated in the London Tower. The investigator knew those initials. They'd appeared on the cheap pamphlets and polemical treatises produced by the Levelers over the past few years of civil war. The Levelers were always being incarcerated for one thing or another, usually for seditious writing. Bartwain asked the boy what the message was and how this W.W. had answered it, but the boy claimed to have forgotten the message and added that he'd never reached the intended recipient — something about a lion distracting him. The investigator doubted this account but went ahead and added William Walwyn to his interview list. Of course, the question of paternity was less significant now than it would have been if the infant had survived. When a bastard child lived, the magistrates could invoke the Poor Law and order the father to pay a stipend to the local church for its upkeep. A non-compliant father could be sentenced to corporal punishment, most likely public whipping alongside the mother. If the child died, only the mother was held responsible. Still, Bartwain thought the lead worth investigating.

From the coroner he had learned that the newborn was female, dead less than three days at time of autopsy, and weighing six pounds and one-quarter ounce. Bartwain wondered about that one-quarter ounce. What part of an infant weighed this amount? A hand? A kneecap? He shuddered and spat into his empty water cup. He detested acts of violence against children. The coroner had said that the lungs were partly inflated, meaning the child had breathed outside the womb before it expired. The body was starting to decompose by the time of the autopsy. The earthworms had covered its little limbs, and moles had chewed through the cloth in which it was wrapped, while beetles had settled in the orifices. The coroner also reported a ring of bluish bruises around the infant's neck, possibly made by string or twine. In his view, this suggested strangulation. But if someone was planning to lay a hand on a newborn, why clothe it first in a carefully sewn yellow dress?

Bartwain tried to imagine what had happened, tried to theorize what had befallen the infant in the minutes or hours before

5

it passed. He considered most women to be deceptive and unreliable by nature, so for him, the challenge in such cases was to leave room for some sliver of innocence, for some possibility that a criminal act had *not* taken place. Still, if the woman was innocent, why would she hide the body?

The night before, the investigator's wife had asked why this case vexed him so. She had seen him preparing his research notes and poring over the autopsy report. Start with the pregnancy and build the investigation from there, she had said. If only it were so simple, Bartwain had replied. In situations like these, identifying the mother could be a vexing challenge. Whether or not an unmarried woman had been pregnant remained difficult to prove after the fact. Some maids were sly and cunning and wore wide skirts to conceal their condition; Bartwain knew of a servant in Worcester who'd told her mistress her swelling belly was not pregnancy but colic. The mistress believed her tale until the servant showed up lean and weeping one Sunday with a dead babe in her arms, saying she'd found it in the alley. Other times women would plead they had not realized their condition until the pangs of labor started. Bartwain found this argument from ignorance persuasive only in exceptional instances, as in a case last year of a thirteen-year-old maid whose master had dallied with her as she moved past the point of her maturation; she had no way to recognize the signs that followed. The same plea would not suffice for a woman like Rachel Lockyer, a woman at the waning edge of the child-bearing years.

At half past nine the Huguenot glover Mary du Gard entered the investigator's chambers. She looked a weary thirty. She wore a gray dress and a kerchief knotted around her shoulders. Her dark eyebrows almost touched.

"Sit." The investigator motioned from behind his desk. "Tell me your name for the record."

She perched on the witness stool, visibly uncomfortable. "Mary du Gard, sir. I am a widow. I would rather not be on the record."

"You would rather not be on the record? You were the one who brought this case to the coroner's attention. Have you grown shy? Have you changed your opinion?"

She blinked. Bartwain's cheeks rounded into what on another face might have passed for a smile.

"Now," he said, leaning forward, leaning all the way across his desk, "if you are here to make my task harder, Widow du Gard, you may leave, and I shall send you back to whatever stinking village in France from which you came. But if you are here to obey the law, and to be a good Christian, then stay seated and tell me what you saw. I do not have all day."

So Mary began, reluctantly, to talk. She had managed Du Gard Gloves since her husband had died in battle; a few months after that, she'd hired Rachel to help in the shop. Together the two women paid a fee to the leather sellers' company to become licensed vendors, though the business remained in the name of Mary's husband. They specialized in military gloves, but because of the war they spent most of their time dyeing gloves black for funerals. Mary's fingers, Bartwain noticed, were stained from dipping the gloves in dye.

Throughout Mary's deposition, which dragged on longer than most, the investigator kept growing distracted from the case; at one point he wandered off in the direction of theology. He found his witness's manner dull and infuriating. She told him point by point about digging up a newborn in the woods behind the Smithfield slaughterhouse, but she took no initiative to explain what happened after. Bartwain wanted to know how Rachel had reacted when Mary returned to Warwick Lane and put the bundle into her arms. He wanted to know why Mary had banned Rachel from the glove shop that same day. Mary stared at him blankly and pretended not to understand. "My English is not good," she said, in perfect English. So Bartwain, intuitively shifting tactics, devoted the next thirty minutes to engaging her in a discussion of ideas. He wanted to catch her off-guard so she would talk. Also, he harbored a hobbyist's interest in the study of things religious. Although Mary was a Huguenot, or French Calvinist, her late husband had adopted the Particular Baptist faith when he moved to England, so Mary knew both factions. Bartwain asked her why the Particular Baptists believed Christ had died for some men only and not for the generality of them. She replied that Christ could not have died for all men because not all men were going to heaven. It made no sense for Him to die for someone if that person was going to spurn Him. Therefore, Christ must have died only for those He foreknew would respond positively. At this point Mary fell silent and eyed the floor.

"Can you confirm that what you unearthed was your assistant's?" the investigator abruptly asked. "Are you quite certain the child belonged to her?" All he needed was one credible confirmation. The evidence required to indict a woman in such investigations was not stringent, not very stringent at all.

"Oh," she said slowly, "I could never be *completely* certain. But I lived with her, so I saw things."

"Things? What kind of things?"

"To recount them would be too tedious."

"I'm a criminal investigator. I specialize in the tedious."

"Well," she said, warming slightly, "I thought I heard Rachel the night before, in her room. She was in the throes of what sounded to me like a painful indigestion or labor. She would not let me in."

"Did you knock?"

Mary hesitated. "I called her name."

"Did she hear you?"

"I am sure she did. I asked what she was doing. She had stuffed a cloth in the keyhole so I could not peek inside. She did not answer the door, so I went back to my room."

"This was the night of November second?"

"No, sir. It was the night before. I told you. It was late; it was around one o'clock. And I did not see anything for certain. I only heard the sounds."

"Did you see her the next morning?"

"Yes, sir, she came down to breakfast, but she was later than usual."

"Did you see signs of a delivery?"

"Not then. But I went into her room later, while she was outside sweeping."

"She swept the walk the morning after she gave birth?"

"She swept it the morning after I heard those sounds, yes, sir."

Bartwain considered this. "What did you see while she was outside?"

"Her bedclothes all in a heap on the floor, and blood staining them, though it looked as if she had attempted to clean them."

"Did you confront her?"

"I tried."

"What did she say?"

"Only that she was in her monthly time, and that was where the stains came from. She said she was feeling faint."

"And what was her appearance?"

"Unseemly and pale. And leaner than she had been the previous weeks."

I guess she would be, Bartwain thought.

"She didn't eat all day," Mary went on with some feeling, "even though we were having her favorite, ham and apple bake."

I'd like some of that now, he said to himself. Where was White with his breakfast? "Why did you decide to go to the slaughterhouse?"

"I was following her."

"The same night you heard the sounds?"

"No, sir, the next night. I heard her moving around in her chambers again, and I was curious. So I followed her out the door. She crept out in the middle of the night."

"What did you see?"

"She was carrying something small and close to her chest. She walked fast all the way to the Smithfield market. She buried the bundle by moonlight near the trees, and then I suppose she ran away."

"So you stayed behind to uncover what she had buried?"

"No, sir. I went home. Rachel returned home too, later that night, very ill and in a fit, it seemed, so I helped her to bed. She would not speak a word. I returned to the market the next morning."

"Why did you wait until the next day to go back?"

"Because those woods are not safe at night."

"Ah. You think those woods are haunted."

Mary reddened.

"I wonder what your late husband would think of your superstitions."

"That isn't fair," she told him.

"Nothing is fair." Bartwain's lungs were threatening to spasm. He coughed into his handkerchief, discreetly checked the contents.

From research he had learned that Mary's Huguenot parents had died by fire for their faith when their daughter was ten; a man named Johannes du Gard had taken Mary under his care in the days following. The same man married her three years later, for her protection, he said, and then went off to war against the Holy Roman Empire. He was gone off and on for twelve years, from what Bartwain could gather. When he returned, he found both his business and his place of worship destroyed, so he crossed the British Sea, wife in tow, to open a glove shop and die for Oliver Cromwell, who believed in the same God he did. Mary never had any children.

White knocked on the door. "Your next witness is here."

"You may go," Bartwain said to Mary. "But be prepared to testify if there is a trial. And I think there will be." She excused herself and left, and he rose from his desk, wheezing, to find his pipe.

The investigator appreciated, at least in theory, why a woman might not want to come forward if she'd given birth to a *living* bastard. But why would a woman stay silent if she'd given birth to a child that died? Where dead illegitimates were concerned, the law turned on concealment. Bartwain lit his pipe, pondering. The reasonable thing for a woman to do in such situations was to come forward and confess she had delivered an illegitimate, explain it had died while she was in labor or shortly thereafter, and present it to the authorities for inspection. But time and again he'd seen women who acted contrary to common sense, women who insisted on disposing of the infants in their own secret way and who then tried to deny any wrongdoing when they were discovered. They failed to grasp that the 1624 Act to Prevent the Destroying and Murdering of Bastard Children declined to distinguish between murder and concealment. The law did not care about such details any more than it cared about the identity of the father. It kept things simple. Any unmarried woman who concealed her child's death could be declared guilty of its murder—why else would she need to hide it? If the death was hidden and the woman unmarried, she could be charged, tried, and executed. Accordingly, all Bartwain needed to indict Rachel Lockyer for the crime of infant murder was proof she'd tried to hide a bastard's death and a reasonable assumption the child was hers. Whether or not she meant to harm it was not important; at least, not in the eyes of the law.

He could hear someone banging around in the hallway. "White!" he called out. "Where's my breakfast?"

His secretary appeared with a platter of duck eggs. Bartwain reached for two and shook them to test for doneness; they were hard-boiled, which made him unhappy, as he preferred his yolks runny. But he was ravenous, so he ate them all anyway, not troubling to remove the shells, stuffing the eggs one after the other into his mouth. "Bring my next interview in," he said between bites. "I will get to the bottom of this case today or I am not Thomas Bartwain." White inclined his head, though his subservience was unconvincing; he went into the corridor to fetch the next witness.

Preparing for his depositions had led Bartwain to investigate the background of each of his interview subjects. Concerning the next woman on his list, however, he knew more about the husband. Everyone knew about Elizabeth Lilburne's husband. They called him Freeborn John, and when he was not earning a meager living as a soap maker, he was working alongside William Walwyn—that W.W. whose full name appeared farther down on Bartwain's list—to organize a group of fiery apprentices, soldiers, and agitators in and around London and the Parliamentary army.

Their enemies had given this group its name, accusing John and his friends of trying to "level" men's estates and share all things in common. The Levelers had supported the Good Old Cause, the dream of a free republic, when civil war first broke out in 1642, and they had continued to support it in succeeding years as Parliament's army warred against the king, or against royal tyranny, as some men—never Bartwain—described it. When Charles I was beheaded in January of 1649, some people blamed the Levelers and called them regicides. But Bartwain knew they did not have it in them to do anything so decisive or matter-of-fact. Since the Parliamentarians' victory, the Leveler crusade had begun to lose momentum—no one could quite tell which side the group was on, Bartwain thought.

He glanced down at his notes. Several years ago, when John Lilburne had spent time in Newgate Prison for harassing the Speaker of the House of Commons, his wife, Elizabeth, had joined him there. As a prisoner of the state, John had received the royal treatment. Elizabeth had received a toothless midwife, ordered down from the women's ward, to assist her as she birthed their daughter on the sticking straw. Bartwain shook his head; that was the sort of thing Leveler women did, stay with their husbands in prison. This past summer, he read on, Elizabeth had lost her two sons to smallpox.

He was picking the last of the eggshells from his teeth when his witness burst into the chambers, her yellow curls angry and springing. Before he could say a word, Elizabeth Lilburne supplied her name, place of birth, and current residence, then sat down on the witness stool. He barely had time to wipe his mouth, pick up his quill, and dunk it in the inkwell before she started attacking.

"You are in bed with the devil," she told him. "You report to the Council of State, which is an illegitimate government. You find women who are poor and vulnerable and accuse them of this and that, and then once you have convicted them you wash your hands and accept your payment. You are the devil's handyman."

"Good morning to you as well," he answered.

She delivered a blistering stare. From the pockmarks pitting her cheek, Bartwain guessed she had contracted the same illness that had taken her young sons. Apart from the scars, she was a handsome woman, he thought.

"You support the work of men who fear the truth. You—"

"I am not here to suppress the truth," he said wearily. "I am here to solicit it. I would be grateful if you would do me the courtesy of allowing me to carry out the work I have been commissioned to do. I am not here to listen to speeches."

"You are a hired dog."

"Please be careful what you say."

"Why, what would you have me say? The justices of the peace have already made up their minds about this case. I know how the courts of London work. They place the burden of proof on the defendant. I am the wife of John Lilburne. I know things."

"Tell me how you became acquainted with the case at hand."

"I have no relation to the case at hand."

"You just said this case was unfair, so clearly you know something about it. You are not a good liar. Your face is blooming red."

"Then you already know how I am acquainted with it, else you would not have called me in here." Elizabeth tapped her heel against the leg of the stool. He noticed her black boot, with its high arch and tarnished buckle.

"You are friends with the woman under investigation?"

"Yes."

"Tell me what you know, please."

"I have nothing to say."

He waited. He did not think she was the kind of woman who could stay quiet long.

"This is an illegal investigation," she flung at him, confirming Bartwain's hypothesis, "and you are working for an illegal government. The Council of State is a government of the sword, not of the people. So I have no words for you today, Investigator."

"You will have to stop talking for me to believe that."

"You treat me like a fool."

"Be careful, or I will hold you in contempt."

"You already do."

They went back and forth, Bartwain making little headway. Elizabeth Lilburne was as belligerent as her husband. Finally he badgered her into admitting it was *possible* her friend Rachel Lockyer had been with child, and it was *possible* she had tried to hide this pregnancy from others, but he could not provoke her into saying anything definite. When he asked if Rachel could have laid a hand on her infant, Elizabeth's face darkened. Only a savage monster could harm its own young, she said. When he asked if Rachel had confided in her, perhaps confessing to some kind of mishap in childbirth, she retorted, "Why would you care? The law still holds a woman responsible." She went silent, holding the investigator's gaze.

If he could not wrangle information out of her directly, he would have to do so indirectly. "Would you say Rachel Lockyer went into a fit of grief after her brother's execution this past spring?" he asked, trying not to sound suspicious.

"You mean his murder."

"Call it what you will. Would you say she went into a fit of grief?"

Elizabeth was not falling for the question. "I would not. For then you would use my words to paint her as a madwoman, capable of anything, even strangling her child."

"So you admit the child was hers."

"I was speaking hypothetically."

"That is some sleight of hand," he observed. "You have spent too much time in your husband's company. I hear he can make a cunning argument masquerade as a plain one."

"He speaks the truth," she snapped. But her strained expression made Bartwain wonder if Elizabeth Lilburne defended her famous husband more vigorously to others than she did to herself.

"I have read your Leveler pamphlets, with all their prattle about the rights and privileges and freedoms of the people. Did Rachel Lockyer believe those teachings?"

She looked at him, puzzled.

"I never knew any woman to harm her child without pleading some doctrine or justification to excuse herself," he told her. "'The child made me ill,' she will say. 'The child made me poor and wretched.' It is the same principle you rebels and libertines rallied behind as you dragged this country into war. 'The king makes us slaves,' you said. 'The king makes us pay taxes.' Both of these—"

"The Levelers did not kill the king."

Bartwain groaned. By nature he was not a political man. He did not think anyone could claim victory in the aftermath of civil war. How it was possible for a dead king to be the only one left standing at the end of a conflict, he didn't know. But it had happened. He waved Elizabeth's words away. "You're missing my point. Both of these arguments are rooted in self-preservation. Both insist that what matters most is *my* life, *my* survival, even at the expense of others. Even at the expense of a child." He should not have been discussing intellectual matters with a woman. When faced with a moral problem, with a case of conscience, as the casuists called it, women tried to solve their dilemmas by referring to examples and stories. They refused to think abstractly, to seek universal principles of reason.

"You think a woman such as Rachel Lockyer has the leisure to sit around and consider what law or doctrine she will use to justify her behavior?" Elizabeth tossed back. "You think she asks such questions while she is sweeping the walk or rolling out the dough before dawn—while she is up to her elbows in flour?"

"If a woman has no time to think on such things, then why did you and Rachel Lockyer spend so many nights with the Levelers at the Whalebone tavern?" He was genuinely curious. "What could you possibly have wanted that would make you leave the house?"

"We wanted a drink," she said.

The investigator burst into laughter, which metamorphosed into a walloping cough. Spluttering, he called for White, who whisked into the chambers with a pitcher of water; White was used to this.

When Bartwain's cough subsided he dabbed his eyes with a handkerchief. "You are not half bad, Mrs. Lilburne." Then, taking a breath, he returned to his investigation. "Isn't there anything at all you can tell me about these events? You might be called to testify if there is a trial. In the courtroom you will not have so much room to dodge and trim and equivocate."

"I'm not equivocating."

"You are," he said, "but I admire your effort and your talent." He rose from his desk, his stomach tipping it forward as he did. A stack of parchments slid to the floor. Elizabeth did not pause to help him retrieve them. She stepped over the papers with a queenly resolution and bade him good morning as she glided out of the chambers. He watched her leave the courthouse on her high-arched boots, saw her tightening the strings of her hat and shoving her blond curls under the brim.

Two

B Y T H E S T A R T of his third interview, Bartwain's head was
throbbing. He placed his head in his hands and pressed
his fingers against his temples. He did not glance up when
the Leveler William Walwyn entered his chambers.

"Name for the record," Bartwain said into his papers.

"William Walwyn."

"Title, living, lodgings."

"Merchant. Former merchant. Formerly of the Merchant Adventurers Company. My home lies at the eastern end of Moorfields, just north of London."

"Former?"

"Yes. I resigned."

Bartwain raised his head. On first glance he was not impressed.
His witness was silver-haired and lean from nine months in the
Tower of London, with a restive, almost refractory stare. But then
Walwyn turned to the side and Bartwain reconsidered his opinion. William Walwyn was one of those men who looked markedly
different in profile. Viewed directly, his face tended toward the
flat and pallid; he would strike you as the kind of man who rarely
apologizes. From the front he looked quarrelsome, abrupt, and his
full forty-nine years. In profile, everything changed. If you were
to assess him from the side, as Bartwain was doing, he became a

lean and graceful man, a thinking man, a philosopher whose only fear was ignorance.

"I heard you broke your oath to the Merchant Adventurers, that you are now their Judas. Sit down." Bartwain relit his pipe, which on long days gave him solace. "I also hear you are trying your hand at medicine—at physic."

Walwyn remained standing. "Why does my profession concern you? I have no idea why I'm here; your secretary never bothered to tell me. Is this about John Lilburne's latest pamphlet? I don't know how many times I have to explain to you people I had no part in it. That last one was entirely John's."

"I'm not interested in you Levelers and your seditious scribbling. I have brought you here on a serious subject. This is a murder investigation, Mr. Walwyn."

"Murder?"

"Yes. There is always a murder when I am on the case."

"Who has been murdered?"

"We'll get to that."

"Mr. Bartwain," Walwyn said, leaning forward, leaning all the way across the desk—rudely, the investigator thought—"I have been under wrongful imprisonment in the Tower for the past nine months. I was released just a few days ago, and since obtaining my freedom I have been busy with household obligations. I have no knowledge of whatever hideous crime you are investigating." He sat back.

"You Levelers are all the same." Bartwain fought off a paroxysm of coughing. "All of you talk about how busy you are. Too busy to think about doctrines, says one. Too busy to engage in king killing, says another. It's a wonder you have time to do anything. Yet here you are, a prolific writer. You know which one of your works is my favorite? I liked *The Power of Love*. I wonder why you wrote that one. It's not very political, is it?"

Walwyn looked at him.

"Now you see where we are heading? Now will you tell me about Rachel Lockyer?" He picked up his quill.

Walwyn leaned forward again. He laid both hands on Bartwain's desk. If the two men had been playing fox and geese, they would have been well-matched opponents. "Rachel Lockyer is a good woman, an excellent woman, a hard-working woman. What has she to do with any murder?"

"Tell me how you came to be acquainted with her."

"Why in God's name should it matter?"

"Tread carefully, Mr. Walwyn." He is confused, Bartwain thought. He has not spoken to her since his release. He has no idea about the child.

"I met Rachel Lockyer three years ago at the Whalebone."

"Do you still frequent that tavern?"

"Not anymore."

"What is the nature of your relationship?"

"She was among those who spent time at the Whalebone. Again, why is this relevant?"

Bartwain laid down his quill. "Mr. Walwyn." He spoke quietly, for maximum effect. He was halfway enjoying himself. "Your time in the Tower has left you blissfully unaware of current events. Rachel Lockyer, your old friend, is under suspicion of murdering an infant. The poor creature was dug up in the woods near the Smithfield slaughterhouse. Widow du Gard practically saw Rachel bury it with her bare hands. I would like to know if the child was hers. I would like to know if she was involved in a sexual dalliance."

Walwyn took a step backward.

"You should sit down. You look ill."

Walwyn sat.

"Now do you understand why I have called you here? I have called you here because I need your help."

He shook his head. "I cannot help you."

"Cannot or will not?" Pushing back from the desk, Bartwain rose to his feet and stood as tall as he could, which was not very. "Have you seen Rachel Lockyer since you left prison?"

"No. I told you. I have not seen anyone except my family."

"You and your fourteen children, is that what number you've reached?"

"For God's sake, why should that matter?"

"A strapping brood," Bartwain mused. "Any man would be proud. So, let's see if I have it right. You remain in Moorfields to care for your fourteen children while Rachel Lockyer has been busy in London destroying her one."

"Take that back or you will suffer for it."

"Is that a threat?"

"What do you think?" Walwyn reached in and seized the investigator's lace collar. He was so close Bartwain could smell perspiration and wormwood. "And what will you do, Investigator? What? Are you going to call for help from that fledgling Friend out in the hallway who pretends to be your secretary? He will fall like a dead leaf as soon as I blow on him."

"Stop it. I will call the officers of the court," Bartwain bleated. "Stop it, let me go. My lungs are not strong." He coughed, louder than was necessary.

"I will let you go when you apologize."

"I never apologize when I am in the right!"

Walwyn pushed Bartwain away and knocked him into the wall as he headed for the door. "Damn fool," he muttered. "Your investigation will come to nothing. She could not have done what you are insinuating. She is incapable of it."

"Incapable of conceiving a child? Or incapable of harming a child once she had one?"

Walwyn opened the door.

"So you are arguing on the basis of Rachel Lockyer's good character?" Bartwain pressed.

"Yes!"

The investigator's lungs were whistling as he breathed in and out. "There are plenty of women of good character who find themselves in damned and desperate circumstances."

"Rachel Lockyer is neither damned nor desperate."

"I wonder if she knew that." The air in the chambers hovered, squalid and damp. "Did you know the infant was found with a ring of bruises around its neck, Mr. Walwyn? The poor thing's skin had turned purple."

"I will not listen to this." The Leveler was out the door, striding down the corridor.

The investigator shuffled out after him. "For the last time, what was the nature of your relationship?"

"She was a friend and a true Christian."

"You speak as if she's dead. Tell me: were you the father of that poor bastard they found behind the slaughterhouse? Yes or no will suffice."

Walwyn halfway turned. "Say what you will. I don't care about my reputation."

"I see." Bartwain nodded. "Your wife will be pleased, I'm sure. Now she not only has to endure the humiliation of your weakness but also stands to lose you to the high tide of consequences."

"Love is a weakness?"

"You're the philosopher. Answer the question."

"Which one?"

"The one on which your reputation depends, of course."

Walwyn flashed a reckless smile. "Love is no weakness," he said. He took the steps two at a time outside the courthouse and disappeared around the corner.

Bartwain's afternoon interviews went by without incident. He spoke with Jack Dawber, the overseer of the Smithfield slaughterhouse, who had glimpsed a woman digging at the edge of the wood and who seemed obsessed with the color of the moon on the night he witnessed the incident; he said it looked "nefarious." Next Bartwain interviewed a butcher and his wife who lived down the street from Du Gard Gloves. They said Rachel had shown up on their stoop in the middle of the night that same evening. Soil and mud streaked her clothing, they reported, and she seemed disoriented. When the butcher identified her as the glovemaker's assistant, the couple dragged her back to Mary's residence and deposited her on the stoop. They assumed she was intoxicated. Bartwain asked if she had said anything, made any kind of statement or confession. The butcher shook his head: "She did not say a word about it that I remember."

21

Before starting his final interview, Bartwain asked White to have the officers of the court fetch Rachel Lockyer from her temporary lodgings at the Lilburne residence in Southwark, where she had stayed since Mary banned her from the glove shop. "Bring her to me, if she is willing," he said. "I want to interview her."

"Why? You're not obliged to question the suspect." White's houndish brow hung low, leaving his eyes in shadow.

"I want to speak with her. I want to make sure I have all the facts of the case. One can never be too careful."

His last interview of the afternoon was William Kiffin, a man who was balding in earnest. Bartwain had not summoned him to the Sessions House; this witness had invited himself.

Kiffin settled into the investigator's chambers as if preparing for a long and comfortable hibernation. "I am the pastor of the church at Devonshire Square," he declared, crossing one stocking-clad leg over the other. "We are nonconformists; we dissent from the doctrines and polity of the English Church."

"I know what a nonconformist is," Bartwain snapped. He harbored no fondness for the myriad sects and independent groups that kept breaking away from the Church of England. He particularly disliked the Baptists, who refused to baptize their infants. In Bartwain's opinion, baptizing an infant was about the only thing a clergyman was good for nowadays.

"Rachel Lockyer used to be my congregant," Kiffin went on. "I have a wealth, a veritable storehouse, of information concerning her. I have taken the liberty of conducting research to aid your investigation. I have left no stone unturned. You will have all the information you need by the time I am finished. Here are my research notes." He reached inside his vest and withdrew some papers.

"How do you know all this?"

"I told you. Research."

"You mean gossip."

"Never," Kiffin protested.

"Just stay with the facts you observed." Bartwain pressed his hand against his rumbling stomach.

"The day after Rachel Lockyer took the babe out to the woods and buried it, Widow du Gard returned to retrieve what was there. When she carried the child back to the glove shop she demanded an accounting. This caused her—Miss Lockyer—to fall into a mad grief, nearly to faint, and then to grab the infant to her bosom, clutching it and shrieking and saying, 'It is my poor babe you have found; it is mine.'"

"Were you there?" Bartwain's quill hovered over his paper.

"Everyone knows what happened. It is all over the neighborhood."

"Tell me what *you* know, Preacher, or I will strike your testimony."

Kiffin's smile grew acerbic. "Well, some weeks earlier I had spoken with Widow du Gard about what to do if she should discover Rachel Lockyer in a state of childbirth, for it had occurred to some of us that she might be in a pickle."

"A pickle?"

"Yes. With child. That's how the matrons put it. Also, 'the rising of the apron.'"

"I see." You are a matron yourself, Bartwain thought. "And how did you come to hold this suspicion?"

"She wore her skirts too high on the waist."

"Is that all?"

"Mrs. Chidley also inspected her breasts for hardness. I did not inspect her myself, of course."

"Go on."

"When our suspicions turned out to be correct, I traveled to Warwick Lane to assist. This was after the Widow du Gard returned from the woods. She sent for me along with the coroner."

"Did Rachel Lockyer concede the child was hers?"

"She did not have to. It was so obvious. I sat her, Miss Lockyer, down at the sewing table. I had to yank that thing from her arms. She did not want to let go of it. I told her it was nothing to hold on to. I reminded her that souls do not inhabit the body once we die. 'You are holding dust,' I said. Still she would not give it up. She is stubborn and unreasonable."

"Did you ask her what had happened?"

"I did. I asked her to make a confession."

"Did she?"

"No. She cursed me. Twice, in fact."

"What else?"

"We waited for the coroner. While we were waiting, Mrs. Chidley arrived and examined Rachel's physical person to verify she had given birth."

During Bartwain's interview with Katherine Chidley, the haberdasher had reported squeezing milk from Rachel's breasts and pulling up her skirts to find significant staining of the undergarments. Bartwain starred this note in his papers. It was as good a confirmation of pregnancy as he generally got in these cases. "Go on."

"When Mrs. Chidley finished her examination, I tried one more time to get Miss Lockyer to say the truth."

"Did you learn anything?"

"Nothing. Mr. Bartwain, it is so obvious what happened I cannot comprehend why you have waited ten days to issue an indictment. Clearly the woman murdered it. Else why would she be so secretive?"

Bartwain, pondering, chewed the inside of his cheek. "That is for me to determine. I will interview her myself this evening."

"If you speak with her, she will try to seduce you. She is cunning. You do not need to interview her to know she is guilty. Look at the facts. The case is open and shut."

"Nothing is ever open and shut." The investigator lumbered to his feet. "You might be called to speak again if there is a trial, Preacher. Be sure you give *your* testimony and not anyone else's."

After Kiffin left, Bartwain picked up his papers, opened a bottle of brandy cordial, and settled in to wait for the woman herself, the lady of the hour, the cause of his present indigestion.

Three

WILLIAM WALWYN STUMBLED around the corner of the Sessions House, dropped to his knees, and vomited into a ditch.

Rachel Lockyer's child. His mind spun like a top around those words.

He stayed on his knees, palms in the gravel. When he regained control of his stomach, he reached for his fallen hat, dragged himself to his feet, retrieved a flask from his cloak, and swigged. The wormwood burned the roof of his mouth. He began walking. As he walked he counted backward — he counted the months on his hands. How could he not have known? How could she not have told him? She must have been with child the last time he saw her. She had tried to visit him in prison, in the Tower, attempting to pass herself off as the wife of Leveler Richard Overton, a fine ruse, since no one ever seemed to remember what Mrs. Overton looked like and only wives were allowed to visit. She made it part of the way, past the drawbridge and the first set of guards. She continued unchallenged into the courtyard, and then a warden's aide observed her striding toward the Bell Tower, checked his list, turned to the warden, and said, "That is not Mrs. Overton." Her walk did her in. The real Mrs. Overton did not move with such confidence. The guards hauled Rachel out. They sent her back over the bridge.

Now Walwyn could hear footsteps behind him. He turned. It was his wife, Anne, following him. She must have waited outside the courthouse in Old Bailey, waited the entire time while he was swatting at the investigator's questions. She would not meet his eye, even as he approached.

"You're going home," she said—it was not a question.

"Yes," he replied.

Anne Walwyn adjusted the deep-brimmed black hat she wore every day. She wore this hat despite the dozen ribbon-trimmed bonnets and high-crowned hats her husband had given her over twenty years of matrimony. The ones Walwyn had bought remained stacked at the top of their wardrobe, as if in waiting.

"You had business in the city?" Her tiny face was pinched. Her fingers hooked protectively around the handle of her basket.

"Yes," he said quietly. "I'm nearly done. I'll be back at the house soon." The Walwyns' home in Moorfields lay just north of the city wall that had shielded villagers from invasion during Roman times.

"Fourteen needs his shoes picked up from the cobbler," she told him.

When their youngest child, Richard, was born, Anne had taken to calling him Fourteen, replacing his Christian name with a numerical one as she had done with the rest of her children. Walwyn used to tease her about this, about her excessive fondness for numbers, but Anne told him numbers were more manageable than names. Number One was her firstborn, for example, and had married Humphrey Brooke, a physician who would have the world view him as an independent man. Walwyn would have liked to view him as an independent man, but this was Brooke's second year as an unpaying lodger in his father-in-law's house. Number Two, their second-born, was nineteen and a linen draper.

"I'll get the shoes," he promised.

"I don't want you running into anyone from the Whalebone

while you're out. I don't want you getting sidetracked by those men." She delivered a scowl especially reserved for John Lilburne, Richard Overton, Thomas Prince, Gilbert Mabbott, and all the other longhaired Levelers whose names she knew from the pamphlets, petitions, treatises, declarations, and Agreements of the People Walwyn had helped to write.

"I have no plan to visit the Whalebone," he said. "I've told you. My time with them is—"

"All that bloodshed and a king's head besides," Anne went on, not listening. "And now you want to run an apothecary? You, the philosopher?"

He tried to touch her shoulder. "Dear heart—"

Anne reached for the ratty chin band that held her old hat in place, as if his proximity were going to wreck something. "Don't." She turned and left him standing in the middle of the carriageway near the waste kennel.

She knew, of course.

Walwyn did not travel directly home. He went to the cobbler and picked up his son's shoes, and then he went to the river. He had no reason for walking there except it was not far from the cobbler's and his thoughts were refusing to cooperate with him. For three hours he sat, feet dangling, on a fishing dock called Broken Wharf, a rattly embankment whose pier was no longer reliable save for tempting old men to totter out on its uneven boards and, from there, to observe that the river was darker than they remembered it, or the waterway more throttled by commerce. To the east lay Salt Wharf and Three Cranes Wharf. Above, hundreds of gulls were flying. The gulls avoided Broken Wharf. They preferred the barnacled posts and fishermen's buckets studding the water's edge at Salt Wharf. The gulls were wise, he decided. He sat and watched them skim the water's surface, his son's shoes in his lap. Not until the afternoon sun began ceding ground to a slinking fog did he remember the time and begin making his way north. He hailed a carriage. When the driver asked where to, he said

Moorfields. The driver said he didn't go north of the city wall at night.

"It's not night yet," Walwyn said.

"It is. The sun is setting."

"Not yet. I can still see it."

"It will be down in a quarter-hour."

The two men bickered until Walwyn offered to pay above the usual fare, and then the driver became accommodating. Walwyn climbed into the back of the carriage, facing away from the horses; a minute later they were off, crawling for home, Walwyn watching the empty street and, behind it, the muddy line of the Thames receding. He pulled his steep-crowned hat low over his forehead. The sun reddened and sank below the horizon. His thoughts returned to Rachel. He remembered squinting through a narrow slit in his Tower cell, transfixed, as she had pleaded her case with the warden below. He had willed her to remain still, not to move, to remain in his sight; but his field of vision was too narrow, and when the guards pulled her arms, she vanished. When she did not come back, he had pressed his fingers against his eyelids, imprinting her reflection on the back of them. Later that night, while his three friends were sleeping, he had retrieved it. He saw the outline of Rachel's hip curving against her skirt where the wind had gusseted it. He traced the line of her jaw when she yielded her face to the light.

Then William Walwyn had become like a fox that will gnaw off its leg to escape a trap. He missed her. He missed the sound of her. He stormed the walls; he threw himself at the door, rousing his companions. He cursed the guards; he bribed the guards; when that failed he swung his fist at them. The guards swung back. He drank himself into a stupor with Overton's wine, became sick, went to sleep, became sick again; his stomach churned for hours. He sensed Rachel was in trouble but did not know what kind. He felt the trouble in his body; his bones told him. The next morning he had called his three companions around. He said they must work together to get themselves out of the Tower, preferably right away. "I am rotting in here," he cried. When Thomas Prince pointed out that the rest of them were rotting in there too, Walwyn said they must try harder. He cursed their lackadaisicalness. Richard Overton whispered to Prince that Walwyn was developing a habit of too much wine. John Lilburne suggested Walwyn was developing a fear of confined spaces.

Four months had passed since then. Walwyn had not seen Rachel.

Four

WITHIN AN HOUR of Bartwain's order, two officers of the court had retrieved Rachel Lockyer from her temporary lodgings in Southwark and delivered her to the Sessions House. She accompanied them freely. Bartwain let them in and showed her to his chambers.

His suspect was no more remarkable in feature than any of a thousand other women he had seen, though if pressed he would have conceded she was attractive enough for her age. Her green eyes compelled him forward. She stood taller than he preferred in a member of the feminine sex—of course, that was not her fault. A fringe of dark ringlets escaped her head covering. She wore a tradeswoman's gloves, the fingers of them cut off for sewing.

He ushered her inside and closed the door. Two candles provided the only light. Motioning toward the stool, he invited her to sit. "I assume you know why I have asked you here."

"Yes." She tucked her skirt and sat. "Elizabeth Lilburne told me about you." She did not seem to know what to do with her hands. Bartwain looked on as she fidgeted and plucked at her sleeves, pulling the material over her wrists until her hands nearly disappeared.

"I would like you to tell me what you did on the nights of November first and second. If you do not, and I think you know this, the law compels me to charge you under the Act to Prevent the Destroying and Murdering of Bastard Children."

"You will do what you want whether I speak to you or not." She tilted her head to the side as she spoke so that a vein in her forehead stood out.

Bartwain was having a hard time reading her expression. "I have brought you here as a courtesy," he told her. "I am giving you the opportunity to tell me why I should *not* have you arrested and charged. The evidence does not fall in your favor."

"By evidence you mean gossip and rumor."

"You are the one to address that. Go ahead. Set the record straight." Bartwain did not feel like matching wits with anyone that evening, let alone another woman, let alone an unmarried woman of a certain age with a vein in her forehead and a tilt of the head that confused him.

"I have been wrongly accused," she told him.

"Of what? Of harming that poor infant?"

"I tell you I have been wrongly accused!"

"Was the child yours?"

"I had not been well in months."

"Were you with child?"

Silence.

"Was that child yours?"

"God gave it to me."

Was this an admission? "You know what I mean," he said. "Were you in labor on November the first?"

"Sir, I have labored my whole life," she said.

He frowned. "So you will not tell me what happened?"

"I cannot say what happened!"

"You cannot say, or you cannot remember?"

"I cannot say! I cannot make it out." She looked ill, or at least ill at ease.

"Did you bury an infant outside the slaughterhouse, and if so, was it yours?"

"I found a child," she told him, growing hoarse. "I buried the child that I found."

"Whose was it?"

"It belonged to God."

"Every child belongs to God," Bartwain muttered.

"Do you think so, sir? I hope so." She leaned toward him; she leaned so close Bartwain leaned backward. He hoped she was not about to begin weeping. He could not bear it when his suspects dissolved into tears.

"Was it of your womb?"

"My womb is old and decrepit."

"You have some trimmer's mouth," he grumbled. "Your answers are slipperier than a rock at the bottom of the creek."

She bowed her head. Bartwain did not trust the posture.

"You might be interested to learn I saw the Leveler William Walwyn this morning. He was certainly uneasy when I mentioned your name."

Her back stiffened but she said nothing.

"I interviewed him," Bartwain went on, trying to gauge her reaction. "Do you want to know what he said? You have not seen him in nine months, from what I gather. You must be desperate for a word from the magnificent William Walwyn, even though he has not been able to leave his house long enough to inquire after your welfare. Something about fourteen children to care for now that he is out of the Tower."

"He lives his own life," she said quietly.

"You know him well, then. And you would prefer to be in the middle of his life?"

"Sir, you are not kind!"

"And you, miss, are a liar. You have not said one word without its meaning something else."

"Sir, take pity," she pleaded. "I am only a woman."

"Only?" he sputtered, before he could stop himself. "I have been talking to women all day long. I deserve more pity than you do. For God's sake, tell me what happened!"

She sprang from the stool. "I cannot. Do you understand me? I cannot explain! I cannot explain what happened to her!"

"So you know the infant was a girl."

She covered her face with her gloved hands.

"So she was yours, then," he pressed.

Face still covered, she nodded.

"Good—now we are getting somewhere." He eyed her over the candle. How long had it been since the birth? Twelve or thirteen days at most. She was pale and more drawn now than at the interview's start. She looked as if she wanted to go home, pull off her boots, and climb into bed without another word. Or was that what Bartwain wanted? His toes had begun aching.

"Miss Lockyer," he said, more gently, "these things are not very complicated. To indict you, all I need is proof you tried to hide the newborn's death and some credible witness indicating the child was yours. Your acknowledgment just now together with the Widow du Gard's testimony about your behavior in the woods and the haberdasher's report that she examined your physical person for evidence of childbirth are sufficient to meet these criteria. If you do not intend to provide some correction or counter to what I have learned thus far, this meeting does not need to continue."

She lowered her hands and met his look. "Have mercy on me," she whispered.

"I cannot have mercy unless you tell me what happened."

Silence.

"Have you lost your memory?"

"I don't think so, sir." She stood very still.

"What is it, then? Don't you know what happened?"

"I cannot say. Can't you understand? I cannot say what happened! I have not yet resolved what took place."

"Haven't *resolved*? What, do the events require interpretation?"

Swiftly she turned away from him.

Bartwain, frustrated, changed tactics. "Do you believe in free will, Rachel Lockyer?"

All the Levelers professed it. John Lilburne, William Walwyn, the others—all swore on their mothers' graves that human actions remained voluntary, freely chosen. But when something happened for which they did not want to take responsibility or for which they feared reprisal, they attributed the event to providence. Bartwain detested such double-mindedness.

"Yes." Rachel was studying his bookshelves. "Yes, Investigator, I believe in free will."

The air in the chamber refused to stir. Even his two candles would not flicker. Bartwain cleared his chest, fumbling in the gloom for his pipe. "Do you also believe in self-preservation?"

"Yes." She moved to face him, stepping closer, her skirt brushing the side of his desk. She was slighter than he had anticipated, and without adornment, like a tree that has cast off its leaves for want of rain. "Yes. What is there to believe? It is a law of nature."

Bartwain did not want to find this woman arresting. She had said little that was useful. He did not find her beautiful. Her pale coloring did not go well with her eyes or dark hair, and her mouth was so wide it drowned out her other features. But she captured the attention.

"If you believe in self-preservation, then perhaps you also think it is acceptable to take a life in self-defense?" He knew he was wandering away from the material evidence.

Her emerald eyes passed through him. "No," she returned. "Self-defense is no sin, but taking a life is wrong in the eyes of God."

"You cannot have it both ways." He stood, swaying, planting his hands on his desk. "Do you think you can have it both ways? Did you harm your child? Did you conceal that poor bastard's death?"

"No," she said again, delivering a look the investigator had not seen before. But Bartwain could not tell which question she was answering.

He could not fall asleep that night. Each time he started to drift off, something his suspect had said would spring into his mind, snapping him back to consciousness. Bartwain resented Rachel Lockyer's impingement on his rest. He possessed neither the youthful idealism nor the digestion to lie awake at night reflecting. Yet here he was.

His suspect had not answered his questions, he complained to his wife, Mathilda, who had rolled on her side in their narrow bed, facing away.

"What did you expect her to say?" she mumbled. "Let me sleep."

"I expected her to deny any wrongdoing. Or to confess and beg for leniency." Bartwain sighed and punched his pillow into a more accommodating position. To bury a child in secret was to conceal its death, which according to the statute was a crime equivalent to murder. But what was the difference between a burial no one attended and a burial conducted in secret? That is, what if someone buried a bastard and no one attended because no one *wanted* to attend? Did that, too, count as concealment? "Bother," he exclaimed, loud enough that his wife jumped.

"Probably she knew you were going to pounce on her no matter what she told you," Mathilda said through the covers. "So why should she say anything?"

"I'm a murder investigator." He was sitting up now, his back against the wall; he was talking to himself more than to his wife. "I'm impartial. I listen to my witnesses. I don't ask why. Neither does the law. I only ask what. That's all the law requires! I follow the law."

"Maybe you *should* ask why, for once," she replied. "You're old and tired, that's what you are. Old, tired, and never got a promotion."

Four hours passed. Bartwain's eyes stayed maddeningly open. He wondered if he should take a cup of cream to induce drowsiness. He tried—it accomplished nothing. Maybe he would be able to sleep if he went ahead and wrote the indictment. Yes, that was it. That was the key. He just needed to finish things up, wash his hands, and be done with it. This strategy had worked well enough in the past. Then he could rest. Yes, yes, he would do it right now. Do it and be done with it. Do what was right. He rose in the dark and patted around for a candle.

"What are you doing?" Mathilda wanted to know. But Bartwain was already tiptoeing down the stairs to his study.

He sat in his ancient velvet chair. He read his interview notes again, all the way through. Then he opened his statute book and read the 1624 Act to Prevent the Destroying and Murdering of Bastard Children. He read it through three times, even though he could have recited it by heart. Nothing new announced itself to him. His eyelids were drooping. His eyelids were begging to fall. His mouth was hanging slack, and he was breathing through it—that was how tired he was.

"Enough," he said out loud. He rose and padded over to his water basin, washed his face, and dried himself with a mildewing towel. He moved to the kitchen, where he drank the hot buttered ale he took each evening purely for medicinal purposes. There, seated at the table in his stocking feet, he wrote and signed an official order of indictment in the case of Rachel Lockyer. The entire process took less than an hour, not counting the five hours of tossing and turning that had gone before.

"Well, that's over with," he said to himself as he signed and stamped the order.

He went back to his bed, relieved. After the trial he would have to submit a final report to the Council of State, but that was nothing—he could do that in his sleep. He chuckled, burrowing under his quilt, delighting in his little wordplay. He closed his eyes and rested.

Possibly an hour later, he awoke to Mathilda shaking his shoulder.

"Morning!" his wife chirped. "It's past sunrise! What were you fussing about all night long?" Mathilda Bartwain adored mornings.

The investigator groaned and pulled himself out of the bed. Had he slept at all?

Within an hour he was heading back to the courthouse, the sun so bright it offended him. When he arrived at the Sessions House in Old Bailey, he handed White the order of indictment and instructed him to deliver it to the Council of State.

A gloom descended on his secretary. "This is not right," White said. In nearly three decades of working together on criminal investigations, Bartwain and his secretary had overseen no fewer than twenty-five bastard cases. Each time an indictment came through, White delivered this same declaration; each time, he wore the same mournful expression.

"My good Friend," Bartwain entreated. "Give me leave to do what the law requires."

Three hours later, Rachel Lockyer was arrested for the murder of her newborn child. Her trial was scheduled to begin the first week of December, the opening day of the winter assizes. Until then, the indictment read, the defendant would wait it out in Newgate, in the third-floor ward for female felons.

Five

❧

S HE WAS AN ordinary woman.

She grew up thinking her life would be one thing, and when it turned out to be something else, for a while the difference between the two, between the life she'd imagined and the life she lived, needled her. When she grew older she realized these things were not anyone's fault. She learned to stop antagonizing her life, stop picking at it. Some nights were still difficult. But in the mornings Rachel Lockyer would rise before dawn suffused with a weary yet vital radiance. She was relieved. She accepted things.

She made gloves and swept floors for a living. Every morning the inside and outside of Mary's shop had to be swept clean to ward off pests, and the piles placed out for the gunge farmers. Rachel always tried to be back inside by the time those men arrived. They would careen onto Warwick Lane around the noon hour, the bells of their carts jangling. If she missed the bells, or if she heard them and promptly forgot—which she was likely to do, because the sound was so regular, because it took them so long to make their way down the street—then before she knew it their carts would be on top of her, pushed by bent men with eyes that rolled red and white, with mange where hair should have been, men who had tongues but no teeth, jowls without shape, sounds without words, mouths without sounds. These were the scavengers, paid to remove the waste that others created.

Rachel accepted her life but did not resign herself to it. She leaned into her life like she leaned into her broom. She pushed. She watched the mist curl over the streets while she swept. In winter she would wrap her head in a woolen scarf as she worked, her view framed by threads that came from creatures who climbed peaks so staggeringly high she could not fathom what they saw before they started descending. She loved scarves and she hated heights. She loved gloves also. She loved what the gloves were made of—goatskin and sheepskin, the finest around. The hides smelled of salt and wind and sky.

Most people who met Rachel Lockyer made up their minds about her quickly. They constructed their images of her the same way a jeweler uses intaglio to carve a gem, cutting below the surface of the stone so the resulting design is not a raised relief or cameo but a recessed portrait, a negative space. This was how most people incised their portraits of her, from the surface down; they knew her less for who she was than for who and what she was not. She was not a matron. She was not a mother. She was not well educated. She was not much of a Christian. Sometimes a well-meaning matron would point these things out to her. But Rachel already knew who and what she was not. She did not need a reminder.

Rachel's father, who died when she was fifteen, had worshiped as a Particular Baptist, meaning he believed God ordained and ordered all things for His good, up to and including the damnation of the lost. Rachel's mother pretended to follow her husband's faith while he was alive, but when he died Martha Lockyer reverted to Romanism. So Rachel grew up wedged between two gods—the God of the Particular Baptists, who snatched liberty out of her hands, having predestined everything; and the God of the Roman Catholics, who offered just enough free will to ensure a continual culpability. Half of Rachel—the half that belonged to her father—assumed God had already made up His mind about her. The other half, that half that belonged to her mother, did as she pleased and then repented.

As a child she would attend weekly services with her father, who could read no better than she could. Crammed onto a backless wooden bench alongside other dissenters from the established Church of England, she would listen to the preacher proclaim the primacy of the Word and the sovereignty of God and Parliament. Once or twice a year, however, she would attend secret Roman masses with her mother. These took place in a neighbor's cellar and consisted of an exiled Jesuit priest lifting the Eucharistic cup, which he did not share with the laity, and whispering something in Latin about the substance and the accidents. After receiving the bread, Rachel and her mother would slip out, returning home before her father noticed they'd gone.

When her father died, Rachel's mother, then pregnant with Robert, barricaded herself in the bedroom of their two-room house for three nights and three days, during which time she chanted the song of the martyrs from the book of Revelation, "How Long, O Lord, Holy and True." When she emerged she said, "Never again." "Never again what?" Rachel said. She was frightened; she was only fifteen. Her mother did not respond. If there had been a way to join the saints under the altar, Martha Lockyer would have. Instead she had to go right on being a mother.

Later, when Rachel moved on her own to London, she attended William Kiffin's Devonshire Square church, which followed the Baptist way. Kiffin told his congregants that God held all things in His hand, even the smallest of creatures; he promised his listeners that in God's eyes everyone mattered, everyone counted; every living being had its place and purpose. But then Rachel took a job as Mary's assistant and had to sweep out the floors of the glove shop, and her days grew longer and continually busy; it became harder to find time to contemplate her place in God's ordering. After a while she stopped going to Kiffin's services. Once or twice a year she tried to locate a secret mass, but those were not easy to find—you had to know the right people to get into one, and it turned out Rachel did not know any of the right people in London.

She was brought to Newgate on a bright and windless morning under a sky spilling with starlings and thrushes. A windmill was bolted to the roof, its revolving blades designed to pull air into the prison. Starlings soared over the blades as Rachel passed through the iron gates. Their wings flashed silver and white.

Her first act as prisoner was to pay garnish—to bribe the warden for a blanket and a nettle-filled pallet. Then she paid two more farthings for the right not to be violated. An aide walked her to the third floor, which housed the women's ward. The place was a shipwreck. Destitute women lay strewn and hulking across the soiled floors. The aide directed her to a dry patch along the southern wall, where she crouched gingerly, clutching the edge of her pallet as she laid it down.

No one talked to her, so for a while she talked to herself—that is, she talked to her brother. Not for long, and not so anyone else could hear. Just long enough to distract herself. She explained she was sorry to be troubling him, but she had no one else.

No one else for what, she imagined Robert replying.

"To talk with."

Why don't you talk with Walwyn? he sniped, peevish.

So Rachel defended Walwyn to her deceased sibling, which meant, of course, that she defended Walwyn to herself.

"He has a great deal to be doing now that he is out of the Tower," she said. "He will come when he can." This explanation failed to satisfy her brother. Robert began talking back to her, as any dream will when we have tried too hard to contain it. Several prisoners lying nearby glanced up, but the guards paid no attention. It was not unusual, a woman talking to herself in Newgate.

In the afternoon, she had a flesh-and-blood visitor. Unable to find Rachel at Warwick Lane, Walwyn had traveled south to the Lilburnes' lodgings in Southwark. She was not there either, so he'd wound up retracing his steps to the investigator's chambers in Old Bailey, where he'd demanded to know Rachel's whereabouts.

"You're late," Bartwain had said, not without pleasure, when Walwyn barged in. "You should have looked after her sooner. They've taken her to Newgate." At this point Walwyn threatened to beat him, but the investigator snorted and waved him off. "There is no love of violence in you," Bartwain said, which was true. Walwyn left the courthouse, crossed Newgate Street, and made his way the short distance to the prison, where he bribed the warden to be allowed inside. Everything at Newgate cost something. Water cost the most. Halfway up the stairs he remembered he had forgotten to bring any. Delayed yet again, he ran downstairs, exited the gates, and hurried for the nearest public tap, which piped water from Tyburn Springs to Cheapside. He emptied his flask of wormwood, refilled it with water, and returned to the prison. He paid the same bribe a second time — in his absence the guards had changed posts — and retraced his steps to the third floor, where an inebriated aide gave him thirty supervised minutes on the women's ward.

When Walwyn saw Rachel he did not ask what had happened. The question did not occur to him. He was not concerned with her guilt. He was consumed with his own. "There you are," she said, over and over. "You were gone so long." She pushed him away when he tried to gather her close. "I cannot help myself," he whispered, "I am so terribly glad to see you." "You abandoned me," she said. She spoke as if they were all alone, as if they were arguing in the bed of the travelers' inn near Warwick Lane, the travelers' inn having been their place. He could still see her there, how the light from the thick panes used to fall on her, used to catch in her hair. He used to try to persuade her to stay with him a little longer. She would say, briskly, as she yanked the blankets off his body, forcing him to rise, shivering, his white buttocks exposed: "You are the one who has to go; you are the one who has a household." "But you are the one who keeps leaving," he would point out as she reached for the door.

Now she was grasping his wrists. "I think I have committed an awful sin."

"What sin is that?" Her nails were in his flesh.

She was shaking her head. "It is the worst thing a person can do."

"Now, this is my entire—"

"You don't know what happened," she said savagely, reading his thoughts. "How can you think this is your fault when you don't know what happened?"

"It's the truth. I'm responsible. They had me locked up nine months in the Tower. I failed to help you."

"You had no hand in this," she uttered so low he could hardly hear. "This one was mine. It belonged to me."

"So there was a child," he said before he could think better of it.

With those words she pulled away and smacked her head against the limestone wall. The first time it happened he was too stunned to react. The second time it happened he was angry. He grabbed her, wrestling her from the wall as she scratched and fought, the thin cords of her neck straining. A welt bloomed along her brow. He held her, hard and unrelenting. Even as she tried to pry his fingers away, she seemed to be waiting for him, expecting him to say something, so he whispered, "Losing something is no sin, Rachel. It is loss. Loss is not the same as sin."

"But what if it is," she cried, and buried her face in his cloak. They were seated on the floor, under the burners, observed by women in the shadows, women nursing children, women standing and squatting and sleeping, the stronger ones rifling through the goods of those who had fallen.

"How do you go to prison for six hours and already have flea stings," Walwyn murmured, studying the bite marks on her exposed neck.

"It's been nine hours," she said into his cloak, as if that settled it.

He wanted to kiss her. He didn't think he should. He was wrong, of course. "Why haven't you kissed me," she plaintively said. But when he went to brush her lips, she said it was too late, said *he* was too late, and pushed his face away. He held her hands instead. He held them and he kissed each one of her fingers, each of the rough knuckles, and was finished too fast. He went in the reverse direction and kissed all ten knuckles again, though Rachel did not appear to be paying attention. Her thoughts were wandering; her thoughts had limped off somewhere, over his shoulder.

Walwyn stayed beside her on the rancid floors and shared the flask of wormwood. When she discovered it held water, she called him a silly old man. He promised to bring her something stronger. He rubbed liniment into her ankles where the leg irons were tearing into them. He did not speak again about the child. When he massaged her wrists, she cried. "I have missed you," she said.

That night John Lilburne refused to draft a Leveler petition advocating for Rachel's release. He said his conscience would not allow him to defend a murdering mother. Elizabeth Lilburne shouted obscenities at her husband's back as he retreated to the privy.

Elizabeth visited Rachel in the morning. She thought ahead before she made the trip; she came better equipped than Walwyn. She brought a handful of shillings, a rye loaf, a blanket, and wine. When she returned home to Southwark, her skin crawled with lice. Her daughter, five-year-old Elizabeth, whom they called Young Elizabeth to distinguish her from her mother, was awake and waiting for her, playing with two spoons in the kitchen. John was still sleeping.

After Elizabeth left, Rachel tried to block out her surroundings by pulling the blanket over her head. The stench of the women's ward was overpowering, the air stifling and warm. Finally she tossed aside the blanket and sat, her back against the wall. This was not the time to be thinking. This was not the time, not the place, to be reflecting on anything. Yet here she was.

The investigator's questions had come so fast, and harder than she'd anticipated. It was like the game Walwyn had described to her—tennis. Rachel had never seen that sport, but Walwyn had visited Hampton Court once and observed a match; this was before the Puritans condemned sports on the Sabbath. He told her the players hit the ball so fast they sometimes struck each other in the face with it. That was how Rachel had felt sitting across from Thomas Bartwain in his chambers trying to return his volley of questions.

She glanced up to find a prisoner crawling toward her, a cloth rag trailing between her legs. The woman gave her name as Nell. She was missing most of her teeth, which caused the lower half of her face to fold in around itself, like a weasel curling into a ball.

Nell was kind to Rachel. She showed her the cleanest place to relieve herself—a slop bucket in the west corner of the ward—and she told her which women and guards to avoid. She offered water from her own supply. "They make you pay for it otherwise," she explained.

That afternoon the two women lay side by side on their mats and whispered to each other, trying not to attract attention. During the night, Nell warned, the ward would take on a bitter chill, and the guards would creep up and down looking for any woman grown too cold or weak to move. When they found such a woman, they would go through all her clothing. Then they would go through all her children, if she had brought them.

"Did you bring yours?" Nell wondered.

"My clothing or my children?"

"Your children."

"No," Rachel managed to say.

Nell cocked her head. "You don't have them, or you didn't bring them?"

"I don't have them."

"Lucky." She nodded vigorously. "Lucky you do not, for then what would you do with them?"

In the evening the guards came for Nell and hauled her away. The whole thing went so fast it took a minute for Rachel to grasp what had happened.

Later she realized the guards hadn't gone about their task correctly. At midnight on the day of a prisoner's execution, the bellman was supposed to stand outside the condemned's cell and ring a hand bell. Then someone would read a sermon or recite Scripture, and in the morning the guards would escort the prisoner to a mule cart that would take the person to the colossal scaffold at Tyburn, stopping along the way for crowds to gawk and spit, and pausing to toll the bells of St. Sepulchre. No one had remembered to do these things for Nell. When the guards came for her, she was so startled she soiled herself. Rachel was lying beside her when it happened. She called out right away when she saw the helmets coming; she tried to warn her. But the guards dragged Nell out by her hair. "Filthy slut, it is time to meet your maker," they said.

How could they neglect the chimes and forget the final sermon? Just an hour earlier Nell was telling Rachel how much she wanted one. She wanted the deacon of Newgate to place his hands on her head, to say God would love her in the next life as long as she repented in this. But the guards swept her off before she could ask.

Alone again, Rachel dragged her pallet to the warmest corner of the ward, under a spitting burner, away from the other women. She tried talking to her brother, but he was not paying attention. After a while she curled up on top of the lice and stopped talking altogether.

She'd first met William Walwyn more than three years before, during an evening of pelting rain that turned to rime along the windowpanes before the night was through. She met him because she was in a fight with her brother. At the time, Robert was nineteen and a private in the Parliamentary army. Robert had ideas. When he announced he was going to the Whalebone tavern to join the Levelers and fight for the poor and the workingman, Rachel had gone along to argue him out of it. She was fifteen years his senior and worried about his safety. He elbowed her; he told her to stop acting like his mother. "I am your mother," she had said. Brother and sister were inseparable.

When they reached the tavern where the Levelers held their meetings, Rachel had stopped to marvel at the massive jawbone of a sperm whale hanging over the entrance, then followed Robert into a narrow passageway that opened onto a lively eating and drinking area. The first thing she noticed was the display of turtles. They were everywhere, trapped in rectangular tanks stationed around the dining room. Some were swimming, others climbing up the glass and sliding down as patrons wandered by and decided which ones they wanted to eat. Once singled out by a diner, the designated reptile would be carried by its shell, head receding, into the kitchen, where the cook would plunge it in boiling water, then discard the head in the alley behind the tavern. He would serve the meat with butter or in a soup with leeks and parsnips.

"I'm going in," Robert said. He was headed into a side room off the dining area that everyone knew was reserved for Levelers.

"Don't you dare," Rachel replied; of course this did no good. Furious, she went in after him.

Inside, five men were leaning in a collective scowl around the center table, surrounded by puddling candles, folio sheets, inkwells, half-empty bottles of wine, and the remains of two roasted capons. Two men, whom Rachel would later know as John Lilburne and Richard Overton, were arguing with a third, the newsman Gilbert Mabbott. It was wintertime; they were cold; the wine made them all angry. Robert introduced himself, extending his hand to whoever would take it. No one seemed impressed with him; John and Mabbott continued to argue. Nobody paid much attention to Robert at all. Rachel was glad. Nobody paid attention to Rachel either, until William Walwyn did. He was leaning over the table, his elbows resting on the parchment, his sleeves rolled up to his forearms, his silver hair falling low over his eyes, ink staining the pads of his fingers, and when he glanced up to think, to catch a word that eluded him, he discovered her instead. He set down his quill. As soon as he did, the other men around the table went silent. Something was afoot. Elizabeth Lilburne and Mary Overton, seated at a smaller table in the corner, looked up and went still, like two weasels when a lantern shines on their foraging in the night.

"What is it?" John said, reaching for the spectacles he had needed since he'd sustained a pike wound to his eye several years earlier. He did not know Walwyn had forgotten his own name. He did not know Walwyn had forgotten his past, his children, his wife, his friends, his faith, his house, even his legs on which he stood. Walwyn didn't hear what John was saying. He was too busy making his way across the room to Rachel, who watched him walking toward her, who knew trouble when she saw it. There it comes, she thought as the Leveler approached. There is trouble if ever I saw it. She held her ground, sized him up. She thought: Magnificent. Before she could think anything else, Walwyn was standing so close she could study the lines of his neck as he spoke. He was saying hello, welcoming her. She said hello back. Only the word did not come out of her mouth the way it should have. It did not come out as a greeting, as the deferential murmur of a trades-woman. It came out like a torch. She said hello and ignited him. She gave him her hand. In the instant it happened, she could not fathom why she did it. It was one of only two hands she had; it be-longed to her. So she pulled back, but only in her mind; her hand stayed where it was. His fingers were sticky with drying ink. He was warm and taut, and in his wrist she could feel the architecture of ligaments and joints. He was holding her hand. Rachel glanced up. Just as she suspected, her brother was fuming—though not because of anything Rachel was doing. He was fuming because the Levelers were not paying him any attention. She returned her gaze to Walwyn. Her eyes were relieved to go back to him. It had been too long already. He was speaking to her. He was speaking only to her. "You are welcome here," he was saying with a lopsided grin. He said some other things she could not remember even five seconds later. Then he leaned in and inhaled her. Everyone in the room saw him do it. Across the table, John's head shot up from his papers. Overton rolled his eyes.

"An embarrassment," John muttered.

"Too much wine," Overton commented. The newsman Mab-bott harbored more sympathy. Walwyn, he grasped, was finished from the first.

The next four nights running, Robert insisted on returning to the tavern. "They will take me if I persist," he said to his sister. He did not want to concede that the Levelers had not noticed him, had not caught his name. He did not know that in those days the

Levelers saw one hundred Roberts a month, one hundred a week if they wanted. The whole world was filled with Roberts—guileless young men eager to give their lives for liberty's sake, though few of them could have said what, besides a hero's death, liberty was good for anymore. Rachel didn't argue when he insisted on trying again. She went back to the tavern with him. She was the faithful elder sister; she joined him every night. True, she had an ulterior motive. Her brother did not need to know. He was too young to need to know. She said this to herself several times.

When the commanders of the Parliamentary New Model Army ordered Robert and a thousand other rank-and-files back to the battlefields outside London, baiting the starving soldiers with promises of warm bread, new boots, and functioning muskets, declaring that a king who levied unfair taxes must be stopped by force, Rachel continued going to the Whalebone. She went on her own. She walked alone, without a brother to elbow her. She swung her arms full and wide as she walked. She laughed out loud as the street sweepers watched her pass. It was ridiculous and fine and undignified and ordinary and wonderful. She felt young and old both. All her life she had assumed she was not subject to the normal laws of attraction; she had assumed this was not her road. It turned out it was.

Rachel's closest friend became Elizabeth, whom she'd also met through the Whalebone. Initially the two women could not decide what to make of each other, but then Rachel had said something that made Elizabeth laugh, and they were off and running. At one point during their first meeting, Elizabeth had hooted so boisterously that her husband turned around in his seat at the men's table and urged her to pipe down. Later, Walwyn overheard Rachel explaining to her new friend that she sewed gloves and pieced hides for a living, heard Elizabeth asking if this was her husband's trade and heard Rachel replying no, for there was none. Elizabeth, sounding aggrieved, had asked, "Well, how does he earn his keep?" and Rachel replied, "No *husband*, I mean," and both women had chuckled.

From time to time, she and Elizabeth would lean their heads close and share opinions about the war and politics. Rachel spent most of these conversations listening. From Elizabeth she learned that the Levelers were principally against snobbery. Beyond that, they believed in hard work, self-preservation, no standing army in peacetime, and the right to a fair trial. They believed in extending voting privileges to men who did not own property. They believed in talking things out. Sometimes they forgot that church was for the next life while government was for this and tried to reverse the equation, but they were not alone in this tendency. Everyone wanted to be a prophet—Elizabeth said this loudly, so her husband could hear her—everyone wanted to create the kingdom of God on earth during a time of civil war.

From Elizabeth, Rachel also learned that the Levelers were not the atheists their enemies made them out to be. Most were good congregational Independents and Baptists, with a few philosophical Seekers, such as Walwyn, thrown in. When Rachel wanted to know what that word meant, Elizabeth sniffed and said Seekers were people who found questions more satisfying than answers. "They are not practical," she said.

Rachel liked to slip away from the meeting room to study the turtles. She used to make her way into the darkened dining area after the kitchen had closed and would stand over the largest of the tanks, peering down at the occupants. Once she scooped a turtle from the top of the pool, where he was swimming. He did just fine at first as she carried him in both hands around the silent tavern. She was giving him a tour; she was showing him things. He did fine, that is, until he poked his head out and glimpsed his tour guide, saw her strange and giant face. He retreated into his shell with an offended look. Rachel returned him to the tank.

Another time, one of the turtles got himself caught trying to squeeze through the rocks at the bottom of his tank. He had flipped sideways to angle through what to his eyes must have appeared as an opening, but his shell had grown; his shell had matured without his noticing. He kicked for a minute, stopped, kicked again, stopped again. Some minutes passed. He was running out of air; nature was taking its course. Watching him, Rachel became unable to breathe. She reached into the tank to dislodge one of the rocks, but her arm was not long enough; the rocks lay at the bottom. The other turtles swam in circles; they did not notice any crisis except the milky white hand intruding into their living quarters. Rachel dragged over a chair, stood on it, and plunged her hand into the tank from this higher position, soaking the bodice of her dress as she reached down to free him. She would dry off later. She pushed the rocks apart, and the turtle swam up. He popped to the surface, his tiny mouth parting, the upper half in the shape of a beak, the lower half soft and petulant. He shut his mouth, eyed her reproachfully, and rejoined his companions, who were still swimming in circles.

She considered rescuing all of the turtles and setting them free at the creek, but this impulse did not seem sensible. The tavern owner was trying to earn a living. Everywhere people were hungry. She supposed it was a case of competing goods. She had heard the Levelers say they were on the side of the poor and hard-working Englishman, and the tavern owner fairly fit that description. Still, she could not eat when the turtles seemed to be watching her. She especially avoided the soup.

One night she wandered into the darkened dining room to press her nose against one of the glass tanks, steaming the view, when a hand came to rest on her shoulder. She knew whose it was before she turned. She had not forgotten that hand. Walwyn was smiling into her eyes. He had left the others in the back room quarreling about property and taxation. They were alone.

Rachel had no idea what to do with him, so she turned back to the turtles, of which she counted five.

"They're something, aren't they?" Walwyn said.

She was not sure how to talk to him, so she said whatever came to mind. It was the strangest thing. It was easy. Once she started talking, it became impossible to stop. She tried to stop, to speak less directly, but that cat was out of the bag. "I don't understand how they can swim and swim like that." She pointed to the tank. "They go around and around in circles."

"They do have that tendency." He was looking at her, not the turtles.

"They never seem to notice. But they have to notice. Don't you think? Don't you think they're going around and around all the time thinking, 'This is the same thing I just saw'?"

He confessed he didn't know, had never thought about it.

She glanced at him, aggrieved. He had failed to wonder the same thing she did. "Would *you* keep swimming around and around if you knew there would never be anything else? They don't have to do it. Here is a dry spot of ground—here, on these rocks. Why aren't they resting?"

"I can't think why," he admitted.

"I can think of two reasons."

"Tell me."

His lopsided smile had returned and was threatening to distract her. She did her best to ignore it. She had a point to make. "One, the turtle doesn't know he is living in the tank. So each revolution he makes, he thinks he has traveled to a new place. He never notices."

"And two?"

"Two, he knows. He knows but he still swims."

"Why would he do that?"

She scrutinized the turtles. Walwyn leaned in and regarded them with her, and together they studied the intricate patterning of each shell. The creatures propelled their ungainly bodies through gray water that had not been cleaned. Each pushed against an invisible current, neck ugly and straining as it thrust itself forward.

"You've studied them for some time, I think," Walwyn observed. "I see you wandering in here. You must be an expert in the lives of turtles."

She reddened. "The other room was too warm."

"It's just as warm in this room."

"Well, it wasn't earlier."

"Well, indeed."

His skin seemed to be throwing off heat—she could not tell the precise source.

"I am afraid I will be of no help to you in your contemplations," he went on, "for I've never examined these creatures myself, at least no longer than it takes for the cook to bring them to me in a soup pot."

Why was his skin so warm? She could not concentrate. Why was he talking so much? "You are some jester," she murmured.

"I suppose I am . . . " He trailed off. "Some silly old fellow."

She was curious about him then. She began to interview him. "Where did you come from?"

He said he came from Moorfields.

"No, not where you live now, but where you lived before."

"Before what?"

A good question, she thought. She had heard of his large household. She changed the subject. "Did you write all those pamphlets and Agreements of the People that the other Levelers are always talking about?"

"Some of them. But not lately. Lately I have not written much."

"Why not?"

"I'm tired."

"Of what? Writing?"

He nodded.

Rachel could not imagine tiring from something that could be done while seated. For a second time that evening she detested him. "How can you be tired of such a thing?" It was too intimate a question, and she apologized.

"Don't be sorry," he replied. "I suppose writing the same things over and over again becomes disheartening when nothing changes."

She considered this. Then she said, "Maybe you know more about the lives of turtles than you think." To hide her smile, she dipped her head. It was the wrong move, or maybe it was the right one, because he reached over and cupped her face in his hand, raising her chin to meet him, his thumb against the underside of her jaw, pressing up on that soft place surrounded by bone.

"Never do that," he was telling her. "Never lower your face for anyone."

"Sir" was all she could say.

"Don't. Don't call me that. I am not that. I am not anyone."

She stiffened. "If *you* are not anyone, what does that make *me*?"

"That's not what I meant," he protested. Then he added, before he could reel himself in, "You are very fair."

Rachel hesitated. She saw she had a fork in the road coming. She didn't want a fork in the road just yet. In her experience they could be tiresome. Sometimes one got to the fork and the road closed. So she said, simply, "I am fair enough, I expect," and then—briefly—rested her cheek against his hand. She didn't leave it there long, but it was enough. Walwyn was discovering her; he was noticing her body. His eyes were dark and a wordless heaviness lingered in them. His palm against her cheek was searing. So this was where the heat was coming from, she thought. She should have known it would be the hand. She could hear the bell clock outside the meeting room chiming.

When a few minutes later John strolled in wanting to know what was going on, what he was missing, neither Rachel nor Walwyn could explain. Walwyn made up something, some cockamamie story, and this set them both smiling. They could not stop looking at each other even after they had returned to the meeting room. Rachel caught his eye across the table and tilted her chin ridiculously high, surveying the world like a propertied woman. She was making fun of him, of his little admonition. She gave it up a few seconds in, but while it lasted her pose allowed him to follow the line of her jaw to where it joined her neck, just below her earlobe. With that sight, every tissue and fiber in Walwyn's body began to heave and flounder toward her, against a dogged current.

Six

B ARTWAIN WAS LEAVING the home of his physician
when he spied Walwyn across the street and heard him
calling.

Bother, Bartwain thought. He ducked into an alley, but a maid
was emptying a slop bucket from an upstairs window and a tor-
rent of dirty water chased him back into the street. "What do you
want?" he demanded as Walwyn approached. Wind was blowing
the morning rain sideways, and water beaded under both men's
hats.

"I need to speak with you."

"Let go of my arm. You're wet and I'm unwell. I have no time to
talk to you today." He did not like to be pulled by the sleeve as the
Leveler was doing.

"You must listen to me. I need your help."

"If you needed my help, you should have asked for it during
your deposition. I am no longer in as fine a mood." Bartwain had
not slept well the night before — or the two nights prior to that, if
he thought about it. It was a complete coincidence that the three
nights he had slept poorly were the same three nights Rachel
Lockyer had been in Newgate awaiting trial. He blamed his lack
of rest on the mice he had discovered in his kitchen cupboards.

The mice were the reason, he assured himself. While searching for a midnight snack, for something to ease his muttering stomach, the investigator had spied four tails scampering for cover behind a sack of flour. Trembling, he had set out cheese and eggs in elaborate traps—he did not own a cat. He stayed up late, holding the lantern, listening for a snap. He gave up and went to bed, where he scarcely slept. At dawn he leaped from his coverlets and descended to the kitchen, where he had counted four piles of droppings but no mice in his handmade traps.

"I'm not asking your help for my sake. I'm asking for Miss Lockyer's," Walwyn said.

You look old, Bartwain thought. Old and frantic. "I'm off the case," he said tersely. "All that's left for me to do is write a summary and report once the trial is finished. Whatever you need now, I can't help you." He shivered and clutched his cloak tighter. He could see the abbey of Westminster from where they were standing. Bartwain's tiny thatched-roof house lay just beyond. His house was so close he could almost smell his wife's cranberry biscuits baking over the fire. His toes were hurting. His bed was calling his name—he was that tired.

"You don't understand. I—"

"I do understand, and so do you. She is no longer my jurisdiction. You will have to find someone else to take pity on you." Bartwain's morning visit to his physician had supplied no good news. The doctor could do nothing to ease his gouty foot. Worse, he had been unable to ease Bartwain's stomach, which was continuing to announce its displeasure with some of his more recent indulgences—stewed boysenberries, boiled crab, and an undercooked custard. Then there was the black, steady rain now pouring over the brim of his hat, silting the folds of his neck as he watched Walwyn shivering in his cloak; he suspected sleet would arrive later. Probably it would start just as the investigator was heading out again, and he would slip and fall and be trampled by a throng. Bartwain disliked both crowds and weather, and especially their convergence.

"Please!" Walwyn shouted. A gust of wind robbed him of sound; Bartwain had to strain to hear him. "I must speak with you frankly. You see, I am responsible. I cannot leave her."

"You are responsible, yes. But she is not your only duty. Even if I wanted to intervene, which I do not, I have no power. I told you. My involvement ended three days ago. The law says I am to step back and write my final report. If you wanted to speak with me, you should have done so during your interview. Excuse me, please — my wife is waiting."

"You don't—"

"I understand well enough, Mr. Walwyn," Bartwain interrupted, his patience fraying. "For all the blithering denials you issued during your deposition, it is quite clear what your relationship has been with that woman. Your time for helping her is over. If you wanted to help her, you should not have allowed her to fall into this situation; you should have known better. You should not have compromised her virtue."

"For God's sake, do you think a woman's virtue lives or dies by what a man—"

"I do not care to discuss philosophy in the rain with a Leveler."

"It's not philosophy. It's a woman's life. It's a woman's life you are tampering with!"

"Forgive me, but last time I checked I was not the one doing the tampering." Bartwain hated the wind; he hated the rain; he hated this man making him stand in the rain; he hated the day, period. "Do you know how fortunate you are, Mr. Walwyn? You are exceptionally fortunate. God must be watching over you."

Walwyn eyed him warily.

"If that child had lived, you could have been dragged to the whipping post alongside its mother. And if all this were happening several months in the future, I predict you would not even be so *fortunate* as to receive a whipping. In a few months' time, our self-proclaimed saints in the House of Commons are going to make good on one of their threats — they're going to make adultery an offense punishable by death. You're aware of that likelihood, aren't you, now that the Puritans have seized the reins of government?" The investigator cleared his throat; he missed the days of King Charles. "So don't forget to say your evening prayers, Mr. Walwyn, because if all this were happening at some other time, you would not be getting off the hook so quickly. They could drag *you* to the scaffold too, if they wanted." One advantage to reaching the age of sixty-one, the investigator had learned, was the insight—or hindsight—that life consisted of a limited number of stories. These stories circled around and around and repeated themselves. There was nothing new, nothing at all new under the sun; even the sun was bored. "You should have known better," he repeated.

Walwyn proceeded to offer Bartwain sixty-five pounds, payable immediately, if the investigator would take the legal action of formally withdrawing his murder indictment. It was a large enough sum that Bartwain actually had to think about it. He could tell his wife he had received his long-postponed promotion. No, she would never believe that. Rain spattered his chin. He brushed it away impatiently. "Mr. Walwyn," he said, blinking and blinking to keep his vision clear. The more he blinked, the faster the rain fell on him. "I might be just an old shoe in this courthouse, but this is one shoe who doesn't track mud where he walks. You cannot bribe me."

"It's not a bribe. An innocent woman is going to be put on trial. You know it and I know it. Whatever happened to her that night was unintentional."

"Happened *to* her? It is impossible to assign intentionality, or the lack thereof, to an act that happened *to* someone, sir, in case your logic is weakening out there in the countryside. Or were you referring to the child as opposed to its mother?"

"Don't play your word games with me. Rachel is innocent."

"Innocent people are put on trial all the time. That's why there is such a thing as a jury."

"You know as well as I do that any jury is going to convict her. You know as well as I what kind of system of justice we suffer."

"Oh, I don't know," Bartwain said slyly. "It's not as bad as all that, is it? Things can turn out all right. They do for some people. They did for you." He studied the Leveler. "It's odd, isn't it? You're getting out of prison just as she is going in. You're changing places."

"The Tower is nothing like Newgate. John Lilburne spent nine months in the Tower and he was fatter when he left than when he entered. Whereas Rachel—do you know what they call that place? Hell on earth."

Bartwain nodded; he had visited Newgate once. He did not care to go back. "Why don't you call on some of your Leveling friends to petition on her behalf? Surely they can write something, get a movement going. They used to wield a powerful influence."

"They are refusing to get involved."

"Ah. Well, that's too bad. But you see, Mr. Walwyn, I do not feel quite so upset as you about these things. My sympathies lie with the child."

"And you think mine do not?" The Leveler's face was blotchy, almost curdled.

"You will excuse me, please," the investigator said primly. "I have nothing more to say." But his stomach twisted with worry.

When he arrived home, he discovered his wife had made no cranberry biscuits and had no plans to do so in the near future. Opening the cabinet to make his own snack, he discovered that the mice had paid a return visit. They had devoured the bait, leaving the traps empty.

Walwyn spent the evening working alone in his makeshift apothecary behind the house. He labored six hours and produced nothing.

He had not picked up a physician's manual until the age of forty, had not seriously studied the subject until he left his post with the Merchant Adventurers over a dispute concerning monopolies and came away with time on his hands. He did not like to talk about his newfound love of physic. What was there to say? How was he to explain such a late-arriving passion? Any serious attempt to justify it would make him look ridiculous. Had he always loved medicine yet lacked the courage to pursue it? Or was he a perpetual malcontent? He did not go inside for supper.

He had no words to explain to Anne why he loved the apothecary, why he spent hours in this dingy shed with its shining instruments and stacks of books that contained anatomic etchings pointing the way to a seamless interior world, a universe of vessels and joints, one in which the rules for health were as simple and symmetrical as the rules for love laid out by Saint Paul. *Though I speak with the tongues of men and of angels, and have not charity, I am become as sounding brass, or a tinkling cymbal. And though I have the gift of prophecy, and understand all mysteries, and all knowledge; and though I have all faith, so that I could remove mountains, and have not charity, I am nothing.*

In 1641, shortly before the civil war started, Walwyn had moved his family from London to Moorfields, with its sprawling green fields and fens drained for men's leisure and women's labor. He could no longer bear the stench of the city. In London, a butcher's shop had been crammed against one side of the Walwyns' narrow house and a tallow chandler's had boxed them in on the other, so that the odor of animal flesh would drift in from the east and animal fat used for candles would choke them from the west. In Moorfields, Walwyn had promised, there would be no vile odors, no more distractions. Anne had warned against this reasoning. Moving north of the city wall was asking trouble to pay a visit, she told him. Sure enough, once they moved, things grew complicated, and Walwyn remained unsettled. Some days he swore he could hear sounds coming all the way from Bedlam — Bethlehem Hospital in Bishopsgate — and would not be able to do his work. Other days his ears picked up the cries coming from the dog skinner's house a quarter of a mile away; these sounds were even worse. He began taking frequent trips by himself into the city.

On the way home after his encounter with the investigator, Walwyn had reached the Roman wall separating London from Moorfields and instinctively increased his pace. The wall stood a few hundred yards from the dog skinner's house. He glanced up at the clearing sky. It was almost noon. His feet moved faster. From the north came a high-pitched yelp, followed by a burst of braying and barking. The dog skinner's work was starting. Walwyn's walk became a run. But the sound overtook him, as it always did.

To Walwyn the sound of those dogs was the sound of every creature that ever saw its end coming and fought back, that knew it would not win, would not survive, that understood it would fall, but that fought on, held on. To Walwyn that sound was the war, which he hated, which he mourned before it began, while his friends maintained with remarkable certainty that armed conflict for the sake of the people was necessary once in a while; armed conflict, they said, was propitious. He nodded when they said these things but he did not write any of their words down; he began to spit on their words in his sleep. To him their arguments marked some elemental failure, some corrosion of nature and imagination against which only love could possibly prevail, against which only love could be thrown, like a sparrow flings itself up against the sooty sky on its first flight, panicked and weightless, yet beating. Walwyn no longer trusted the ends to which the word *necessary* was applied. This was another reason he had stopped writing pamphlets.

When the sound of the dogs continued, he came to a halt at the side of the carriageway and bent over, hands covering his ears, as patchwork horses carrying out-of-work soldiers steered around him, the rank-and-files shouting at him, calling him an old man, telling him to move out of the way, as the hooves of their beasts clopped past. Walwyn ignored them. He kept his ears covered with his gloved hands, with those gloves that never left him. He leaned against those ancient Roman stones and waited for the sound to stop. What bothered him, he once tried to explain to Anne, whose gray eyes silently followed his gesturing hands, what bothered him was not just the sound of the dogs dying but the sound that came before it, of awareness.

In the few days since his release from the Tower, Walwyn had taken to reading his youngest, Richard—or Fourteen, as Anne called him—to sleep in the evenings. More than once Anne had awakened in the morning to find the two of them curled on a pile of blankets in the passageway, Walwyn's hand cupping the four-year-old's neck, the child's hot face nestled in his father's shoulder. Walwyn's physician son-in-law, who had studied William Harvey's *De Motu Cordis*, or *On the Motion of the Heart and Blood in Living Creatures*, had diagnosed the boy with poor circulation of the blood. He was born with a faulty heart—Fourteen, that is.

When he could not concentrate on his studies, Walwyn paced the length of the apothecary. He also cleaned. He sorted through instruments and vials. He sat on a stack of anatomy books and drank from a bottle of wine. Recently his son-in-law, Brooke, had compiled a manual of physic titled *A Conservatory of Health* and had left an early version in the work shed. Walwyn picked it up now and flipped through it. The book sought to explain how the world of science operated at the level of the individual human. It claimed to cover "the six particulars necessary to a man's life." These included (1) air, (2) meat and drink, (3) motion and rest, (4) sleep and wakefulness, (5) the excrements, and (6) the passions of the mind, in that order.

When Walwyn finished the book he studied the frontispiece before setting it back on the stack. Then he leaned his head against the wall and considered those particulars Brooke had not covered.

No one had seen them leaving the first time he and Rachel slipped out of the Whalebone. John and Elizabeth were finishing a plate of salted cod and arguing about a domestic matter. The others were drinking and squabbling about the limits of Parliament's power during wartime. It was a good argument; it would keep them going for hours. First Rachel and then Walwyn had ducked out of the meeting room. No one noticed their departure.

The reason they had given each other, the reason that had pushed them, whispering like conspirators, outside in the cold in the first place, was Rachel's offer to show him the glove shop on Warwick Lane. They had known each other only a few months. This was how she'd phrased it as they'd sat in front of the fire at the Whalebone: Would you like to see the glove shop? "Yes," Walwyn had replied. "Why, yes, of course I would." Until that moment he had never given glove making a second thought. "The sewing of gloves fascinates me," he said. "For example, how long do the fingers need to be? Who supplies the hides?" He went on to ask about the layout of the store, about the organization of inventory. He posed innumerable pointless questions. It would be easier if she just showed him, she suggested, her words forming more slowly than usual, as if her lips were cold. Were her lips cold? Of course not. She was seated two feet from the fire. Ridiculous falsehoods had tumbled from her mouth, and he had returned them. Their lies were steppingstones; it was impossible to go where they wanted without them.

They took the shortest route to the glove shop, following a cottage-lined carriageway in the dark as fumes from nearby cooking fires stung their eyes and noses. When they reached Warwick Lane, Rachel stopped in the middle of the carriageway. "My head hurts," she said, and tried to untie her bonnet, but during the brief journey her ties had tangled and she could not unknot them. She wound up shucking the bonnet from her head, embarrassed, yanking out several hairs in the process. She balled the bonnet up and pitched it in the kennel, the trough that collected rain and waste, on the edge of the street. "That's better," she said daringly, though in the morning she would repent of her recklessness and go back to retrieve it.

Not until they approached the darkened storefront did she reach for Walwyn's hand. It occurred to her then that she trusted him. She was not sure why. He was not her husband. He did not belong to her, nor she to him. It was his hands, she later decided. She trusted his hands. She trusted how they appeared, callused and scrubbed, with ink staining his fingers. She trusted how they touched her.

For Walwyn, that first night was a humiliating experience, yet simultaneously a renewal, as if a layer had been peeled off his body, leaving him stripped, sheared, rebaptized. When they entered the glove shop they did not look over the inventories. She did not show him the ledgers. He did not ask to peruse the shelves. He did not ask to see anything. He saw no hides. He saw no account books. He received no glove-making tutorials. He did notice one sheepskin, recently cleaned, but that was only because he laid Rachel down on it. He slid it onto the floor in the back room, the workroom, next to the sewing desk. It was not a calculated action. It was just—there is a sheepskin, take it off the wall, it is better on the floor—here; and he was gently lowering her onto it, and then lying on his side, absorbing the sight of her, and she on her side as well, looking up. Around them hung freshly dyed gloves, suspended from ribbons Mary had strung across the frame of the door. They hung from the ceiling. "Where is your employer?" he whispered.

"Upstairs," Rachel whispered back, pointing straight up at the gloves, which pointed back at her. He should have asked permission for what happened next, but they had bypassed permissions by this point; they were a mile down the road, past the first fork. He reached out and traced the line of her jaw with two fingers. A scarlet blush sprang up on her like a trail. He followed the slope of her neck, unfastened her bodice; the blush wandered south. Interesting, he thought. Where does this go? He was on a mission now. He was a merchant adventurer. The trail plunged to her navel. It followed the line of his thoughts. He leaned down and kissed it. He kissed each way station along it. He invented way stations where none previously existed. Every dip and curve startled him. As soon as his mouth touched her skin, he knew two things at once: he was going to love this woman, and he was going to be held responsible. For what? He did not ask. He did not know; he did not want to know; he was already old with it. When he reached her mouth, reason left his side, or more to the point, he left reason's side. He abandoned reason at the front door of the glove shop. He left it out in the cold, under the swinging sign. He wanted to try one night in his life without it. Even as he left reason behind, however, he could hear it outside, at the door, calling for him.

For her part, Rachel pitied him. Odd to pity a man as he lowered you to the floor and prepared to climb and bob on top of you, yet there it was. He was like no man she had had before. He was hopelessly vulnerable. She reached out and tickled at his breeches until he lurched and let out a muffled sigh and collapsed onto her, like a tent whose stakes have been pulled up in the storm, leaving her pinned. She pushed him off and rolled back over on her side, though still on the sheepskin. There with him, face to face, eye to eye, hip to hip, hand to hand, she pushed everything aside but him and smiled into his eyes; she swept all questions and doubts out the door; she set her thoughts out for the scavengers.

His hand slid under her skirt. I am going too fast, he thought.

She pulled his hand higher. What took you so long, she thought back.

He entered her, at first gently, apologetically, a cowed dog. He had never done this before, not in this way; he had never been confronted with such a sensual woman. Rachel was not having the same thought. Her thought was: He is too slow! She had to speed things up. She bit down on his finger, hard, and held his gaze. It worked. She had not even taken a breath before he began hardening and stiffening. He turned her onto her back, arching her spine, making her laugh; she did not know why; she could not help it. She lifted her head higher to watch him, and as she took him into her sight her laugh dropped an octave, coming to rest near the base of her stomach. He was thrusting away, would have seemed angry were it not for the pink ears and earnest enthusiasm, which endeared him to her. He held her close; he kept one hand under the back of her neck, his gaze never faltering. She prayed to God that Mary du Gard would not hear them. She did not pray to Christ, for Christ too had been human and so He could not help them this time. Then she was rocking and he was expostulating, her mouth cracking wide, he delivering his point. His eyes squeezed shut; the upper and lower lashes joined. He ran over her as a carriage rattles over a hole in the middle of the street; he came to a rough and clattering halt. "What is it? What's wrong?" Rachel whispered, beaming, and he, over and over, gasping, "Dear Christ."

After, they lay silent. They stayed on their backs, looking up at the ribbons that crossed the workroom, the ribbons that held the gloves. He supposed the two of them might have lain there longer save that Rachel's powers of hearing worked exceptionally well, and she sprang up from the floor a minute later, swearing she could hear Mary trundling about upstairs. She pushed his clothing into his arms and told him to hop to. As Walwyn tried to remember how to pull on his breeches, tried to remember what purpose breeches served, she drove him toward the door, whispering goodbye for now, watching him struggle for his footing. "My legs haven't returned to me," he confessed. He started to say something else, leaning toward her, very silly grin, really, but she rushed him off; she didn't have time; she wanted him to hurry. Mary would have her head, she told him. Walwyn could not have hurried if he'd tried. He could not have hurried if two hundred soldiers were firing cannonballs at his buttocks. His thighs had mutinied on him, his thighs and also his calves. "I am undone," he rejoiced. Yes, yes, she nodded, as am I; now go. Briskly she pushed him out the door, where he shuffled like an arthritic beggar into a lane that had no light except two candles winking from the windows of a travelers' inn one block over. He kept turning around, even after she closed the door.

In the days that had followed, they tried to be careful. They would time things according to her monthly cycle; they would take all the usual precautions.

But then weeks turned into months, and months into a year, until finally three years had grown vines around their love, with hidden cords keeping them safe, and suffocating. They became both comfortable and reckless. If it is possible to be so at one, so intertwined with another person's life, that you hurl yourself onto the rocks daily, then that is what they did.

She had decided to keep him. In her own mind, at least, she was completely in the clear. She was not sure what obligations she had to him. In the absence of a definite list, she would bring him oranges from the market and then eat half of them. She did not bring him by the glove shop. She did not tell Mary about him. Once in a while she would visit the church where Walwyn brought his family. She would sit across the aisle, two rows back. It was a good view, not of the preacher but of Walwyn, who was hard and lean and silver and weather-beaten and everything else that caused strife in a woman. During the sermon she would count the heads of all his children. Afterward, she would despise herself; she would despise him; she would resolve to throw him out. But then he would come to her; he would invent preposterous problems that required him to skip his Leveler meetings and go see her, even as his friends started wondering about him. "You are not writing like you should," John scolded. Walwyn didn't care. The real problem, for him, the problem that vexed him, plagued him daily as he washed his teeth and studied his watery reflection in the basin, was this: How shall I make love to her next? He spent a good deal of time considering the question. He nearly wrote an essay on it. When he saw Rachel he would forget everything he had planned and pull her to his chest, planting his chin on top of her head while they embraced—he was that tall. She didn't mind his being tall, she would say. "What do you mind then?" he asked once. She said she minded going without a window. When she spoke her head moved and his chin moved with it. "All right," he replied. "A window it is." That much, at least, he could promise. She could hear his heart scudding beneath the cage of his chest. The sound made her almost forgive him. They would stay for a few hours at the travelers' inn; the plan was to make love but more often Walwyn wound up listening and Rachel wound up talking. He would lie at her feet in the rented room as she told him about her life. She did not know she had so much to tell until Walwyn started listening. She had more stories than he had time. She astounded herself. She had never been a talker, and look now.

He asked about other men, about former loves or lovers; he wanted to know why she had no husband. She replied that many women had no husbands during a civil war. It was the fault of the times, she said. She adopted her haughtiest expression, lifting her chin high as she informed him of this, though really she was evading the question. Of course there had been other men, here and there in her past, but none of them had wanted to keep her. She saw no reason to speak of them, to bless them with words. And she had not conceived a child in the past, she thought, she reasoned with herself; why should she now? So, as the months went by, she began to take precautions only when she thought of it, when the weather was chilled or the hearth not lit, when the river's edge was caulked with fog.

She told no one about him except Elizabeth, who, on hearing the news, groaned and struck her forehead.

Their second winter together, Rachel and Walwyn had traveled to see Robert, whose company of New Model Army foot soldiers was waiting out the winter in Hounslow.

Visiting a soldier in the field was not unusual—many women did it. Elizabeth had done it for John during his active service as a lieutenant colonel in Parliament's army. She had warmed his stews and mended his boots while John watched her with eyes rebellious and needy. When Walwyn found out Rachel was going to pay her brother a similar visit, he offered to accompany her. She reminded him it was the middle of December and especially bitter that winter. You will be sleeping on frozen ground, she warned. I know, he said with a grin. He was almost giddy about it. The two of them had never spent a full night together.

They set up camp in a dead meadow. They were staying a quarter mile south of Captain Savage's company, adjacent to a small campsite set up by women who were following their soldiering husbands and sons and fathers. In the mornings these women would rise before dawn, emerge yawning from canvas tents, light the fires as they spoke to their younger children in hushed voices, and then haul pots of steaming broth into the men's camp, distributing breakfast. Rachel waited to see her brother until late in the day, when these women were not around. She suspected they would not approve.

At night, she and Walwyn would lie on their backs under blankets that failed to warm, and they would listen as winter drifted over the top of the tent. Hours before sunrise, they would hear three hundred rank-and-file soldiers in the distance, chanting and praying in unison. When the sun broke over the foothills, the troops would practice marching, and after breakfast they would clean their pikes or count their premade cartridges. On blustery days the soldiers' fingers would go numb, and some would fumble their ammunition, breaking the cartridges open, so that they had to separate the gunpowder from the snow. Double shafts of steam blew from their nostrils as they worked. Near the end of the day Rachel would carry soup to her brother. She walked beside Walwyn as she went to find him, their faces shielded by scarves; the cold rendered them both anonymous. They grew lightheaded with imagined freedoms. Walwyn's shoulders loosened; his hand constantly sought hers. She said she could not hold his hand and a pot of soup too. Give me the pot, he said; I will carry it. But she lifted her face up to him as he spoke so he would kiss her.

After they saw Robert, they would return to lie shivering again under the canvas tent. They spoke of birds, and sometimes of Scripture, and sometimes the two conversations would coalesce and turn into one and they would wind up discussing all the places where Scripture spoke of birds, or all the ways birds reminded them of Scripture. Rachel was interested in these things. She told Walwyn that she was not able to read. He replied that he would help her learn, starting tomorrow if she wanted. He had been waiting for her to say something about this so he could offer his help. But she buried her face in the blanket and said she did not want to talk about it. Trying to reassure her, he said she had not missed much. The world is better than a book, he said; most books by my reckoning are useless. Rachel pulled down the blanket just far enough so her green eyes showed. I would like the chance to decide that for myself, she told him — but Walwyn was no longer paying very close attention. His hands were taking over. They were wandering. They burrowed under her petticoat. When she closed her eyes he put his mouth on her eyelids. He rose up, and then again, there it was; there was this thing, this lightness, between them, and even though it was patently absurd — *it* being everything—and the cold was whipping them both to shreds, still they pressed forward, and there followed a great lumbering and heaving, with gasps of stifled laughter back and forth. I don't want to wake those other women, Rachel kept whispering. What other women? Walwyn said. The outer world did not exist for him in that moment. He pulled and plucked at her clothing and then, reaching under her skirts with a vigorous and ingenious blind navigational system, he warmed his hands on her thighs and traveled northward; she cursed his hands for being so cold, though at the same time she was waiting, writhing, unable to see, unable to stomach another second without him taking her, which he did. They kept their eyes on each other in the dark. When she cried out he withdrew and rolled onto his back and pretended to be dead, pretended to be unyielding and aloof, until she slapped and straddled him and he revived, tickling her, she pulling at his wrists to get him to stop, her skirt crowning both their hips, while underneath great acrobatic feats of mischief took place. You are mine, he whispered up at her. No, she said regally; no, you belong to me. You are my property. She was right, at least in that one moment. When he teased her, she said, I insist; and she moved harder and faster; she was strategic about all this. I must tell you something, he breathed; I want to tell you something. Hush, she said, and covered his mouth with her hand. The faint line of her breasts rose and fell beneath her dress. There was no way she was going to take off her clothing in the middle of December. Around them, snow fell. Before he could get out another syllable he was undone; it was all over for him.

After, Rachel was the one to fall asleep. She could not help it, could not fight it, could not begin to resist the urge. She didn't sleep; she slumbered. She had never known such quiet. There was nothing to hear, nothing to say, no one to watch over. There was no walk to sweep, no brother to feed, no gloves to sew, no Mary. Just this.

While she slept, Walwyn lay on his side and watched her. During the quietest part of the night, the snow ceased falling and he thought about the pieces of his life. He did not have to ask what it meant to be an honorable man to know how far short he had fallen. He did not have to ask what it meant to be in debt to understand he owed more than he could afford. The Levelers believed in prompt repayment of all outstanding accounts, however rashly incurred. But what if a person owed multiple debts at once? Did those assumed in the past take precedence over those shouldered most recently? What counted as an imprudent obligation, and what counted as a wise one? He remembered telling Mabbott the newsman that God had given him back his life the night he first saw Rachel. "I didn't know your life had been taken from you," Mabbott had replied as the two men watched the darkening silhouette of St. Sepulchre's, the bell of which tolled for the condemned. Walwyn did not reply.

He recalled the time he and Rachel, passing through St. Paul's churchyard, had come across a group of soldiers forming a circle around what was called a wooden horse, a device used by the army for punishing thieves and blackguards. The horse consisted of a wooden board elevated horizontally six feet aboveground and lashed with leather ties to two standing beams, each split at the base for balance; these held the suspended plank aloft. Two soldiers with muskets tied across their chests were hoisting a shivering boy, no more than thirteen or fourteen, onto the horse, forcing him to straddle it, tying his wrists with rope. The boy wore a soldier's breeches, but his chest was bare; Walwyn could count his ribs from twenty paces. The soldiers tied their muskets to the boy's ankles with a rope that began to twist and snarl, causing the weapons to rotate. The boy tried to stay still, but the guns began revolving of their own accord, cutting a red swath into his ankles. Walwyn remembered how one of the soldiers had flung a bloody hide over the boy's shoulders, which gleamed as pale as Guernsey flowers. "To warm you," the soldier had shouted as a gathering crowd applauded. Another soldier slung a writing board on a necklace of twine over the young thief's head. FOR STEALING AND ENDEAVORING BY FORCE TO STEAL DEER, the sign read.

Turning to Walwyn, Rachel asked how long the boy would stay that way. "Two hours," he replied. "I cannot believe the army continues this practice. It is barbaric and humiliating. This boy is one of their own."

"He stole," she countered. "He took something that wasn't his. This is his punishment."

"But he is starving!"

"He took what he did not own," she insisted.

"You would condemn a man for filling his stomach?" he asked, incredulous.

"Well, no," she replied, conflicting emotions flickering across her face. "No, but I would wonder how hard a man tried to earn his food before he fell to stealing it."

On their last morning at the winter camp in Hounslow, Rachel climbed outside the tent before dawn and Walwyn rose to join her. Together they made their way through the snowy meadow to see her brother one last time; the next day they would return to London. At first Robert seemed embarrassed to receive another visit from his sister. "I thought you left yesterday," he complained as she bent down and inspected his failing boots. "I'm a grown man. I'm twenty. I don't need you mothering me." But he got over the mothering when he saw how the other soldiers were responding to Walwyn. In 1647 the Levelers were still giants; they were still on the winning side. When Walwyn unwrapped his scarf, finally revealing his face, some of the soldiers recognized him, and his name spread in whispers through the camp. They lionized him. Walwyn had quite a time that morning. Clapping the youngest troops on the back, he said hello to everyone; he gave away all his tobacco, all his spare coins. He admired the soldiers' strength of will and he thanked them for their courage. He did not thank them for their sacrifices. These were men who had joined the army because they were destitute, because they needed a day's wage. So when he thanked them, he said *courage*; he did not say *sacrifices*. Meanwhile Rachel restitched her brother's boots and told Robert not to do anything foolish.

Later Walwyn supposed he should not have let all those rank-and-file soldiers see him with a woman who was not his wife. But it had been one of those mornings where the air hung so crystalline and suspended, so still and clear as the lapwings whipped and carved the light, their wings like straight-edged blades, that he could feel no shame. He looked over as Rachel threw her arms around her brother. In that moment her name eluded him. She was winter and spring alike; who was she? Her name was written all over his body. His body was saying her name for him. That night he fell asleep still trying to remember it, still trying to get her name back on his lips. He continued the struggle in sleep. In the morning as they packed their few belongings and prepared to return to London he listened to starlings rooting and vying for whatever green shoots might by some accident of providence have thrust their spindly arms up from the barren soil overnight, and he found the word at last, waiting for him.

Seven

B ARTWAIN HAD A VISIT from the prosecutor. Edmund Griffin was twenty-four years old and silky as a nesting dove. He was the kind of man who kept one eye on his complexion in the mirror and another on a possible Parliament seat.

The younger man traipsed down the Sessions House corridor after Bartwain. "I need your notes, Investigator. The trial starts in three days."

Bartwain pulled a bound book and a stack of papers from his shelf and handed over both items. "These are my depositions. In the papers lies the coroner's report." Reaching behind his desk, he retrieved a wooden box. "Material evidence," he stated flatly. The box included the infant's yellow dress as well as several tiny caps and cloth boots taken by the coroner from Rachel's box made of wainscot. The coroner had removed the child's body by the time Bartwain started his investigation. He was glad he did not have to see it. He hoped someone gave the poor thing a decent burial. Rachel had not been allowed to take possession of it.

"Is everything accounted for?" Griffin asked.

Bartwain had never found whatever thread or string had caused the blue bruising, but the prosecutor would not need that item to make his case. "The coroner's report and witness testimonials should be enough," he said.

The younger man nodded cheerfully. "This case is open and shut."

The Baptist William Kiffin had used the same phrase. Bartwain fought off a surge of irritation. "Be careful. You are new to these situations. They have a way of becoming complicated."

"They are not complicated. The law is plain and simple. The law asks only if she hid the bastard's death and if the child was hers. You are the one who taught me that. Did Rachel Lockyer conceal its death?"

"Yes."

"Was the child hers?"

"Yes. Though she has not come right out and said exactly what happened."

"What she did or didn't say doesn't matter now. This case is effectively closed, wouldn't you agree, Investigator? It is a fait accompli. I appreciate all of your labors on my behalf. You have worked industriously."

Bartwain did not care for his tone.

"I'll take the evidence box with me," the prosecutor went on. "If nothing else, it will be good for giving the jury a show. Everyone likes a good show." He snatched the infant's yellow dress out of the box and laid it against his slender chest, pretending to wear it. He twirled around in a circle.

Bartwain did not like young counselors. He did not like young men, period. When he regarded them — Such white teeth! Such arrogance! — he remembered all the promotions for which he had been passed over.

"Mr. Griffin," he said brusquely. "I am well aware what the parameters are in this case. I have devoted my professional life to the law and to its upholding. I have investigated over twenty-five bastard cases during my thirty years as investigator. And I am reminding you to be careful."

"Yes, yes, of course. I'll take your notes and review them. You're certain she didn't tell you anything useful?"

"She said that she had not yet resolved what happened."

Griffin snorted. "Then it is up to me to resolve it for her—and for the jury."

"I'm not sure it's that simple." What was he saying? It *was* that simple. But Bartwain was in a terrible mood and needed to dispel it. "The statute against bastard murder does allow for one possible escape," he told the prosecutor. "Surely you know this?"

Griffin's face remained blank. You are green, Bartwain thought. Green and stupid. The investigator reached for his statute book and flipped through the pages until he landed on the relevant section of the 1624 Act to Prevent the Destroying and Murdering of Bastard Children. "Here it is. Listen." He cleared his throat. "'If any Women . . . be delivered of any Issue of her body, Male or Female, which being born alive, should by the Laws of this Realm be a bastard, and that she endeavor privately either by drowning or secret burying thereof, or any other way, either by her self or the procuring of others, so to conceal the death thereof, as that it may not come to light, whether it were born alive or not, but be concealed, In every such case, the said Mother so offending shall suffer Death, as in case of murder—'"

"I know all this."

"Hold on. I'm getting there." Why were the young such imbeciles? "'Except such Mother can make proof by one Witness at the least, that the Child (whose death by her so intended to be concealed) was born dead.' There. Now you see what I am getting at?"

Griffin scratched his head.

"The defendant needs one witness, one *credible* witness, to come forward and persuade the jury that she—Rachel Lockyer—gave birth in the presence of another person. She needs someone to swear that the child came out of the womb stillborn."

"I see no cause for concern."

"I do," Bartwain told him. "I would not put it past Elizabeth Lilburne."

"If Mrs. Lilburne didn't say anything of that nature in her interview with you, what makes you think she would try it in a court of law?"

"Mrs. Lilburne was too busy dodging my questions to be sufficiently cunning in her interview. By the time the trial starts she might be thinking more clearly."

"Then I won't call her to the stand."

"You don't have to call her to the stand," Bartwain said with grim satisfaction. "She can call herself to the stand. Witnesses with relevant information can volunteer their testimony."

Griffin shrugged. "She'll be intimidated up there. She'll faint in front of all those spectators."

"You have not met Elizabeth Lilburne."

"I tell you I'm not concerned. Whatever that woman tries to do, whatever *either* woman tries to do, will be without a counselor's help." The prosecutor reminded Bartwain that the Council of State did not permit defendants to bring legal representation into the courtroom. Rachel was going to have to defend herself.

You have never eaten too much boiled crab or undercooked custard in your life, Bartwain thought. You have never been outwitted in your kitchen by a mouse. You have no idea about the world. "Don't underestimate your opponent," he said. "You recall Freeborn John Lilburne's recent achievement in the courtroom at Guildhall?"

"Yes. He defended himself against charges of treason and won a full acquittal."

"Exactly. And his wife doesn't gripe and carry on like he does. If I were you I would be careful." It was the first time Thomas Bartwain had spoken highly of any woman besides his wife.

Griffin stepped into the sunlit street. "I appreciate your help, Investigator," he called over his shoulder. "I mean, think of it: you're more than twice my age but still taking on cases. You're an inspiration."

Bartwain delivered a black cloud of a look.

The investigator returned home to a wife who had remembered her earlier interest in Rachel's case — or, more precisely, her earlier interest in her husband's *handling* of the case. He did not feel like answering her latest questions, so he told her to go ahead and read his transcript notes if she was that interested. She surprised him by doing so. Afterward, padding into the kitchen, her white hair frizzing out of her nightcap, Mathilda proceeded to stand and wave the court papers over him as Bartwain sat on the kitchen floor and repaired one of his mousetraps.

"You have no idea what to do with this woman," she declared.

"I have ideas aplenty," he retorted. "But what I think doesn't count anymore. My part is over, except for my final report. The rest is up to the jury."

She folded her arms and fixed him with a glare.

"What?" He could not stand it when she stared him down that way.

"You are making a mockery of the law."

This was too much. "I do not mock the law," he shouted, rising to his feet one stiff leg at a time, abandoning his mousetrap. "I follow every jot and tittle!"

"But that is your problem. You never bother to check the jots and tittles. You never ask if they still make sense."

"And what do *you* know?" he growled, his nose reddening. "I'll tell you, Mrs. Bartwain, if you get sidetracked into asking such questions, you will lose your bearings. Trust me; I have learned this from experience. The law protects us from the insidious and irrational aspects of human nature by asking us to determine only *if* the suspect in question committed the hideous deed. To ask *why* she did it, to wonder about her life, to circumvent the parameters of law by probing whatever secret and inward instincts lie beneath each human surface, is to show pity where none has been merited; it is to place a higher value on the perpetrator's life than on the victim's!"

"You're frightened, aren't you?" Mathilda said, not unkindly. "You're frightened and you're tired."

Then she wheeled around and marched back up to her bedchamber, leaving Bartwain red-nosed and wordless.

Eight

R ACHEL HAD DISCOVERED she was with child on the
morning of her brother's execution. She was standing in
a sea green dress at the edge of a crowd when the revelation came. She was watching the soldiers circling, the way they
breathed and blew like eager little gods, creating clouds that min-
gled with the mist and clung to the churchyard grounds, the tents
of Captain Savage's company snapping their colors in the distance.
She was listening to six musketeers begging Robert Lockyer to
wear a blindfold because they did not want to look their friend
in the eye when they shot him. She was studying Robert, who
looked even younger than he had the previous winter; she could
see his shoulders shivering. She stood on the flattened grass, missing Walwyn, waiting; all these things were spinning around her,
and suddenly, there it was. Rachel knew.

Conception is a strange word. One conceives in different ways.
An idea can be conceived. So can a plan for a cathedral. A philosophy student conceives a way through a logic problem. A spider
conceives a web. Conceiving is creation, but before it is creation it
is mischief. And before it is mischief it is faith.

For Rachel the discovery had taken place in St. Paul's churchyard, Elizabeth holding her up on one side, Mary bracing her on
the other. It was late spring, nearly four weeks past Easter, and she

had not seen her brother in months. Two days before, a mutiny had broken out among the lower ranks of Robert's company, and a dozen soldiers, Robert among them, had snatched their captain's flag and holed up in an abandoned church, refusing to return the colors until they received their past-due wages. Our families are starving, they had said; give us what we are owed. Their superiors replied: You will get what you are owed when you are dead. Robert lost his temper and started shouting. Then General Oliver Cromwell had shown up, "breathing forth nothing but death to them all," as John Lilburne later wrote, and quelled the skirmish. He let most of the mutinying troops go with a warning, but he kept Robert back. He wanted to teach his men a lesson. This is the ringleader, he said; this one supports the Levelers' Agreement of the Free People of England. Cromwell did not know that the Levelers had never paid any attention to Robert. Cromwell did not know that Robert never led anything in his life except his sister by the elbow, and even then he was not too successful.

As Rachel watched the musketeers forming a reluctant line in the churchyard, she happened to glance down at her abdomen, and the universe shifted. Either that, or her place in the universe shifted. It was nothing she saw or physically felt. It bore no relation to the senses. She simply knew. She talked to God. She said: God, is this what is happening now? And God said, *Yes.* So she asked what God wanted. She said: There is no place for this kind of gift, if that is what You are giving. And God said, *Find one.* It was her mother's God talking to her.

She sagged and buckled.

"Rachel," Elizabeth whispered urgently through the spitting mist, through the squall of the gathering throng. "Let us take you home."

She pushed herself up. No. I will stay with my brother. She said it without saying it. She gripped Elizabeth's hot hand and the words traveled that way instead, through their fingers. Elizabeth always said the real truths were the simple ones; the real truths consisted of deeds, not words. So Rachel pressed her friend's hand

and Elizabeth crushed hers back and they talked to each other that way. And when Mary, who did not speak their language, tried to pull them out of the crowd, back toward Warwick Lane and the safety of the glove shop, Elizabeth snarled, "Let her be; she does not want to go." And Mary shook her head and was angry with both of them.

Five times that morning the musketeers asked Robert to wear a blindfold, and five times Robert declined. First he said he wanted to see his executioners with his own eyes. Then he declared his cause was just and he need not be ashamed. The third time they asked, he said he welcomed death and did not fear its face; the fourth, that he could not believe so small a thing as demanding an honest wage should give the army occasion to take his life. He was doing the Levelers proud. The last time they asked, he said nothing, only gave the sign to fire, raising two scrawny arms over his head and throwing his gaze skyward, so that the final sight to greet his eyes was the space where the cathedral used to have a spire before lightning had razed it. In the same moment Rachel lowered her head into Elizabeth's neck, and six muskets sputtered and roared. She kept herself still and she counted backward from fifteen, which was how long Walwyn once told her it took God to welcome by name any innocent who had suffered. She remembered asking why it took fifteen seconds, why God could not name the soul immediately. And he had grazed her cheek with his finger and said, Because there is always a line of souls waiting.

The soldiers laid Robert's body on the grass. Elizabeth and Mary let go of Rachel's arms, and she pushed through the throng to say goodbye to him. She sank to her hands and knees in front of him. But that was not enough; that was not close enough. She laid herself on top of him. She blanketed Robert with her body. She rested her forehead against his forehead and stared into his open eyes; she whispered in his ear as the soil around his head went dark and wet. I told you not to do anything foolish, she cried. I told you. Look what has happened. You said you did not need a mother and now look. She begged him not to go. Do not leave me, she said; don't you dare leave me alone with my life. Walwyn is locked up in the Tower. I cannot lose you and him both.

Then Elizabeth was grasping her, rocking and pulling her off Robert's body. As the two women struggled to their feet they came upon a circle of soldiers sucking on long pipes, and Rachel looked for the man with the finest uniform. When she found him she told him she wanted her brother's body. "Let me have it," she pleaded, plucking at his felted sleeve, "so I may give him a good burial." The colonel shook with suppressed laughter. He said he could not give her anything—the Levelers had commandeered the corpse. They are taking it away, he told her. It is theirs; they have bargained for it.

"For what?" Elizabeth interjected. "I know the Levelers. They would do no such thing."

"They would," the colonel replied. "It is useful to them. They specialize in the art of agitation. They are taking Robert for their symbol, their hero. They are going to turn his death into a martyrdom."

Elizabeth, furious: "On whose orders?"

"John Lilburne's," another soldier said. "He sent a message from the Tower."

Elizabeth turned a mottled red.

Rachel exploded. "How dare you use a young man's death for political gain!" she shouted at the colonel, though she should have been shouting at John Lilburne.

The soldiers howled. They said some people were more valuable in death than in life, and Robert was one of them. "He mutinied against his captain," one said. "He forgot his place. We have no use for him in a professionally trained force. But the Levelers will make him live forever. The Levelers would immortalize a half-wit if it suited their purpose. They would turn a bastard into the Christ child if they could."

With those words Rachel remembered her discovery, and her knees buckled again.

Elizabeth intervened. "Please forgive her, sir, she is struck dumb with grief and has no husband to help her," she implored, pulling

82

Rachel back to her feet and in the same moment tugging loose the ties under her friend's bonnet so she could breathe. The soldiers let them leave. As the women slipped out of the churchyard, Mary trailing behind, one of the soldiers noticed that the dark-haired one, the one with the brother, had green eyes that could clear right through a man; she had eyes, he said, that bruised.

The next morning Rachel rose before dawn to the sound of trees. A cold April wind was tearing through the poplars, and moonlight revealed a carriageway slick with fallen flowers. Some of the petals had escaped into the ditches and kennels that lined either side of Warwick Lane. There, swirling in circles, they joined the rainwater and detritus of the city on a slow southward journey that would end where it always did, in the waiting Thames.

Rachel washed her face and neck in the basin she and Mary shared. She returned the bowl to the shelf that sat between their upstairs sleeping quarters, tied her hat tight to keep the wind from snatching it, and slid downstairs, passing through the darkened shop and slipping out the door before Mary could call for her. She bent her body against the wind. She was in the dark, marching. She bit the inside of her cheek to keep from noticing the cold. She tried not to look down at her abdomen, tried not to think about the previous day's revelation. This did not work.

A few weeks before, armed officers in the service of the new Puritan government had dragged William Walwyn from his bed in Moorfields in the middle of the night. They pulled a screaming Richard out of his father's arms and passed the boy over to Anne, who took him without a word, her eyes never leaving her husband. "What have you done this time?" was what she said to him. The soldiers hauled Walwyn off to the Tower to await charges of treasonous writing, though the pamphlet in question was John's. Rachel learned of the arrest a few days later from Elizabeth, whose husband was also taken. Elizabeth's left eyebrow rose very high as she delivered the news. "It is best if you do not try to contact any of them," she told Rachel, by which she meant that only wives were supposed to visit.

The funeral procession had its starting point near the vacant stalls at the western end of the Smithfield market. Behind the stalls Rachel could see the slaughterhouse and, beyond that, a shadowy woods with elm and beech trees still thin and white from winter. For a moment she considered escaping the morning's events by hiding in the quiet of those elms. She did not want a processional. But Robert had not died privately, so he was not going to be buried privately either. She guessed he would have been proud. It had taken three years, but the Levelers had finally adopted him.

First ten, then twenty, then thirty figures gathered in the semidarkness around a horse-drawn cart that carried Robert's body. Rachel saw Katherine Chidley, the haberdasher. She saw Gilbert Mabbott, the newsman, who arrived as the processional was starting. Mabbott waved when he saw her coming; he joined her for the first half mile. She was grateful to him. She asked if he had any news from the Levelers in the Tower. She was referring to Walwyn, though she did not say his name. She was wondering how she was going tell Walwyn she was with child. "They are all right," Mabbott said, "but angry." He was referring to Walwyn too. The newsman stayed by Rachel's side until someone told them women were supposed to be at the rear of the processional, and Rachel dropped back, disappearing before Mabbott could explain that she was the dead man's sister. The leaders of the march did not recognize her. Robert belonged to them now.

She saw William Kiffin, her former pastor, scraping dung off his boots at the side of the carriageway. She hid her face in her scarf and waited for him to pass.

Overnight the wind had swept away all clouds. When the sun broke over the tops of the vendors' stalls it peeled the shadows off the mourners' faces. The processional began coiling, a long leviathan, heading south to Newgate Street, then east toward Cheapside, gathering momentum and onlookers as six trumpeters sounded the call up front. Many in the crowd wore ribbons and scarves of the same sea green color as Rachel's dress. To make the color, they dipped a piece of cloth in blue dye taken from the woad plant, and then they dipped the same cloth in a solution of alum and urine, because it cost nothing. The onlookers might not know Robert, but they knew the Leveler color; they knew what the color represented. They emptied out of their flats and boarding-house rooms and thatched-roof houses and joined the funeral walk. They saw the coffin draped in the hue of the ocean and they understood.

From Walwyn Rachel had learned that the sea green of the Levelers stood for all those places in Scripture where the poor, the meek, the hungry, and the desolate are said to be wider and vaster than all the waters in the ocean. He had explained this to her amid a crushing din of apprentices and agitators who had gathered, stamping and singing, around John's table at the Whalebone, cups of wine and ale lifted high and spilling as John and Overton shouted out their latest victories, called for freemen to be given the vote, demanded just wages for soldiers, denounced passive obedience, and ridiculed the divine right of kings. This was back when the Levelers still thought they were winning. As the men sang and whooped, Walwyn leaned over to her table and murmured nonsensical things; her ears burned, and she studied his mouth as he delivered the words. Sometimes she could not even hear what he said, but she watched his lips in earnest. The others around them cheered and chattered. All the while Rachel waited for the wry grin that would creep up on him unnoticed, and the red curve of his lips, almost like a girl's; she waited for the those lips to touch the rim of his cup; she wanted to watch him swallow. Her ears would sizzle; her ears would suggest she sat too close to the fire. Near the end of that evening she asked him if Scripture ever said that the poor being so vast in number was something to be corrected. She wanted to know if Scripture said the poor should be made rich. Walwyn looked at her and his brown eyes softened. He said he supposed the writers of Scripture didn't always know what they meant. They wanted the poor to be raised high, to defend themselves; but they also thought only the meek would inherit the earth. So there is a problem, Rachel had said. Yes, Walwyn had replied, his smile broadening; yes, there is a problem. And though the other Levelers roared and drank and crashed all over them, she and Walwyn did not notice.

After the funeral marchers passed Newgate Street, they began the long climb north toward Moorfields. The processional would finish up in New Churchyard with a hastily dug grave, a reading of Scripture, and impassioned political speeches. By the end of the day, Freeborn John would be writing a martyrdom pamphlet in Robert's honor from the Tower. As Rachel walked, she could see flung out before her a great expanse of humankind, two thousand now or more, a tide of green streaming through the carriageway, causing more doors and shutters to open. Onlookers pointed and waved from their second- and third-floor windows. These were candle makers and butchers and salt-and-pepper grinders and tanners and tailors and match vendors, men and women who toiled and labored for their living, all marching. Children thrust their heads out of boarding-house doors to marvel at the sea of people and to test their elders with questions. *Who is it? Who is the man that has died?* And the answer, thrown up from the swell of bodies, again and again, with a different voice each time, *A martyr of the people.* And though Rachel did not want her brother's death used for political gain, her heart could not help but pound harder and faster as they neared the end of the march. When they passed the Roman wall and crossed into the rolling farms of Moorfields, the mourners had grown to three thousand strong, their scarves and ribbons flapping against the fields, flashing like iridescent scales on a sea snake as it passes through shallow water. In that moment she felt herself to be almost a new woman, and London almost a new city.

In the days that had followed, Rachel began talking to the child.

First silently, cautiously, in her head, while she was sewing a glove. She would loop a stitch and drop it, her hand falling slack. Then Mary would stare crossly at her until she returned to her task. She wondered how long it would take Mary to cast her out once she learned what her assistant was hiding.

86

Next she started speaking to the child out loud. She wanted to see how she sounded as a mother, even though at the time she was only a few months along. She experimented while sweeping the walk. She was trying not to worry about the future. Whenever the future invaded her thoughts, she despaired. Staying in the day was not too encouraging either, but at least it did not send her into the abyss; at least it did not pitch her into the pit like the future did. She asked the child its name; of course it didn't answer. She asked again, pushing her broom harder. If she listened hard enough, she could pretend she heard it gabbling. She told the child who she was. "I am Rachel Lockyer, glovemaker," she announced, then glanced around, expecting Mary to laugh at her. But Mary was not outside.

She told the child about the world. She talked about the turtles. She talked about owls. Recently Rachel had noticed a pair of screech owls nesting near the Smithfield market. They called one way when they were mating and another way when they were hunting moles. She mimicked their sounds for the child's benefit. She explained the difference between calfskin and sheepskin in the design and manufacture of gloves. She told the child she was too old to be a mother. She did not give her exact age, but that was because she had lost count. She said she was born and reared in London and was sick to death of war and all it had wreaked on those she loved. She explained the war to the child. She said the reason no one understood the war was that it had two parts. The first part had been between the king and the army, and the army had won. The second part was between the army and the people, and the people were losing. Between parts one and two, the Levelers had changed sides. So while they'd been on the winning side in the war against the king, they were now on the losing side in the war against the army.

She talked about her brother.

She did not mention Walwyn, not at first. She had no idea what to say about him; she suspected the child would judge her. But when she whispered Walwyn's name, she thought she could hear the child burbling with laughter. And as she swept she listened to the tinkling sounds of distant bells coming in her direction, sounds that coursed up and down her spine, and the laughter of the child joined with the laughter of the bells and left her weak-kneed with joy. It was the first time since Walwyn had gone to the Tower that Rachel did not feel alone. And even when the sound of the bells became transformed into the ringing of the scavengers' carts as they lurched down the street in her direction, still she felt no fear. She glanced up at the rusted sign hanging over Du Gard Gloves, a large glove with a gold-trimmed cuff, and she smiled; the child comforted her.

When thoughts of the future returned, she fought them off as best she could. She took up arms against the future. Her weapons were thread and needle. She began sewing baby clothes. They were so small — woolly hats and boots no larger than three fingers. She asked the child what color it wanted and the child said, *Not green*. So she sewed in yellow. She made a dress in yellow brocade from a row of fabric at the bottom of Mary's window covering. She hoped Mary would not notice the missing piece. Again she asked the child its name; again it did not answer. But at night it would squeal with giggles that she could feel cascading up and down her body. She shook with its sound. She longed to write it down, to describe it, to send the sound to Walwyn in a letter. She found some old news pamphlets, and several times she tried to trace the alphabet from them. I can do this, she said to herself. This is not beyond me. But then Mary would come in to remind Rachel a customer was waiting.

During the same weeks, word reached London that the few Levelers still active in the Parliamentary army had managed to blunder another uprising. Cromwell had begun disbanding large sectors of his winning troops without troubling to pay their arrears, and a heavy-drinking corporal and Leveler sympathizer named Will Thompson grew enraged with this decision. Thompson organized several hundred soldiers to protest the policies of the general for whom they had fought. This sort of thing went on all the time now that England had no sovereign; this was what victory looked like. Thompson and his men marched forward, confident God was on the side of the poor; they were met, slaughtered, and left as carrion by another company in Cromwell's army. Rachel heard the news from Elizabeth. Thompson and his ringleaders were executed in front of their men in a churchyard. The following night, Cromwell received an honorary degree from Oxford; two days later, he went bowling on the green at Magdalene College. Rachel wondered if Will Thompson had refused to wear a blindfold.

Several days after that, Mary mentioned in a brisk voice that she had seen Rachel making a dress out of a curtain. "Whose are those tiny clothes and why are you sewing them?" she demanded. Rachel said Mary should not be spying. Mary blushed but held her ground. Rachel listened, astonished, as a lie whistled out of her own mouth. She told Mary these were clothes for her expectant sister who lived in Essex. Rachel had no sister in Essex, but Mary did not know this. The two women did not divulge biographical details. They shared only the essentials. Rachel knew the precise dampness of air that caused Mary's thumb joints to ache and what was required to ease them. Mary knew Rachel could not sleep when the moon was waxing. Rachel knew Mary attended the Church of the Refuge on Threadneedle Street, where the Huguenot pastor preached to his immigrant congregation that the higher powers of this world were being thrown down. Thrown where exactly, he never specified. He explained that Christ would be returning any day now, and the faithful must be careful lest they miss Him. And Rachel knew Mary was disappointed, for though she was very careful, Christ had not returned yet.

That night she began stuffing the corner of her shawl into the keyhole of her bedroom door so Mary could not peek through it. When she slept, she dreamed her brother called her a coward.

She tried to heed Elizabeth's caution against contacting Walwyn. She understood it was not allowed; a woman in her position was not supposed to declare herself, to make public her situation. But she was growing angry. The future was continuing to intrude. It kept barging into her sleeping quarters at night, vexing her to no end; to make matters worse, dread had started sliding under the door with it. So, disregarding Elizabeth's advice, she went ahead and tried to send Walwyn a message. Doing so required the help of Thom, the messenger boy who huddled in the alley behind Du Gard Gloves and who sometimes slept in the storeroom without Mary's knowledge. Rachel did not disclose her condition to the boy; she suspected he would gossip. "Tell Mr. Walwyn I am in need of aid for myself and for Fifteen" was all she said. "And hurry." She knew Walwyn's wife referred to her children by numbers; she knew how many children the Walwyn household had. She prayed Walwyn would grasp what she meant; she prayed he would put fourteen and one together.

Thom made his way to the Tower, where Walwyn had remained with John, Overton, and Prince since the publication of John's *Second Part of England's New Chains Discovered*, which criticized the new government for being too much like the old government. Walwyn continued to deny any involvement in the pamphlet's production. I am not the author, he said over and over to anyone who would listen; I am out of the Leveling business. At the same time, Walwyn *was* the author because he was John's teacher; John's wardrobe of ideas consisted almost entirely of hand-me-downs from Walwyn.

When a week passed with no word from Thom, a line appeared between Rachel's eyebrows that did not soften when she slept. I will be whipped, she thought. Once I have this child, I will be whipped and cast into prison if I refuse to name the father. And if I do name the father, Walwyn's wife and fourteen children will be publicly disgraced and humiliated. Their shame will be even worse than mine, because they are not expecting it.

In the mornings, ravenous and nauseated, she would pace from the hearth to the cupboard as she hunted for something to eat. From the doorway Mary would watch this performance, unimpressed. "If you spent as much time stitching gloves as circling the kitchen, we would be caught up on our orders," she said. Rachel told Mary to mind her own business, which was not entirely fair. But she felt herself to be falling into some kind of a well or shaft, stony and bottomless, without a rope.

Several times she tried to tell Elizabeth she was with child. Whenever she started to speak, however, her friend interrupted. It turned out Elizabeth had a good deal to say now that her husband was in the Tower. Rachel could not squeeze in a word, could not find the right moment to tell her. Also, she was nervous; she feared how Elizabeth might react. Though she displayed little interest in the moral shortcomings of others, Elizabeth never hesitated to pass judgment on people she viewed as careless. In Elizabeth's opinion, there was only one real sin, and that was irresponsibility.

From Elizabeth, Rachel learned that several hundred matrons sympathetic to the Levelers had besieged Parliament with a petition for the four Levelers' release from the Tower. The officers had turned them away, told them to go home and wash their dishes: the law took no notice of married women. "You are your husbands' property," they said, and pushed them off the premises. The Levelers remained imprisoned. This fact did not seem to discourage Elizabeth.

"We will organize another petition," she said one evening to Rachel. "We will put one thousand women's signatures to it this time. Here—would you take him?" After handing her infant son to Rachel, who was sitting at the table, she opened the front door to air out her smoke-filled kitchen. The Lilburnes rented a three-room, three-floor lodging in seamy Southwark, south of the Thames and close to the Bishop's stews, those brothels the church used to regulate. "If there is one thing the Levelers still have," Elizabeth went on, returning to the table and beginning to chop onions, "it is our loyalty to family and our reputation as honest householders. The Council of State will not be able to slander *us*. They will not be able to ignore an army of God-fearing wives and matrons."

"Not all of us are wives and matrons," Rachel reminded her.

Elizabeth leaned into her knife. "What's the matter? Have you gone missing your good humor today?"

Rachel started to speak, started to confess her situation, but again faltered. Her eyes had to say it for her.

"Why, what in the world is the matter?" Elizabeth spoke over the glad squeals of her middle child, two-year-old Tower, named for all the times his father had spent in prison. The boy sang and warbled in his pen in the corner; he was macerating a bowl of cherries with his fists.

Rachel's eyes said: I am in dire straits.

Elizabeth's eyes grew large.

But then Tower knocked his bowl upside down, and pits and purple juice flew everywhere. He began bawling. Elizabeth's newborn, a tiny boy as lumpy and downy as a ripe peach, added his opinion from Rachel's lap. Elizabeth's eyes pulled reluctantly from Rachel to her sons. As she went over to Tower's pen, she called out distractedly, "Aren't you the lucky one, not having all these suckling mouths to run around feeding!"

Rachel's face burned as if the wind had cut her. Elizabeth had not understood what she was trying to tell her. She helped clean up the spilled cherries, and she rocked the youngest one until he quieted. Later she tried to return to the conversation, but the shadows under her friend's eyes suggested the moment had passed. "I'm worn to the bone," Elizabeth said.

Nine

THOMAS BARTWAIN WAS paying a visit to Newgate.
Years had passed since his last time inside this prison.
Normally his direct involvement with a suspect ended
once he had written and signed the order of indictment. His
business belonged in the early stages, he reminded himself;
his business lay in determining if a case should go forward. Yet
here he was, two nights before Rachel's trial, rattling the gates
of his least favorite place in London, announcing his creden-
tials, demanding to be let in. The courtyard stank of gutted fish.

"I will not go to the women's ward," he said to the warden, who
came out to greet him. "Bring her down here, to meet me in the
open. I will not set foot inside that building. It's not safe."

"It's safer for you than for her," the warden returned, though
he did what Bartwain asked. A guard escorted Rachel downstairs
into the courtyard.

When she saw who her visitor was, Rachel pulled her shawl
around her shoulders.

"You're sick," Bartwain said gruffly. "Your eyes are weak and
congested." He shifted his weight—he was trying to stay off his
gouty foot. He had no clear idea what he was doing there, he realized.

"What are you doing here?" Rachel asked.

Maybe it was Griffin's fault. The prosecutor had irritated Bartwain beyond measure, reminding him of all the officers of the court and civil servants Bartwain had known who treated the law as a public means to a private end. "The law is not the means," Bartwain had grumbled to his wife the day before. "The law is itself the end. The law is beautiful; the law is order. If we have not law, we have nothing. We descend to anarchy and noise, and one man will kill another for a roasted hen."

"I'm roasting a hen now," his wife had commented.

"How are you bearing up?" Bartwain said now to Rachel.

She answered with silence, clutching her shawl tight.

She thinks I make this kind of visit for everyone, he fumed. She has no idea how unusual this is, how I am extending myself beyond the bounds of ordinary duty.

"My wife—" he started.

Last night Mathilda had questioned him yet again regarding his handling of the case. "You never gave her a chance," she said. "You never listened to her side."

"I listened for two hours," he'd defended himself. "She would not tell me her side. I pulled her into my chambers and said, Talk; she refused to."

Mathilda gave him the look she usually reserved for children. "Maybe you did not ask her the right questions," she said, and poked him in the belly, which he hated because it tickled. "Make it right, Thomas. Make it right or you are not the man I married."

"But the law does not want me to do anything else. In the law's eyes I have completed my assignment."

"So?" She poked him a second time. "Have you read your Scripture?"

Not this again, he had thought.

"Read the commandment," she urged, her cheeks dimpling as she sought to make her point. "Go back and read the greatest commandment. Then tell me your law is not lacking something."

"The greatest commandment has nothing to do with this case.

94

The greatest commandment is to love the Lord thy God with all thy heart, mind, et cetera."

"I don't mean that one. I mean the *other* one. The one that comes after."

"That's not the greatest commandment. That's the second commandment," he said churlishly.

"They cannot be separated," Mathilda argued. Then she added, loud enough that the mice hiding in the cupboards could hear: "Thomas Bartwain, love thy neighbor."

The investigator pulled himself back to the present as he realized Rachel was speaking to him. "Why are you here?" she asked again.

"My wife sent me," he admitted. "She sent me to see how you are bearing up."

"But you are the one who put me here."

"Yes."

"So now you are returning to see the results of your handiwork? Are you impressed with yourself? Do I look sufficiently beaten?"

"That's not what I—"

"You would like for me to die, wouldn't you?"

"I do not want anyone to die. I simply fulfill my duty."

"And what is that?" she burst out. "What is that word, *duty*, Investigator? Tell me that. Tell me how you do it. Maybe you learn it in books. For myself, I have had so many hands and fingers clawing at me my whole life long, telling me this and that and the other is my duty, telling me fifteen duties in a row and then reminding me nothing I do matters because God has already made up His mind about me, because God has already decided one way or another, that I can hardly see what I am obliged to do or not do in this life; I can hardly lay all my duties on the table!" It was her longest speech to him.

"Are you ready for your trial?" he said quietly. "You know you will have no counselor to help you."

"No, sir!" she shouted. "No, sir, I am not."

"You are better than this, Rachel Lockyer," he said, surprised by his own words. Since when had his wife started talking through him?

"I was once," Rachel replied tersely. Then she called for the warden and told him she wanted to go back to the women's ward. She left Bartwain standing by himself in the courtyard, listening to the groan of the windmill.

By ten o'clock that night the third floor of the prison was quiet except for the shuddering sobs of one young woman who had arrived a few hours earlier. The other inmates had been talking about her. This was a country girl, they said, who went mad after losing her infant, one her stepfather had sired. She stabbed the man with a knife, after which she tried to steal his silver. Her stepfather survived the assault and recovered his silver, for his wife's daughter had poor aim and had opened up his shinbone rather than his stomach. He sent for the authorities and washed his hands of her, thereby ruining the same girl twice.

When an hour had passed and the girl was still hiccupping, Rachel left her pallet and crept over to her. She could hear the guards playing a drinking game outside in the corridor. The newcomer was lying thin and flat under a dirty shawl. There was little Rachel could do. Should she say something? She had no words of comfort. So she sat beside her. She thought about that story in the book of Daniel, about the den of lions and how God shut the lions' mouths. She supposed God did that so Daniel would not be harmed. But Rachel was less concerned about Daniel than she was about the lions. Daniel made his way out and became a famous prophet. Of course he did. But what about the lions? What was it like for them, running headlong into God like that? He sewed their mouths shut, so their roar had no sound.

The girl poked her head out. "What's your name?" Her thinning hair revealed a patchy scalp. She was possibly thirteen.

"Rachel."

"Mine's Eve." She sat up, cross-legged. The two of them looked at each other in the shadows from the wall burners. Each could barely make the other out.

Eve told Rachel she came from farms where they bred horses for a living.

"Where do you get the horses?" Rachel asked.

"We take them from the moors; we take them wild and we break them." Then she asked if Rachel had ever seen a Wiltshire mare caught and brought to the farms for breeding. When Rachel said no, the girl's eyes seemed to darken. She said once a man had ridden a mare long enough, the mare would accept things as they were during the day.

Rachel looked up to see two night watchmen patrolling, clicking their sticks.

But at night, Eve went on, when the other horses were sleeping, the mare would rise up on two legs and scream. She had heard the sound, she said. It would scream for an hour.

Then Eve buried her face in her shawl, which was crusty with dried stains, and Rachel guessed this was the covering in which she had wrapped her newborn before she lost it. Swiftly she drew the girl to her. "You will tear me from myself, then," Eve cried out, to no one, to the walls. But her words came too loud, and the next minute the watchmen came. They took Eve away; they pulled her from Rachel's arms. They took her to ease their boredom. They were not well paid, these guards; they were not in line for raises. So they cut their losses with girls. Being young and of the rural sort, Eve did not have money to fend them off. Snarling, Rachel tore into them, using her teeth and the rusted hinges of her wrist irons; she fought to drive them off. When that did not work she lifted her own skirts and offered herself as a distraction. Through it all Eve kept squalling. The guards muzzled her with a rag another woman had used to stanch the monthlies. They spat on her balding head and shoved her to the floor. Then they dragged her by the arms and hair outside the ward and into the passageway, behind the black storage barrels. When they finished with Eve they came back for Rachel, who by that time had found a wooden torch with a jagged three-inch splinter on the end of it; she lit it and shook it at them, shaking uncontrollably. They laughed and let her be; they tossed Eve in a heap at her feet.

Rachel did what she could. She dabbed the swellings and cuts and swaddled the girl in her shawl. She talked about everything; she talked nonsense. She counted to fifteen and back. She stroked the girl's hair. And when Eve started hemorrhaging, she tried to stanch the bleeding. But Eve was not even a week out of childbirth. Her body was not well healed. Her womb gushed, angry and sobbing; her womb emptied itself all over the floor. She bled continuously, for an hour. There was nothing Rachel could do.

She lay beside the girl's body until dawn.

Rachel's mother was the first person Elizabeth Lilburne had written to when she learned of her friend's arrest. In the letter, she asked Martha Lockyer to come to London and testify before the jury on behalf of Rachel's good character. Martha Lockyer had not responded. Her silence enraged Elizabeth but did not surprise Rachel, who understood her mother did not like London.

The last time she had seen her mother, Rachel was five months pregnant and frantic. The visit did not go well. Half a week's wages had allowed Rachel to board a coach and travel two days north to a tumbledown farm where Martha Lockyer resided with her brother, Rachel's uncle, whom Rachel had never met.

For her mother to reside *anywhere* came as something of a surprise to Rachel. For years following the death of her husband, Martha Lockyer had roamed from village to village. She would tell people she was searching for work, but really she was searching for other Roman Catholics. For a while Rachel and Robert traveled with her, but when they grew older Rachel declared her intention to return to London. "I am tired of wandering," she had said to her mother, who replied that the true Christian had no earthly home and should expect continual uprooting. This observation did not stop Rachel, who packed her brother's bag and took Robert to the city with her. He was so small then, with riotous curls that tumbled down his back and tangled in the strap over his shoulder. Their mother let them go. With no more children to impede her, Martha Lockyer had roamed still farther north, until she arrived at a farm that turned out to be the home of her long-lost brother and his nine children, none of whom was Protestant. She did not move again. After a while she became like a servant in her brother's house. She retained a bulldog's grip on her faith, practicing with great fervor and secrecy, although her brother and his wife reminded her she did not need to hide anything from them. Where the sacraments were concerned, Rachel's mother seemed to prefer a whiff of illegality.

When Rachel arrived at her uncle's house, she asked her mother to consider moving back to London. "Come live with me," she entreated. "You can stay in my room, over the glove shop. I will sleep in the workroom." Martha Lockyer refused. London rained too much, she said.

Rachel asked if she could come live with her mother instead. "Will you take me in?" she begged. "I promise I would not be any trouble to you or to Uncle." Again her mother refused, only this time she could not blame the weather.

Rachel made a pointed reference to her own state: "Mother, I have not experienced the normal course of women for some five months."

With this news her mother's eyes had hardened into beads, and she said she would not play nursemaid to a foundling.

"It would not be a foundling."

"Then it will be a bastard," Martha Lockyer replied, shaking her head. "Don't you know what it will be? It will be a son of nobody. It will be *of spurious issue*," which was a phrase used in the parish registers to indicate a child who had no father.

Rachel asked her mother to have mercy on her, please, in memory of Robert if for no other reason. "I cannot do this alone," she pleaded.

"Do not say his name!" Martha Lockyer had shouted, the veins in her temples deepening and darkening. "I do not want *his* name coming out of *your* mouth." She said that Robert was a martyr, God's chosen, whom Rachel had stolen away, whereas Rachel was a—she snapped her lips shut. She seized her rosary under her tented sleeve and fingered the beads, looking the other way.

When Rachel's uncle interrupted, calling for help plucking a goose, Martha Lockyer groaned up from her chair as if her limbs were about to splinter. She brushed past her daughter, commenting, "God forgive you, child, you never could do anything the way I asked." Rachel returned to Warwick Lane alone.

Even before that failed journey north, she had begun dreading the child's arrival. Rivers of sweat coursed between her breasts each night. She hardly slept, and when she did sleep, she turned into an accountant. Rachel's dreams became bookkeeping sessions. She weighed and tallied the child's cost. If the magistrates took notice of her situation, she knew, she would be forced into a public confession of the father's name. Walwyn's family would face scandal and embarrassment, and if he ever left the Tower, Walwyn himself would be flogged or, more likely, ordered to pay a monthly fine to the Church of England. If she refused to give the name, if she stayed silent, she would be whipped or sent to a house of correction or both. Who would care for the child then?

During the day, Rachel fanned out gloves on the showing table and let her mind wander to stories of women driven to restore their monthlies before it was too late. Her great-aunt, now long passed, used to frighten her with tales. Rachel remembered one account of a maidservant who went to a midwife for a bloodletting and emerged with her feet bound in red rags but her regular cycle restored. Then there was the mother of eleven who had tied her undergarments devilishly tight and pressed and flattened her stomach with a rolling pin. The next day her monthlies returned, though for weeks afterward her limbs spasmed and stiffened at inopportune moments, like a prisoner's stretched on an invisible rack. Rachel remembered asking if it was a sin, what these women had done. Her great-aunt had waved this question off, her wooden spoon in her hand. She said women had neither the time nor the luxury to quibble over what was and was not a sin. "We are not casuists," she said.

Rachel tried repeatedly to track down Thom the messenger. When she found him, he shamefacedly confessed he'd never delivered her message to Walwyn. "Never delivered!" she shouted and smacked him. Immediately she regretted her action and handed him a farthing, which the boy deigned to accept as payment for his pains. He proceeded to tell her what had happened. While preparing to charm his way into the Tower, Thom said, he had seen a horse-drawn cart crossing the moat. The cart carried a chained and starving lion wearing a ruby collar. Soldiers were wheeling it into the belly of the prison for the warden's entertainment. Thom gaped and gawked. It was his first lion and so he had nothing with which to compare it, but in his eyes that cat stood equal to any apocalyptic vision in the book of Revelation, even though its tail was bald and its hipbones nearly punctured its mangy coat as it staggered the length of its movable prison. When the lion's chain dragged along the cart's boards, the two geldings pulling the cart flared their nostrils, their ears flicking back. They could not believe they were harnessed to this thing, to this predator; they could not fathom how they'd wound up bound to it. Thom stood for so long watching this spectacle pass, gnawing his fingernails with the zeal of the truly curious, that by the time the old cat vanished into the inner courtyard he had forgotten the task with which Rachel had charged him. He remembered only that he had a shiny coin in his pocket and it was nearly suppertime — and his poor stomach was growling. He made his way north to the Gray Swan tavern, bought a loaf, and bragged about what he'd seen to anyone who would listen. Rachel's message to Walwyn went undelivered.

"Go back and try again," she ordered when he finished his story. "And if you see a lion, ignore it."

Someone she knew, a seller of fruits and vegetables, had been in her situation not a year earlier. Rachel remembered hearing the matrons say that this woman had given birth to a "natural child," meaning a child out of wedlock. Lacking the means to support it, the fruit seller had fallen on the charity of William Kiffin's congregation, but Kiffin had declined to help until she named the father; he'd also threatened to send her to Bridewell or some other house of correction. The woman refused to give the name. Weeping hot tears, she had stood in silence before the congregation, her arms crossed over her breasts, which still sought the child, who had come out sickly. They never did force a confession out of her; she never did apologize. Rachel had no idea what happened afterward. She suspected the child had died. She had heard that its name was not added to the membership rolls.

That night, after she saw Thom, she began binding her breasts to minimize the appearance of swelling.

About a week later she learned that the Council of State had declared a day of celebration in honor of the Levelers' recent defeat at Burford. Elizabeth said it would be a day for the wolves to celebrate slaughtering the sheep; the saints had defeated the poor. Rachel said she thought the poor and the saints were one and the same. Elizabeth shook her head, bouncing two-year-old Tower as he swatted at the strings of her white linen cap. "They used to be," she replied, "but now it appears that to be one of the Elect one must have property."

On June 7, the Council of State made good on its promise and held a day of thanksgiving in honor of the suppression of Leveler agitators. The same day, Rachel let out the waist on all her skirts. She could hear the child babbling as she ripped and stitched. The sound no longer comforted her.

On June 11, in a fit of despondency, Rachel traveled to the midwifery on Poultry Street and paid a week's wages to procure the herb savin, which the midwife promised would restore the monthlies to a woman in her condition. This was the same day that a group of enraged landowners disguised as women attacked a homeless community called the Diggers for the crime of planting a vegetable garden on public land.

On June 18, John Lilburne published from prison *The Legal Fundamental Liberties of the People of England,* in which he inveighed against capricious government and offered an extended account of his own sufferings. Cheap copies started arriving in the booksellers' stalls the next week. Elizabeth passed by those stalls, passed by those copies of her husband's latest, on her way to the Newgate market. She was headed to buy her boys beets. While she and the vendor haggled, a Digger, an old homeless woman from

Surrey, lurched toward the pyramid of root vegetables but missed her target, collapsing in Elizabeth's arms, slack-jawed, diseased, and pox-ridden. Elizabeth gave her the beets.

On June 22, Parliament expanded Oliver Cromwell's powers by appointing him governor-general and commander in chief of the army, now charged with invading Ireland. The same day, Rachel self-administered a dose of savin, a halfhearted attempt to restore her menstrual cycle. But she could not keep the herb down, and the attempt failed. She decided to visit her mother.

On July 5, Rachel returned from her travels to learn that Elizabeth had fallen ill with a rash and vicious fever. Her friend had contracted smallpox from the Digger woman and was close to death. Her two sons were also feverish. Rachel rushed to Southwark as soon as she heard the news. She returned a few days before John. The guards released him soon after, on compassionate grounds. They forced him out of the Tower over his protests; they told him to go home and care for his wife and children. The guards knew what smallpox was. They knew his children had no time. John did not want to know. He crossed the Thames in a rented wherry on a Sunday morning through a thick fog. He returned in time to bid his sons goodbye.

That night, Rachel sat on one side of the bed and John buried his head in his hands on the other as Tower and his tiny brother died in their mother's arms. Elizabeth, her face a rash of blisters, could not weep, for her eyes had swelled shut. Rachel had to guide their downy heads to their mother's mouth so she could kiss them. John rose and staggered alone up the stairs, blind for a different reason.

When she returned to Warwick Lane, Rachel burned the rest of the savin.

Ten

JOHN AND ELIZABETH fell asleep early on the night before Rachel's trial, by eight o'clock. John had planned to work on the ending of his latest antigovernment pamphlet. But he slept through the night and wrote nothing.

Anne and William Walwyn also turned in early, though not quite so early as the Lilburnes—she to her bed at nine, he to a blanket with Fourteen at half past the hour. Neither slept.

Over the glove shop on Warwick Lane, Mary du Gard tossed fitfully. She could hear the shop sign hitting the outside wall when the wind gusted.

Tucked inside their thatched-roof house, Thomas and Mathilda Bartwain rested quietly for three hours, until a noise downstairs roused the investigator. The sound was coming from the kitchen.

Bartwain sat up straight, clutching his nightcap. He had heard a rustling, a kind of exhilarated scuttle. There had followed a single crack, like a twig snapping. The hairs on the back of his neck rose. His wife heard nothing; his wife was snoring. He lit a candle on the bedside table. As he lumbered to his feet, pulling his night robe around his sloping abdomen, he happened to catch his reflection in the water basin on the floor. His chest resembled the teats of an old sow. Bartwain tried to remember when his body had begun its long downhill shuffle. No one had alerted him. No one had said: *This* is the day you will stop being the young one, the one on the rise, the one everyone watches. No one had warned him that the next generation of investigators would be waiting for him to go away, would be lining up to see the day, not to bid him farewell or thank him for his service but to take his place, to leap onto his desk, empty his shelves, claim his chair, cast aside his life's work, and build over whatever had gone before, planting their shiny boots in the face of the old days, of the old giants who had fallen.

He should not be looking at himself in the washbasin, he decided.

He descended the narrow stairs to the kitchen. He kept an eye on his stocking-clad feet. He did not want to fall. He could not bear the thought of falling. When he made it to the kitchen he placed his candle on the table, but it did not throw off enough light to see, so he lit a second one. His hand was trembling. He put the candle down and regarded his hand. Odd, he thought. He picked the candle back up. Work with me, he said to his hand. We are not done yet.

Bartwain pulled open the cupboard. He saw shadows; he saw flour spilling out of its sack. Grainy powder was everywhere. He thrust his head halfway into the cupboard and peered inside. He wielded the candle high, by his nose, singeing his nostril hairs.

Then the investigator saw it. It was in the very far back, under his handmade trap, its neck broken. It was not a rat. It was not a mouse. It was too tiny to be a mouse. Yet there it was. It was the son of the son of a mouse. Bartwain had never seen a mouse so small. It was no larger than an ear. He stared. Each fine whisker was dusted with flour.

He recalled the hours he had spent preparing for this moment.

Suddenly Bartwain felt weak in the chest. He pulled his head out and shut the cupboard door. He blew out the candle in his hand, which was still trembling. Then he used his fingers to snuff out the one on the table, though the wick kept smoking.

December 1649

Eleven

THE SESSIONS HOUSE in Old Bailey opened its doors early that first week of December for the convening of the winter assizes. By eight o'clock the benches closest to the front had filled, and dozens of spectators were crowding and jamming the balcony.

Bartwain arrived at a quarter past the hour and made his way to the top riser. From this height he could gaze down on the proceedings like a bird of prey. Years had passed since his last time attending a trial of this nature — he no longer had the stomach for it. But he loved this ramshackle courtroom. During the months between sessions, activity around the Old Bailey would groan to a halt, except in the rafters, which provided seasonal accommodations to bats, barred owls, pine martens, and mice. When the sessions resumed, a gaggle of cleaning maids would preen and fluff the courtroom to life, evicting the squatters and throwing open the doors to that species which prides itself on its capacity for distributive justice.

Bartwain scrutinized the scene below him. The last time London had seen a courthouse this crowded, John Lilburne was the defendant. This time, Freeborn John would have to remain a spectator. The jurors were filing onto their benches, and the court clerks followed, wearing red caps over their shaggy hair. The bailiff entered from a side door and announced the judge's arrival.

When the Honorable Marchamont Blakemore stepped out from his chambers, Bartwain emitted a congested snort. The judge failed to inspire confidence. He bobbled in with wig askew, clutching two bouquets of forget-me-nots. A small boy processed ahead of him, strewing the aisle with fresh-cut rosemary and parsley. Both the herbs and the flowers constituted a tradition among Old Bailey judges. The bouquets would be placed on Blakemore's desk so he could bury his nose whenever he desired relief from the fetid air, which was poisoned not only by the hundreds of unwashed bodies cramming into one structure but also by the gagging smell creeping in the windows from nearby Newgate Prison. The herbs, which old Blakemore crushed beneath his slippers as he shuffled to his seat, served in theory to protect His Honor from the plague or whatever diseases of mind and body the people of London happened to be spreading.

Bartwain chewed the end of his pipe. Last month had not been a good one in terms of his personal health. He needed to elevate his foot, but the crowded balcony made this position impossible. He would have to endure it. He reminded himself that most trials of this nature moved quickly, lasting no more than a day.

The clerk called the house to order. The defendant entered through the east door, causing the audience to swivel as one. Her hair hung loose. Manacles clamped her wrists and irons clad her ankles; her irons scraped the floor. Her face displayed no readable emotion. A gibbering roar from the spectators began rising toward the rafters of the courthouse, and Judge Blakemore commanded the crowd to be quiet. From where Bartwain sat, all that was visible of the judge as he admonished the audience was his massive wig, which was powdered so heavily that every time he shook his head or pointed a finger, a gasp of talcum escaped into the gray light, where it lingered in air thick enough to lean up against, like a good friend or the voice of conscience.

The bailiff spoke. "Rachel Lockyer, of Warwick Lane, London, daughter of Jonathan Lockyer, hold up your right hand."

When Rachel held up her right hand, her left hand went up with it. She stood under a reflective mirror that beamed light onto her countenance—the mirror of truth, some called it. Bartwain leaned forward to get a clearer view and felt the riser creaking with his weight.

The bailiff read: "'Rachel Lockyer, daughter of Jonathan Lockyer, you stand indicted for that you, on the first of November, 1649, being great with child, by the providence of God did bring it forth alive, and which child, by the laws of this realm, was a bastard; and that not having the fear of God before your eyes, on the babe feloniously, willfully, and with malice aforethought did make an assault upon it, ending its life, and then carrying the babe to the Smithfield market and burying it in the ground near the slaughterhouse to conceal it, abandoned it to the elements. The infant being discovered the next day, it was examined and evidence of murder found. You are therefore indicted after order of investigation by Thomas Bartwain, called to this courthouse by the Council of State, in this Commonwealth of England without a king or lords, may it please God, this first day of the winter sessions for the first week of December in this year of our Lord 1649.'"

Did I really write all that? Bartwain thought.

"How say you, Rachel Lockyer, are you guilty of this felony and murder whereof you stand indicted, or not guilty?"

Thirty seconds passed. The judge emitted a restless cloud of powder.

"She had better say something," someone called; the voice sounded suspiciously like John Lilburne's.

Judge Blakemore parted the two bouquets on his desk and peered out between them. With a withering glare he repeated the clerk's question.

Rachel remained silent. Blakemore rose to his feet. "Your refusal to plead will send you to the press room. There you will be laid on a board and your chest weighted with stones until you smother or speak. These are the rules of the court. Are you guilty or innocent of that deed of which you have been accused? Speak!"

Still she said nothing. Bartwain noticed Elizabeth Lilburne motioning to the defendant from the witness box.

"What would you have me do?" the judge demanded. "Do you prefer to die today? Ridiculous woman!"

"Answer the question," Elizabeth hissed. The court clerks began snickering.

Lowering her hands, Rachel turned and said something to Elizabeth, Bartwain could not hear what. For reply, Elizabeth stood, left the witness box, strode up to Rachel, and said, plain as day, "Don't you dare do that." The crowd tittered, and then the crowd cackled; as the two women argued on, the crowd grew bored. No one could hear what they were saying to each other. Bartwain was totally absorbed. He forgot his swollen toes. Both women fascinated him.

When Rachel resumed her place under the defendant's mirror, Elizabeth, wearing a dissatisfied look, returned to the witness box. "Your Honor," Rachel said. Her delivery was stronger than Bartwain had anticipated—her voice penetrated the courthouse. He leaned forward again, the riser groaning. "Your Honor," Rachel said again, "I am prepared to plead—"

She stopped short as the scaffolding on which Bartwain and one hundred other people were seated collapsed. Everything fell. Within five seconds the risers had splintered and the entire structure tumbled, four packed rows crashing, one on top of the next, and dozens of bodies crushed beneath. A collective gasp rose from the center of the courthouse, and those who had been spared rushed over to aid those who had fallen. Women crawled out from the pile on their hands and knees, foreheads bleeding; the bailiff and his men rushed in and started tugging at arms and legs, and when that did not work, they tugged at the boards—if they could not pull the people out from the risers, they would pull the risers off the people. They freed the children first where they could—during the winter the poor brought their young inside the courthouse to keep them dry and warm. Somewhere in the bottom of the pile a man was shouting, wailing, for the Holy Spirit to come.

The judge clapped his wigged head, regarded his fallen house, rose, and fled the courtroom.

Such incidents were not unheard-of. A similar catastrophe, more minor in scope, had taken place at Guildhall before the start of John's trial, when too many spectators tried to cram into too few seats. The ensuing delay had given John more time to prepare his opening speech. This time the disaster was worse. But it was no one's fault, or at least that was Bartwain's thought as he'd felt himself falling, tumbling, from his bird-of-prey perch, plummeting nearly fifteen feet.

As he fell, he told himself he was fortunate. Sitting as high as he was, he would be among the last to land. Those who had gone ahead of him could provide a buffer, a cushion. He continued to tell himself he was fortunate even as his spine smacked into one of the benches and he felt a crunch in the bones of his left wrist, even as he looked down and saw his arm pinned beneath a man's leg. Bartwain recalled his anxiety several days earlier about the rain turning to sleet by morning. Now this concern struck him as whimsical, almost endearing. He wondered if he would walk again. If he could not, he would invest in one of those moving chairs that operated like a wheelbarrow. His secretary, White, could push him around in it. He smelled smoke. He hoped he had not dropped his pipe onto something combustible. The bailiff was bellowing for soldiers. Beside Bartwain lay an unconscious elderly woman, her skirts snagged on a riser; he could see her buckled shoes and her bare ankles, oddly twisted. Everyone had forgotten about Rachel Lockyer. For a moment Bartwain forgot about her also. He stayed still, waiting for someone to help him; he wanted someone to reassure him he had not broken anything essential. He could hear the bailiff bellowing that the trial would have to be postponed. They would reconvene in a few days' time, he shouted; right now they needed doctors. "Leave the courthouse unless you are injured or can tend those who are," the bailiff ordered. "And someone send for the coroner."

Then Bartwain did think about Rachel and how it must feel to be told to wait another week to learn if one would live or die. He could no longer move his arm. He thought of Elizabeth Lilburne, and he pitied her; he remembered her two sons were gone. He lifted his head. High up, on one of the rafters, perched a barred owl, a holdover from the summer months that the maids had failed to sweep out with their dusters. Bartwain watched it with everything he had; he concentrated on that owl. It began to fly and screech. It flapped up the crowd and down the aisles; it howled around the scaffolding. It was alone, and overrun; it sounded off on what was coming. The others did not notice; the others were too lathered up. But Bartwain heard it. How could he not? The owl battered the walls.

"God send you a good deliverance," the clerk in his treble voice was saying.

As the officers of the court pushed the uninjured outside and away from the courthouse, the Reverend William Kiffin, his breath smelling of cabbage, made his way over to Rachel's employer, Mary. She was standing apart, squinting through sheets of rain, the spiraled outlines of St. Sepulchre in the distance. Water snaked down the courthouse eaves and lit her up from behind, like colored glass that runs.

"You are going to be the principal witness," Kiffin said, not troubling with a greeting.

"What?" Mary recoiled from the preacher's rank breath.

"You heard what the bailiff said. 'Abandoned it to the elements.'" He clutched her arm. "No one else observed this crime as closely as you did. You must be exceedingly prepared with what you say when the prosecutor calls you to the stand. The jury will need every detail. Leave nothing to chance."

"I will say what I saw," Mary replied, puzzled. She dreaded having to return to the courthouse. She had hoped to get the matter over and done with.

"Of course you will. Just be scrupulous in your reporting."

"What do you mean?"

"You are, after all, a stranger." He delivered these words with

114

a paternal smile. "You are not English. The jury will have to be persuaded to trust you."

"I will do my best, Mr. Kiffin." She stepped away from him, into the rain.

"*Reverend* Kiffin," he corrected, but she was gone.

His admonition remained unnecessary. Mary was not about to say anything less than the truth. What she saw was what she saw; what she knew was what she knew. At first she had tried to tell herself the child might belong to one of those homeless women who slunk around the Smithfield slaughterhouse looking for maggoty meat. But on her way out of the woods that morning she had stumbled across one of those women and motioned her to come see; the poor creature had darted away as soon as she beheld the bundle. Even a toothless Digger, it seemed, did not want what Mary was carrying. A real mother, in contrast, would be unable to keep away from it. Therein lay the proof. At least, that was what Mary thought when she carried her burden back to the glove shop and returned it to the arms of Rachel, who held it.

The look on her assistant's face that day reminded Mary of the time when Rachel's three-legged dog had gone missing. Mary never liked that dog. No one liked that dog except Rachel. It was a speckled runt with a curious habit of whimpering when it was glad and barking ecstatically whenever it suffered an insult. Rachel used to feed it scraps in the alley behind the glove shop and bring it yeast dough from the common oven, something that should have been left for others. That dog ate finer food than Mary did. Then it had disappeared, and Rachel became convinced the dog skinner had taken it. She informed Mary she was going after it. "Going after what?" Mary said. She always forgot that animal as soon as it left her field of vision.

"The dog. It would not just up and leave for no reason." As she spoke, Rachel thrust out her chin in a manner Mary initially interpreted as her having taken offense but later recognized as an attempt to ward off tears. Rachel swept the floors faster than usual and then declared she was going out.

Mary, bewildered, said: "You just lost your poor brother, and now you are going to spend your days grieving a three-legged runt?"

For reply Rachel tromped out. Of course Mary had to follow; she had to find out what happened. Neither woman could afford to take a coach, so they marched single file, twenty yards between them, two miles north to the dog skinner's house, which was an old barn bearing the look of perpetual disappointment. The dog skinner resided there with his younger brother, who had lost his sight double-lighting a cannon in the battle of Marston Moor. Rachel knocked on the front door while Mary watched. When no one responded, Rachel walked around to the back and called for help. The dog skinner was not there, but the blind brother heard her.

From her vantage point at the edge of the property, Mary looked on as the brother escorted Rachel to the dog pens. There sat six starving mongrels crammed inside a wire cage in sludge so thick it buttered the small dogs' stomachs. The blind man said, "That one?" and reached through the wire and touched one of the animals, and sure enough, landed straight on it. It was the three-legged spotter, and Rachel, incredulous, asked how he knew that, and he said it was not hard to pick out a creature that had so much missing.

Rachel paid the brother for his help. She paid him three times what a four-legged dog would be worth. When he had counted her coins, the man smiled, his teeth sinking into their gums like the dogs' paws sank into the sediment. Then Rachel walked the mongrel all the way back to Warwick Lane, stopping twice to carry it. When Mary asked her at supper later why she'd done it, why she'd rescued it, as the dog cried happily, its ratted tail thumping against the twice-swept floors, Rachel looked down at it and said she supposed things didn't feel right without its company. And then she went right on eating her stew, as if everyone naturally loves whatever God places on our doorsteps without our permission.

In the war, Mary's husband had killed three boys, none more than twelve years old. Each of them had straggled, nameless and barefoot, onto the battlefield to join a cause for which their fathers had suffered. For his actions in battle, Johannes du Gard was told to be more careful of whom he shot, but privately he was commended for giving back to God what the army of saints sought. And Mary wondered if it was worse to destroy the thing you do not love or the thing you do.

Back inside the courthouse, a word of good news—Bartwain's back was not broken. He had sustained a fractured ulna, however, and the doctor who delivered this diagnosis placed the investigator's left arm in a sling and told him not to use it. Perspiration irrigated the furrows in the doctor's forehead. "The lower vertebrae in your spine have been injured," he explained. "They have sustained a wrenching." When Bartwain asked what this meant, the doctor said it depended. "But I would not walk for a while yet," he added, as Bartwain stood and walked.

For the first ten minutes of his journey home he felt as giddy as any paralytic who stands and rolls up his mat after Jesus talks to him. After ten minutes, Bartwain understood what the doctor had meant. Taking a step caused radiating pain to course down his spine and buttocks. His fractured wrist was throbbing. He made it home, barely. He collapsed into his favorite chair and called for Mathilda. She was not home, but his secretary came by within the hour—White had heard about the courthouse accident. Bartwain asked him to go fetch one of those wheeled chairs, the kind used by the lame and crippled. White said he had no idea where to find one. Bartwain was unrelenting. "I need it right away. I have to practice rolling."

It would take his secretary several days to locate one.

When at last White returned, he was pushing a wheeled chair with a passing resemblance to a wheelbarrow. Bartwain nodded his approval. "Now you will practice taking me around in it," he said with some excitement; he had a fondness for contraptions. He lowered himself into the chair and instructed White to wheel him up and down the hallway. White rolled his eyes. From her vantage point in the kitchen, Mathilda chuckled.

As White strained to maneuver his employer's substantial

weight down the corridor, he pointed out that no one would think less of Bartwain if he did not attend any more of the proceedings, which were scheduled to resume as soon as the judge declared the courthouse fit for reentry. "You're injured," White said, gasping slightly. "You don't have to go to the trial. You don't have to go anywhere until you feel better."

"I will feel better when this case is over," Bartwain said. "Now push."

Twelve

THE LABOR PAINS had made their first appearance a full month before Rachel thought they would. They dissipated during the day but resumed overnight, so she could not rest. In the morning the pains had vanished again, and she swept the walk as usual.

The week before, Rachel had awakened to the hawkish face of Katherine Chidley leaning over her, fumbling at her nightdress, trying to squeeze her breasts. "This woman is great with child," Chidley trumpeted.

Rachel shoved her away and sat up, pulling the quilt around her. Mary was watching, her arms crossed, a sentinel at the top of the stairs. "Oh, Mary," Rachel cried. "How could you let her into my room?"

"You didn't lock it," Mary said.

Chidley tugged Rachel's hair. "Thick and shining. And skin fresh as a girl's! You will bring shame on this house. Who will pay to maintain your bastard? Do you even know the father?" Again the haberdasher's arm flew out and landed on her target. She groped and mauled Rachel's nightdress. "Aha!"

"What?" Mary leaned in. "What is it? What have you found?"

Rachel pushed back, but Katherine Chidley was a large woman. Enveloping Rachel in a great molesting embrace, she proceeded to palpate and pinch her nipples, forcing her fingers under Rachel's robe and digging into her breasts. "Aha!" she crowed again. "Swollen like a creek in springtime!"

"Let her be," Mary cautioned. "That's enough."

I will be eaten alive, Rachel thought. These women, these matrons who tear chunks of flesh with their beaks, will devour me. "I'm not expecting," she spat. It was a ridiculous lie, but once out of her mouth, she had to stay with it. "I come from a long line of hard-breasted women. My breasts take on extra denseness during my monthly time."

When Chidley questioned her growing girth, Rachel attributed it to a digestive ailment.

When Chidley asked what kind of ailment, Rachel retorted it was none of her business and she did not want to discuss matters of physic in the morning.

When Chidley told Rachel she could discuss the matter with her now or later in front of a justice of the peace, Rachel said she doubted a justice of the peace would have time to interrogate the digestive ailments of a glovemaker's apprentice. There was a war on, after all.

When Chidley reminded her that the war had ended, Rachel said, "Then someone ought to inform the army."

The haberdasher threw up her hands and turned to Mary. "She is unrepentant."

Rachel stood shakily, wrapping the quilt around her shoulders. "These are still my sleeping quarters, and last time I checked I was still the owner of myself. I will not have you marching in here without my permission!"

"No, you are not the owner of yourself," Mary called from the door in a sorrowful voice. "You belong to God, who will do with you as He wishes."

Chidley, nodding, glided to the stairs and descended them with a fat swish. From there she let herself out.

Alone again, Rachel and Mary eyed each other. Mary said she was disappointed in Rachel.

Rachel said *she* was disappointed in Mary. "You let that woman into my chambers. How could you?"

"My husband's good name is the only thing I have," Mary declared. "It is all I possess now that he is gone. I will not have you under this roof if you bring shame to his name. Do you understand? I will not tolerate it! Any woman who gives birth to a bastard will find no safe harbor at Du Gard Gloves. Now go sweep the walk."

Rachel said she would do it right after breakfast.

"Do it now!" her employer shouted, screwing up her thin face. "I cannot tolerate the sight of you."

Again Rachel had hunted down Thom. Again she asked the boy to deliver her message. "What message?" Thom had replied. Again she slapped him. Thom paled with unshed tears. "Tell Mr. Walwyn I am in need of aid," she said, kissing his cheek roughly. "I'm sorry. I'm begging you. Quickly. Get past the moat this time." Thom sped off, his legs churning; he did not like being slapped. He did not come back.

During the same days London descended into a strange stew of smoke and heat and insidious humidity. The air swept in from the south. It invaded the city. Women on their way to market pushed their sleeves high past the elbows, their palms slippery as they balanced baskets of bread and apples on their shoulders. The heat wave made it harder for Rachel to sleep. Nights were the only time she could escape the prying eyes of others, so she would throw her robe open in the dark, her skin parched, her nipples cracked and aching. Long blue veins had begun to spin themselves around her swollen abdomen.

When she was not staying awake brooding about the future, she was staying awake worrying about Elizabeth. For two days after the passing of her sons, Rachel's best friend had lain unmoving, head to the wall, neither eating nor drinking nor rising to use the house of office. On the third morning she had hauled herself up with a single shuddering breath, wrapped herself in her husband's dressing gown, the first thing her hand found in the dark, and crept downstairs to the kitchen, where she stood and boiled a pot of oats for her one remaining child, five-year-old Elizabeth, whose eyes were like free-blown glass, swollen and translucent.

John had done what he could to help. For the remaining days of the summer he had stayed by his wife's side, writing treatises on government at night while she slept and moistening her face with lemon in the daytime to lessen the scarring from the smallpox. But then Elizabeth grew well enough to remember she disliked it when he hovered, and a relieved John returned to his work, pouring everything he had, everything he knew, into his Leveler causes. In record time he had completed a scathing treatise that accused the new republican government of treason against the people of England. John titled it *An Impeachment of High Treason against Oliver Cromwell and His Son-in-Law*, and he dedicated it to his three friends still locked in the Tower. The treatise accomplished what John wanted. Like clocks with perfect weights, five officers arrived right on time at the Lilburnes' door. They left without him, John putting on a show of resistance for the neighbors, but they returned later, as he knew they would. They dragged him, noble and remonstrating, before the attorney general. When John demanded to know the nature of the charges against him, the attorney general said seditious pamphleteering. When John denied that the new Parliament wielded any lawful authority over him, the attorney general recommitted him to the Tower. Rachel assumed this was what John wanted. In the midst his grief, Freeborn John had begun to fester. He missed Walwyn in the Tower. He missed the Tower. At this point he would have settled for a straw mat in Fleet Prison or the Clink, almost any form of imprisonment being preferable to time spent in his own house, where the very walls were weeping.

When he returned to prison John left his wife and daughter behind. Rachel began making trips across the Thames to check on both Elizabeths. She fried eggs in Elizabeth's pan, overcooking everything. It didn't matter. Her friend would not eat. Rachel told her to make the most of this time without her husband. "He'll be back soon enough," she said. "Don't spend your time wallowing. Before you know it he'll be sitting at your table again, waiting for his rye loaf, telling you to fetch the kindling when the fire has gone out, and him in his stocking feet." Several times Rachel came within a whisper of confessing her condition. But if it was hard to say anything earlier, it was twice as hard now. The pen where Tower used to sit and mash his cherries sat empty in the corner of the kitchen.

Rachel did not find the courage to speak until the end of the summer, one afternoon when she had traveled to Southwark to help Elizabeth distribute another petition for the Levelers' release. Elizabeth was rising to gather her daughter's cloak when Rachel flung out an arm to stop her and said, quickly, before she could think better of it, "Elizabeth, please listen to me. I am going to have a child."

Elizabeth stared, then steered an uneven berth around the table to the door, which she yanked open, letting in the sound of gulls and the smell of rot from the river. She had been drinking wine earlier.

"Did you hear me?" Rachel asked, glancing down at Young Elizabeth, who was seated at the table, studying her wooden doll.

"Hear you?" Elizabeth turned. "How could I not? And did you think I failed to notice anything earlier? I am not an idiot. You are larger than a house."

"Then why didn't—"

"What is there to say? What could I possibly say to someone who has lost her mind? You have become the worst thing a woman can be. You have become . . . *impractical*!" The scars left by her fever were blazing. "How are you going to pay for its upkeep? You can hardly provide for yourself. Are you going to ask Walwyn to pay for it? He has fourteen already, and he is no grand landowner!"

Young Elizabeth covered her doll's ears.

Rachel said, "Shhh, your daughter, she doesn't—"

Elizabeth exploded. "What do you know about children? Nothing! Do you know what it is like to have a howling babe feeding and flailing all over you day and night for months at a time? How are you going to manage it? And you sweeping out the store and stitching hides for that Huguenot every hour of day and night, what will you do? Will you strap the child to your shoulders? Will you lug it around like a flour sack? And what happens when they come after you and demand a public penance? They will come after you, you know. What happens when they pull Walwyn to the whipping post too? They will take down the other Levelers with him; they love to paint us all with the same brush and color. Will you carry your bastard on your back when you are sitting in Bridewell? Who will feed it then? How dare you be so reckless!"

Rachel blanched.

"Furthermore," Elizabeth went on, "do you know what it is like to have a child and then lose it? Do you?"

"No," she whispered.

"No. That's right. No, you do not! You would not be so quick to twine your legs around a man if you knew what happens once you become untangled. You would not find him so irresistible then. I tell you, children are a burden and a curse." She glanced over at her daughter, who had laid her head down on the table, its surface scored and grooved from Tower's eager stabbings when he was learning to use a fork. "They are a cross too heavy to bear," she continued hoarsely. "They cough and they retch and they catch fevers. They cry and they cannot breathe and then they die. They fall prey to one hundred wretched fates the world has in store for them. Are you prepared to bury what you love if God decides it is time? How large is your heart?"

"Please. Please, please, don't do this," Rachel begged. "I cannot do this alone."

"Pshaw!" Elizabeth spat, an odd sound that emptied into a sob. "I don't want to hear it. You have been irredeemably careless."

Elizabeth's daughter lifted her head and began to cry, great wretched whoops that turned into hiccups and then into ominous belches. Elizabeth went to the girl, scooped her up, and deposited her on the staircase. "Go upstairs. Go upstairs and stop crying or you will make yourself throw up." Her voice held no sympathy. She turned back to Rachel. "You are in these straits by your own hand. You took something that was not yours. You are the vainest and most self-important person I have known." Her eyes had begun filling. "And that includes my husband!" But as she returned to the table, she placed her hand over Rachel's. Outside, two streetwalkers were arguing over something they had found in an alley.

"How can I bring a child into this world?" Rachel, stricken, finally whispered.

Elizabeth nodded, swiped angrily at her cheeks, nodded again, glanced at the place on the table where Tower used to bang his fists at the sight of beets. "How can you not?" was all she said.

The grand jury did not arraign Elizabeth's husband on charges of treason until the middle of October, finally giving John the date for his long-awaited trial. The same day John was arraigned, Elizabeth received notice that she was to be evicted for failure to pay the rent. She suffered an attack of nerves and retreated to her bed, where Rachel and Young Elizabeth tended her.

On October 25, Freeborn John had his day in court. Delivering an oratory at once deft and long-winded, he wore out his prosecutors; he pummeled them with words. He argued that the jurors should assess the merits of the law by which he was being tried, not limit themselves to the mere facts of the case. He argued that where treason was concerned, intentions mattered more than actions: what counted was the heart. Elizabeth did not attend her husband's trial. When Rachel asked why not, she said she already knew everything he was going to say.

The jurors deliberated John's case for three-quarters of an hour over a generous quart of sack. When they returned from their chambers, weaving on their feet, they acquitted the defendant on all charges. It was a victory for the people, John later said. With the jury's pronouncement, the courthouse at Guildhall erupted, causing the judge and prosecutor to turn pale. The bailiff flung open the doors of the court. Hundreds of townspeople swarmed forward, roaring.

That night the city of London sang and crackled. Unemployed

soldiers waved sea green flags and belted choruses as they emptied their bladders in the kennels. Tradesmen and apprentices waved banners and lit bonfires up and down the riverfront; from Elizabeth's third-floor window in Southwark, the northern bank of the Thames seemed be on fire. At Bishopsgate, metalworkers struck a coin commemorating the victory. At Aldersgate, the owner of the Whalebone threw open his doors and sold ale for half the regular price. Everyone wanted to toast the name of Freeborn John, even those who had never heard of him. The Lilburnes' landlord gave Elizabeth an extension on the rent.

Rachel did not hear about the real conclusion to John's trial until several days later, when Elizabeth stopped by to complain that the judge had sent John back to the Tower, where he remained with his three companions. Elizabeth was of the opinion that Cromwell and his Council of State stood behind the delay in letting him go. Cromwell, she said, was bent on suppressing his former friends the Levelers.

"I thought the Levelers had already been suppressed," Rachel said.

Elizabeth concurred. "But," she added, "they have not asked our opinion about it." She vowed to go to the Tower and demand their freedom in person. She was thinking about the extension on her rent, which would not last long.

At the end of this conversation Rachel revealed to her friend that she was having some beginning labor pains. Elizabeth's mouth tightened. "Yes," she said. "Yes, but it's early yet. Come find me in a few days, when you will be having more of them." That was all she said, though she embraced Rachel tightly as she left.

The next day, the first of November, the clawing hand of labor returned in earnest. Rachel was outside sweeping, wind drying the back of her throat; each time she pushed the waste out to the street, a snarling gust of premature winter scattered the refuse back, blowing it over the threshold. When the pain recommenced, she opened the door to call for Mary, who waved her off. "I'm balancing the accounts," Mary said. So Rachel left the premises. She walked out without telling Mary. She headed south until she could walk no farther, and then she hired a hackney carriage to take her the remaining distance to the Thames. At the river steps, watermen bombarded her with offers. She went with the one who was cheapest, climbing into his rocking rowboat. They pushed off and the waterman began wheeling and dodging, shouting obscenities in a foreign tongue whenever another vessel crossed his path. She told him to take her to Southwark. To Elizabeth, she might have said.

When she made it to her friend's residence, she pounded on the door—no one answered. She knocked again, calling Elizabeth's name, asking to be let in. A neighbor was scraping his boots on the stoop next door. Rachel asked if he knew where Mrs. Lilburne was. "She went off this morning," he said, "storming about something or other. She said she was going to retrieve her husband." Rachel asked if he knew how long she would be gone. The neighbor kicked dried mud from his boots. "However long it takes to get her husband back to soap making," he reported. Rachel nodded. That sounded like Elizabeth. And she had no idea how long her friend was going to be gone.

She returned to Warwick Lane alone.

As she walked, the pains intensified. She turned her back to the wind, breathed as slow and long as she could, wrapped her cloak tight around her midsection, and delivered her first maternal order. She told the child: *Wait*. "You're too early," she said. "It's not time yet."

With those words, the child in her womb chose to rouse itself from its long slumber. It stretched and yawned and bugled. It delivered a swift and deliberate kick: Here I am. Rachel doubled over. The child pounded with both feet: It is time when I say so.

Rachel tried reasoning. She asked the child to stay where it was, for its sake if not for hers. Wait for Walwyn, she proposed. He will be released any hour now, I'm sure of it. They will let him go as soon as they release John. Elizabeth is taking care of things. She knows my situation. She will persuade the Council of State to release them, and then she will come to me, and she and Walwyn will both help me. Together we will come up with a plan.

I am tired of plans, the child said.

Rachel replied: Listen to me. I have not yet resolved how to protect you. If you come now, we will be on the street. Mary will not have me. My mother does not want me. We will wind up homeless or worse.

Tell them who my father is.

No, she said. If I name him, his family will learn of me and will be humiliated by the fact of your existence. His children will be dishonored. He could lose his ability to provide for them.

The child replied that Rachel could worry about some other family's reputation and livelihood if she wanted, but *it* would go live with the Lilburnes.

That will work only so long as John is still in the Tower. John will not have an illegitimate in the house.

The child kicked again.

Rachel, coldly: Why are you in such a hurry? The world is not going to be anything like you expected.

The child, peeved, astonished: Why not?

Rachel stole a glance down at her hands, with their knotted veins and wrinkling knuckles, and could not answer.

Next she tried bargaining. If the child would hold off coming until after Hallowmas, she would have a plan in place, she promised. The child asked what that was. "I'm not sure," she said out loud. "But Walwyn and I will come up with something together."

I wasn't asking about the plan. I was asking about Hallowmas.

Rachel, taken aback: It's today. It's All Saints' Day. It's a day of feasting to honor all the holy people who attained the beatific vision.

What is the beatific vision?

"You ask too many questions," she cried. All Saints' Day took place on November 1. All Souls' Day followed, on November 2. Rachel's father used to refuse to commemorate All Souls' Day because it involved intercessory prayers for the dead in purgatory. Rachel's mother observed both days quietly.

By the time Rachel returned to the glove shop, the child had gone quiet. Rachel did not go inside the shop to Mary. She stayed outside as long as she could. She sat on the stoop and scanned the street as if waiting for someone. No one was coming. She waited anyway. She had no place left to go. The entire afternoon the wind would not let up.

At six o'clock Rachel was still sitting when someone did come, a young match vendor, the poorest of the poor, wearing rags and with a red kerchief knotted into horns on top of her head. She was trying to make a sale, she said. She asked if Rachel wanted to buy something. Cupped in the vendor's apron were matches—spills of wood coated with wax and tipped with sulfur for lighting. With her free hand, Rachel noticed, the young woman was pulling the arm of a child, a spindly boy of three or four who could not stand without his legs buckling. Something was wrong with his knees. He peeked out at Rachel from behind his mother, blowing bubbles of saliva at her, his legs crossing like a pair of opened scissors.

"I'll buy a sheet," Rachel said, not taking her eyes from the child. The young woman handed her a long card of matches. When Rachel went to pay her, she remembered she had given her last coin to the waterman. So she paid with gloves; she peeled off her own gloves and gave them to the young woman, who tried them eagerly. Rachel could not breathe for looking at that boy. As the pair turned to go, he swung around one more time. He smiled and blew bubbles until his mother dragged him forward. She yanked him upright and said something into his ear; she jerked him straight every time his useless legs crumpled. Up and down the little boy went, an unlucky jack-in-the-box, until they reached the corner of Warwick Lane and disappeared.

Then Rachel went inside.

She asked Mary if she could please go upstairs, but Mary said not yet. "Where have you been?" she added, though she did not wait for an answer. She reminded Rachel they still had twenty pairs of funeral gloves to dye; a general or lieutenant colonel, captain of something or other, had passed. So Rachel stayed in the workroom, dipping gloves into an iron bath until they blackened, hanging them from the ribbons crossing the ceiling so they would dry overnight. As she worked, she affixed her thoughts to Walwyn. Their first night together they had lain right there, right there where Mary was standing. He had asked the whereabouts of her employer, and Rachel had pointed up at the ceiling, and the gloves had pointed back at them.

After the last pair was hung, she stuffed the remaining ribbon in her pocket and faced her employer, who was seated in the corner, having returned to her accounts.

"Mary," Rachel whispered.

"No" was all Mary said. "Not now. Not tonight." Her cheeks were gray and papery and she was biting her lip. She would not look up from her ledgers.

Rachel ascended the stairs with excruciating slowness. She felt a clawing and scratching at the base of her abdomen, from the inside out. When she reached the landing she turned one last time, but Mary was still in the workroom. There the good Huguenot proceeded to tear into her hides an hour or more, separating the sheep from the calves.

That night, Rachel locked her door.

Thirteen

S AVE FOR A FEW scattered piles of straw where the scaffolding had stood, the rear of the courthouse was empty the
day Rachel's trial resumed. The straw covered the places
where injured spectators had bled into the floorboards. Then the
doors opened and the crowds returned; the front rows filled, and
people began to stand and sit wherever they could, tossing down
their doublets and cloaks and lowering themselves to the floor.
Some had brought baskets of bread to eat and beer to drink while
they watched the proceedings.

"Come to order," the bailiff called.

Here we go, Bartwain thought from the safety of his wheeling
chair, which White had pushed near the front. This time White
was with him.

In bed the night before, Bartwain's wife had wanted to know
why he had not done more to help the defendant. "It's not my job
to help her," he had said. "The law comes first. Rachel Lockyer
has failed to uphold the law. That much is incontrovertible."

"But what if others failed to uphold her? What about grace?"

"The law *is* grace," Bartwain said irritably. "It gives form and
pattern and order."

Mathilda shook her head. "You know I had a stillborn once."

131

He remembered. He did not like to think about that time. "Yes," he said, more quietly, "but the law does not concern itself with a situation such as yours. The law does not worry about a married woman."

"Why?" she pressed. "Is the married woman incapable of wrongdoing? I'd like to meet the matron who never dreamed of running over her husband with a scavenger cart. I'd like to meet that woman."

He begged her to let him sleep.

"You will sleep when my questions are answered," Mathilda had said.

The clerk was calling Mary du Gard to the witness stand.

Wait a minute, Bartwain thought. Hold on. You are not picking up where we left off last week. Where we left off before that damned scaffolding fell was the plea. The defendant is supposed to plead something. She is supposed to say "Guilty" or "Not guilty." The investigator swiveled in his chair to regard his secretary. White returned his aggrieved look; he, too, had noticed the omission. Bartwain darted a glance at Griffin. This is not where we left off, you half-wit, he thought. Get the defendant back up front and tell her to plead something. If you do not follow procedure you make a mockery of the law. But no one in charge seemed to notice.

Bartwain ordered White to go inform the prosecutor. "I cannot maneuver in this goddamn chair," he fumed. "Go tell him for me."

White slunk up to Griffin, who was reading his notes. The prosecutor listened to the secretary's whispered statement and said something into his ear, then delivered a sophomoric smile in the direction of the investigator. White retraced his steps, kicking the ends of the spectators' benches along the way.

"What did he say?" Bartwain demanded.

"He said for you not to worry; justice will still be served."

"No, it will not," Bartwain raged, fumbling to his feet. He could stand if he must. Keeping one hand on White's shoulder, he declared in his most authoritative voice that the prosecution must stop its proceedings. "Justice cannot be served when the procedure is trampled," he shouted. But no one was paying any attention. If anyone noticed him it was with amusement, Bartwain later thought; probably they saw a fat old man with his arm in a sling wearing a too-tight wig and weaving on his feet. Probably they thought he was a drunkard. The bailiff called for silence.

Bartwain tried to step forward but stumbled over an uneven floorboard, and before he could right himself, White pulled him back into the chair. "Stay still, or you'll hurt yourself."

"I am not an invalid," Bartwain roared, but his defiance went nowhere. The courtroom was becoming a carnival. Someone was selling candied flowers at the Sessions House entrance. Someone else was passing bottles of wine up and down the men's rows. Two women were dispensing wrapped parcels from a basket in the back, and the smell of raw eel wafted forward. This was the state of London under the new republican government, Bartwain thought. We have decapitated our king and disbanded our House of Lords, and now there is no one left who knows the rules; now there is no one left to restore reason and line and order.

Again the bailiff ordered silence.

"The prosecution calls Mary du Gard for its first witness," the clerk repeated.

Rachel's employer approached the jury, wearing a dress the color of turnips. "I am a widow. My husband was Johannes du Gard." She began delivering her testimony in fits and starts; she kept stealing glances at Rachel. "When my husband died I took on his glove business. Rachel Lockyer was apprenticed to me in the trade and served as my assistant. She was a good helper. She earned her keep."

"Go on," Griffin prompted.

"She grew unwell after the death of her brother in April. She would take to her bed early."

"Was she with child?"

"I thought so. I could not be sure. I tried to find the signs but I could not see for certain. She kept to herself and was secretive."

Oh, hurry it up, Widow du Gard, Bartwain thought. I have

heard your testimony before, and it is just as plodding now as last time.

"She would dress with great haste and in the dark. She wore her skirts high on the waist and would not let the matrons inspect her, although Mrs. Chidley tested her breasts for hardness. But she said her mother had the same breasts and they were thick by nature. Then she said her swollen belly was the result of a digestive ailment. Later I asked if a man had taken her in sin. She replied that she had not been taken *in sin*."

"Did you believe her?"

"No."

"What happened the night of November first?"

"She took to her quarters after she finished her work. It was late. She had disappeared a good part of the day, so we were running behind schedule. I stayed downstairs and continued working."

"When did you go upstairs?"

"Around half past ten. I went right to sleep and was awakened later by the wind. Then I heard a cry. I thought it might be her dog. But it was not a dog that I heard. I rose and called to her outside her door and the sound stopped. She would not let me in. I tried to look through the keyhole but it was covered. She never answered my call. I returned to my bed for the remainder of the night. If she wanted my help, she should have asked for it," Mary concluded, directing a helpless glance in the direction of the defendant.

"Did you see inside her sleeping quarters?"

"Not until the next morning. I went inside and saw stains on the floor and in the bed, and the bedclothes all rumpled. I said, Rachel, what have you done? She said it was her monthly time. I did not think so much blood could come from that. She was very pale. She worked in the shop but she did not complete any of her tasks. She went back to her bed at the end of the day and did not take any supper."

"Did she say anything about giving birth?"

"No."

"What happened that night, the night of November second?"

"I woke again to sounds from her chamber. I looked through the keyhole and this time she must have forgotten to cover it. She was taking something out of her wainscot box. I hid in my room when she opened her door. She crept down the stairs. When she left the house I followed her." Mary's slender upper body pressed forward, as if fighting an invisible current. "She walked to the Smithfield market. She did not look behind her. She walked past the old slaughterhouse at the northern end of the market and headed into the woods. I waited near the slaughterhouse. She returned crying and running in the other direction. I went home then. I did not try to follow her."

A juryman: "Why didn't you go into the woods?"

"Because those trees are haunted at night."

Poor Mary du Gard, thought Bartwain. She lives between a dead husband and a haunted forest.

"What then?"

"I heard a sound at the front door later that night. I went downstairs and found her lying on the stoop. She was in a dead faint and did not say a word. I helped her up the stairs and I tried to speak with her but she was in a fit and she fainted again. I went back to my bed. In the morning I returned to the Smithfield market. I went behind the slaughterhouse into the wood. I saw a mound of earth, freshly dug. I scratched at the dirt and saw something and began to pull. I pulled some more." Mary's voice grew hoarse. "And there I saw as mangled and pathetic a little infant as ever there was. It was in piteous condition. Oh, it was so small. It was dressed in yellow brocade and partly wrapped. There were sores and marks on it."

Across the courtroom, Rachel was standing motionless, two spots of red coloring her cheeks.

"Were there signs of violence to it?"

"I think so. I am not sure. I wrapped it in my shawl and walked as fast as I could to Warwick Lane. Rachel was in the back room of the shop, cutting and stitching. Two customers were there also. I pushed them aside and I said to her, 'Is this yours? Is this what you have gone and done?' She seized it from my arms. She moaned and grabbed it to her breast and wept bitterly. The buyers left without making a purchase."

"Who called for the coroner?"

"I called for Mrs. Chidley and Reverend Kiffin. They called for the coroner."

"Why did you call Katherine Chidley and William Kiffin?"

Mary did not hesitate. "Because my husband would have wanted me to."

The prosecution called Mr. Jack Dawber.

"I oversee the slaughterhouse at the Smithfield market," Jack said. "On the night that Frenchwoman was talking about"—he pointed to Mary as she stepped off the stand—"I'm asleep on my cot in the back, to keep away thieves. The middle of the night, I wake to a sound. I walk to the back of the pens and look. There is a crescent moon shining on the elms, lighting them up. A woman is walking into them. I cannot see her face. I watch her kneel down and begin digging. I start to go outside but then I decide not."

"What date was this?"

"All Souls' Day."

"You mean All Saints' Day."

"No, sir, I do not. I mean All Souls'. All Saints' had already passed."

"Why didn't you confront this woman when she intruded onto your property?"

"I did not trust the moon. I have seen a number of moons and I know which ones are not trustworthy."

"Go on."

"So she buries her bundle and leaves and I return to my sleep. Then that Frenchwoman comes to the slaughterhouse first thing the next morning, crashing around so loud she wakes me." He looked balefully at Mary. "I see her pull a dead babe out from the ground. I fall to my knees right there and pray for its soul. Then I pray for the mother."

Griffin asked if he had seen or found anything else.

"I found this. Not far from where she buried it." He pulled out of his pocket a long ribbon inked with inch marks.

Bartwain leaned forward in his chair. What in the name of God was that?

"Is this the same ribbon Rachel Lockyer used to measure hands for a fitting?" Griffin asked, turning to Mary in the row of witnesses.

"Yes," Mary sorrowfully called out. "And for hanging gloves to dry."

The measuring ribbon, Bartwain thought, that's what she must have used around the poor child's neck. It was a damning bit of evidence, and the only item he hadn't located. He should have questioned the slaughterhouse overseer more thoroughly. Why were his witnesses so inconsistent? Every time they spoke it was as if they were inventing their tales anew. Maybe it was his fault. You are getting lax, Thomas, he chastised himself. You are no longer a competent interviewer. They are right to want to retire you.

Suddenly he felt tired, more tired than he had in years. He knew how this was going to end. "Take me home," he said to White. But his secretary pretended not to hear him.

"Is there anything else?" Griffin said with satisfaction.

Stupid sot, Bartwain thought. And to think this is the kind of man who will wind up with a Parliament seat.

"No, sir," Jack Dawber replied. "That was enough for me."

The next witness was the butcher's wife, Mrs. Dalton, a tireless gossip.

"Our shop is four houses down from Du Gard Gloves," she said enthusiastically. "I found Rachel Lockyer on my stoop that night. I did not recognize who she was. My husband figured it out. He said it was the glovemaker's apprentice on our stoop. She wore a dress strung with filth and smelling of bitterroot." Mrs. Dalton paused to direct an accusing stare at the defendant, as if the real crime being tried was a failure of hygiene. "I gave her salts and she revived. We asked her what happened. She did not speak. She had a shifty look."

"What was her comportment?"

"Confused."

"Is that all?"

"That, and she asked for water and lye soap. We brought it and I gave her a basin. She washed her hands and neck and cheeks until they were red and raw. My husband suspected she was an inebriate. We nearly fetched a clergyman. We did not know she had been to bury her babe or we would have called for the justice of the peace."

Judge Blakemore asked: "Why didn't you fetch a clergyman?"

"Because my husband remembered she was a Leveler, and so an atheist."

From the middle of the courthouse John Lilburne called out, "Not true!"

"Please proceed," Griffin said.

"Nothing else happened. We took her back to her lodgings. I had no idea we were providing aid and comfort to a murderess!" Mrs. Dalton trembled with evident pleasure.

Next the prosecutor called Katherine Chidley. Bartwain shifted in his cushionless chair. No one was providing any new information. No one was explaining *why* any of this had happened, why Rachel might have tied that measuring ribbon around the newborn's neck. Of course, such questions were off-limits. But Bartwain's resolve not to ask them was weakening every time Griffin turned to pontificate before the spectators, his velvet cape swirling behind him.

Chidley launched into her testimony with the ease of a seasoned informant. "I have given birth many times and have assisted at many births. When Widow du Gard called for me, I went and saw the infant. We had to pry it from Rachel Lockyer's arms. I called for the coroner to order an examination."

"Did you ask if the child was hers?"

"It was self-evident. I did not need to ask."

"Did you know she had been expecting a child?"

"Yes."

138

"How?"

"I inspected her physical person in the final days of her pregnancy. I checked her breasts and they were hard and distended. She never admitted anything. She is a disorderly woman. She twists the meanings of words. When she swelled up she said it was a digestive ailment."

"Did you examine her physical person after the infant was found?"

"Yes. I pressed her breasts and the milk came. I looked under her dress and her undergarments were stained. I went upstairs and found her bedclothes bloody and wrinkled. I opened the wainscot box and it had a strange odor. I believe she hid the babe in there, and then before it could rot she took it to the woods to bury it."

"Was there anything else in the box?"

"Some velvet baby caps. Also some slippers sized for an infant."

Griffin paraded these items before the jury. He also showed them the yellow brocade dress, passing it around so they could touch it.

A juryman on the left, wearing an eye patch, spoke. "The sewing of garments strikes me as an indication that the woman did not intend harm to her child and was planning to care for it."

Chidley sniffed. "These were flimsy and made all in a rush, like she was not going to use them. They were not well sewn."

Good Christ, Bartwain thought. Are we now going to convict a woman based on the fact that she cannot turn a decent stitch? "Take me home," he said again to his secretary. White continued to ignore him—he would not take his eyes off Rachel.

"Still, velvet seems dear to use as a ruse," the juror persisted.

"All the more reason for her to rely on it," Chidley said.

The bailiff called Dr. Jacob Featherman, the coroner, who approached the bar wearing a black doublet and a ruff with pleats. Bartwain always hated this part of a bastard-murder trial—it was one reason why he generally avoided attending. He could not bear to hear about the state of the corpse.

"I was called by my superiors to examine a dead newborn," Featherman said. "The coroner's office had come into possession of an infant. I was asked to inspect it."

"What did you find?"

"At the time I conducted my examination, the body was in an early state of putrefaction. It was black around the mouth and there were settlings of blood in the limbs. The orifices were infested with small worms. The trunk showed insect marks and bites. The neck had a ring around it, which I took to be chafing from a string or ribbon—like the one that man there showed earlier." He pointed at the slaughterhouse overseer. "When I opened the body I found the blood vessels healthy and the lungs to have some air. The lungs were partially inflated."

Bartwain studied Rachel, who stood motionless under the defendant's mirror. She isn't saying anything, he thought. She needs to speak up. The defendant is supposed to interrupt and challenge the prosecution. She should have taken a few lessons from John Lilburne about how to win over a courtroom.

"What do these findings indicate?" Griffin asked.

"That the child took some breath outside the womb before it died, otherwise the lungs would not have inflated. Therefore, it was not stillborn. Also, the chafing around the neck indicates the high probability of strangulation." It was the same thing the coroner had told Bartwain at the outset of the investigation.

From the juryman on the far left, the one with the eye patch: "Were the lungs only partly inflated?"

"Yes."

"So it is possible the child could have died by natural causes, and still have taken in some air as it passed out of the birth canal?"

"Yes, it is possible. But there is the matter of the bruising."

"Could the bruises have come about by accident?" the same juror persisted. Good point, Bartwain thought. You are a troublemaker, juror-with-the-patch. During trials of this nature, the jurymen could question the witnesses directly, just as the judge, the prosecutor, and the defendant could. Sometimes everyone peppered the witness at once. Bartwain disliked it when that happened.

"Anything is possible." The doctor shrugged. "But in this case I do not think so."

"Then it is your opinion that this child was alive when it was delivered?" The question came from Griffin.

"Yes. Yes, that is my firm and unwavering opinion."

The last witness for the prosecution was William Kiffin. He was wearing thick spectacles that fogged when he exhaled and cleared when he breathed in. "I was called to minister to Rachel Lockyer after the Widow du Gard found the infant," he stated.

"What did the defendant say when you arrived at the house?" asked Griffin.

"Nothing."

"Nothing at all?"

"Nothing that I can repeat. She is an unnatural woman."

"What happened then?"

"I stayed some hours to counsel her. In all that time Miss Lockyer would not speak except to curse me. She held the cloth that had been wrapped around the infant. She clung to it. I told her she ought to tell the truth. I told her she needed to confess. Still she said nothing. She is a monstrous mother. I left that evening persuaded she had murdered it, else why would she need to lie?"

"Are you certain?"

"I have no doubt. It is clear what happened. She gave birth to a child of spurious issue and was ashamed. So she ended its life. She ended its life, in my opinion, to spare herself the shame and inconvenience."

Aha, Bartwain thought. Here was the first attempt on the part of a witness to explain why she might have done it. But the law did not allow such speculations. The law did not care about the reasons prompting the act. Pleading good intentions would get you nowhere, Bartwain thought, unless you were John Lilburne defending yourself against treason.

The investigator sat upright. All his life he had studied the statute books, but until now he had not noticed this discrepancy. Where treason was concerned, what counted was the intention. Where bastard murder was concerned, all that mattered was the act.

Why, the law is flawed, he thought.

Elizabeth Lilburne was stepping onto the witness platform over the objections of the prosecutor.

"I am the wife of John Lilburne," she declared. "I am here on behalf of the defendant. I have known Rachel Lockyer since 1646. And I was with her the night she gave birth." This caught the audience's attention—it caught Bartwain's as well. I knew it, he thought. I warned Griffin. I told him she might try to establish herself as a witness to a stillbirth. At least someone is going to make the prosecutor earn his keep this morning.

Elizabeth proceeded to give her statement. "On the first of November Rachel sent the errand boy to fetch me, around nine o'clock at night. When he arrived at my house he told me she was not well, so I made my way to Warwick Lane. I entered the shop and went to her sleeping quarters. She asked who it was. When I gave my name she let me in. She could hardly move for the pains. She said if she had ten thousand words still she could not say how much it hurt. I told her to kneel in the bed on her hands and knees, and I helped her deliver. It was a difficult birth."

The prosecutor pounced. "Your Honor, I would like to call this boy, this errand boy, to verify her testimony. She is saying she was present at the birth. This is the first I have heard of it. Let us find the boy and see if the witness is telling the truth. Let's see if he was called to her house that evening. My own opinion is she is lying. Her testimony is not credible."

Judge Blakemore said this request for verification seemed reasonable enough.

Elizabeth stated: "That's not going to be possible, Your Honor."

You're almost enjoying yourself up there, Bartwain thought. You're more of a Leveler than your husband.

"What is the boy's name?" asked Blakemore.

"Thom," she swiftly said. "But I do not know his surname or where he resides. He has disappeared."

"Where has he gone?"

"We think he has gone off with the Diggers. Also, he is a thief and not to be trusted."

"And you are?" Griffin retorted. The jurymen laughed. Griffin beckoned to one of his clerks and sent the youth scampering out of the courthouse. "We will hunt down Thom the messenger," he announced. "Don't worry, Mrs. Lilburne. It will not take long to verify your testimony."

Elizabeth held her ground. "Your Honor, he will not be able to find him, for the boy has gone out of town and I do not know when he is coming back."

"I thought you said he had gone off with the Diggers."

"Yes, but who knows where they have wandered?"

"I saw them milling around just last week," one of the jurymen piped up, "tilling that field next to the Crown and Hope tavern."

"I saw them too," said another. The jurymen began conversing amiably with one another. Someone mentioned refreshments.

Judge Blakemore buried his nose in his bouquet. "Go on, witness."

"Tell me this," Griffin interposed before Elizabeth could say more. "Where was the Widow du Gard the night you say you went to Warwick Lane? Can *she* verify your presence in the shop?"

"I did not see Mary that night. I assumed her to be sleeping. I didn't try to wake her—I did not think she would want to be involved. Also, there was a gale. It was hard to hear past the wind."

Griffin told Mary to stand, which she did, though her eyes sought the floor. "Did you see Elizabeth Lilburne that night?"

"No," Mary whispered. "No, I did not. The dog would have barked if anyone came to the door."

Oh, Elizabeth, Bartwain thought. You forgot to account for whatever damned mongrel Mary is talking about. And that matter of Thom is going to come back to haunt you.

While the court awaited word on the messenger boy, one of the jurors asked if Elizabeth had ever given birth. The jurymen were finding Elizabeth Lilburne more interesting to look at than the other witnesses. They didn't mind keeping her on the stand.

"Yes, I have given birth," Elizabeth snapped. "Three times. I know what it is to have a difficult labor. And Rachel's was difficult. She bled a copious amount. There were other problems common to a first delivery. When the infant would not leave the birth canal I examined her. Its shoulders seemed wide, so I took the ribbon and tied it around the neck. The head was mostly out. I tugged one time and that was all we needed. When the child slid into my arms it was full grown but not breathing. I tried for some minutes to clear its lungs. Rachel tried as well," she concluded, gesturing at the defendant, who was staring at her, open-mouthed.

She hasn't agreed to this, Bartwain realized. Elizabeth has not bothered to obtain Rachel's permission before telling this little lie on her behalf. And Rachel does not like what she is hearing.

"Did she harm it?" Blakemore asked.

"No! She sought to revive it. Only a savage monster could harm a child."

"Your Honor, I am telling you, she is lying—she was not present," Griffin protested.

"I *was* present," Elizabeth flared. "When I saw the child would not revive I asked Rachel what she would have me do. She said she wanted to be by herself. I said she should not be by herself under the circumstances. She paid me no heed. She said she would wrap the child in a blanket and bury it the next day. I said I would help her, but she would not listen. She wore a frightful look. I returned home. That was all. Your Honor, she is innocent!"

It was an entertaining tale, and it resembled the truth in places, but it failed to persuade Bartwain. And if it failed to persuade him, it would never persuade the jury, who did not appreciate Elizabeth Lilburne's enterprising spirit as much as he did.

"Are you certain the child was not living when you left?" This question came from the juror with the patch.

"Of course."

"Did you return to check on her, on Miss Lockyer, the next morning?"

Elizabeth hesitated. "No."

"Why not?"

Her lie was growing complicated. "I could not return because my husband was released from the Tower of London shortly thereafter."

"What relation does that have to your attendance at Warwick Lane?"

"I became busy with aiding in his release and caring for him. He was in need of my attention."

The crowd cheered and hooted. From his seat in the middle of the courthouse, John Lilburne muttered a few choice words.

The judge called for order. "It is your opinion then, Mrs. Lilburne, that Rachel Lockyer did not kill her babe?"

"Yes, that is my opinion. It was stillborn. *I am the one credible witness.*"

For a second, Bartwain almost believed her. Maybe Elizabeth had resisted divulging these details earlier because she did not want her name—her husband's name—drawn into scandalous association. No, he decided, recovering his senses. She is trying to atone for having raced off to retrieve her husband and in so doing missing Rachel's hour of need. She is trying to protect her friend. And she is failing.

Before the jurors adjourned, the errand boy Thom was dragged into the courtroom. Griffin's clerk had found the boy sitting outside St. Sepulchre's, enjoying the morning, dining on a plundered oat loaf. Thom had no idea his name was being bandied about inside the Sessions House. He had no idea Rachel Lockyer was on trial until the clerk recognized his orange hair and nabbed him. He was not happy to be pulled into the proceedings. On one side of him was Rachel, who housed him when it was raining. On the other side was the prosecutor, whom the boy feared. "May I go, Your Honor?" were his first words.

The judge asked Thom if he had been sent to find Elizabeth Lilburne and bring her to Warwick Lane on the night of November 1. "This is very important," he cautioned.

Stalling, Thom glanced over at Elizabeth and tried to read her expression, but Elizabeth's eyes were daggers and Thom could not read them. He turned back to the judge. "I don't remember."

"Think harder," Blakemore urged. "We are attempting to confirm or disprove a witness to a stillbirth."

Thom had no idea what they were talking about. He decided to give himself time to think by reviewing his message-delivery schedules out loud for the court, ticking off his list of regular customers as well as their more unusual habits, causing some in the audience to laugh. He began to relax; he grew less intimidated. His inner jester came out. A few minutes later he shouted, "I remember!" He bounced up and down. He hoped what he remembered was the same thing Rachel and Elizabeth wanted him to say. Elizabeth, at least, was nodding vigorously; she looked encouraging.

"What do you remember?" Griffin said.

Thom proceeded to do exactly what he should not have done—he proceeded to tell the truth. "No, sir, no, sir, there was no call to fetch Mrs. Lilburne. I never saw hide nor hair of Mrs. Lilburne that night. I would've remembered that! I did not see anyone that night, sir, no one at all. I mean, I remember it all quite clear now, for there was a crescent moon and I was eating ham and peas east of Poultry. I never saw Mrs. Lilburne, sir. I have not seen that lady in months. I would've remembered that." Eating ham and peas off the trash heap, he might have added, but he kept that detail private. He danced on his toes, relieved to have done his duty.

Elizabeth dropped her head, low and furious, a bull about to charge.

"May I go now, Your Honor?" Thom piped up.

A low hum, a kind of squalid mutter, began reverberating through the courthouse.

Griffin smiled. "Yes, boy, you may go." Thom sprinted down the aisle.

Judge Blakemore addressed Elizabeth. "Woman," he said, "are you aware of the dangers of bearing false witness?"

Bartwain shifted in his chair. Leave her out of this, he thought.

"What I said was true," she insisted. "That boy is lying."

"Your deception will send you to Newgate along with your companion. Is that what you want? Correct your testimony, Mrs. Lilburne, or you too will face a punishment."

Suddenly the defendant spoke up. "Leave her alone," Rachel commanded.

Bartwain groaned. Why now? Why not sooner? She should have been speaking earlier. She should have been cross-examining the prosecution's witnesses. She should have been pounding each link in the chain, looking for weaknesses. Yet she had said nothing—until now.

"Pardon me?" Judge Blakemore had almost forgotten Rachel was in the courthouse.

"I said, leave her alone!" she repeated.

At the rear of the courthouse, William Walwyn was standing, struggling up from the bench, shouting something, trying to speak. Mabbott the newsman was pulling him back, gripping him roughly, reminding the Leveler his testimony could only make things worse. For Walwyn to reveal himself, to stand and proclaim his support, would be to remind the jury that the defendant had a past—that she was an oyster wife, a strumpet, a stealer of good women's husbands. Mabbott pulled Walwyn back to the bench.

"Elizabeth Lilburne had a fever last summer and was not well," Rachel said to the judge. "She lost her two boys to the smallpox. She made a mistake in her testimony. That is all. Please let her be. It was a mistake. She was confused. I will do whatever you want, just let her be."

The judge looked from one woman to the other.

"Your Honor, please," Rachel entreated.

Elizabeth, to Rachel: "Stop it. Stop saying that. I can speak for myself."

Rachel, to the judge: "I tell you, she is not well."

"I am well enough," Elizabeth flung back.

Blakemore called for order. He said Rachel had no permission to speak about the guilt or innocence of others; she must speak only of her own. "What do you have to say in your own defense? Speak now, or your time for speaking is over."

Rachel gazed out over the packed courthouse. Her eyes flickered with recognition as she saw Bartwain, but she did not linger on him. She was not searching for him. She was seeking someone else. Bartwain did not have to turn around to guess whom she wanted. Again the Leveler rose from his bench with a strangled cry; again his friend silenced him, pulled him back. Mabbott the newsman, Mabbott the moderate, was restraining Walwyn, talking in his ear: You cannot help her this way, he was saying.

Then, in a small voice, Rachel said, "I waited too long, Your Honor." That was all. She stepped off the platform.

The judge rose. "Very well. I see you do not wish to speak further. Clerks, put her words in your books. The jury will adjourn."

Bartwain squirmed in his movable chair, craning to get a better look. Say more, he silently urged. Explain what you mean. Don't do this. Give us your side. Tell us something. Tell us anything. Give us a reason. There has to be a reason. Talk to us. Talk to me, at least. Tell me why it happened, so I may sleep again.

The judge sent the jury into the back chambers to dine on roast chicken and to deliberate.

Bartwain smoked his pipe and waited.

Fourteen

NEAR THE END of her trial, Rachel thought she saw her brother standing in the back of the courtroom. For a minute she forgot he had died; she looked for him among the spectators. When she remembered, she searched for Walwyn instead; she sought the one who was living. She concentrated so hard she became nauseated; she thought she might be sick on the stand. She beat back the urge. She found Walwyn in the last row. Fixing her attention on the horizon of his face, she distracted herself by trying to name all the sounds creatures make when they are in trouble. She ran the noises around in her head. She wished she too could roar and whistle and screech and bleat and rattle and all those other noises a woman could not make unless she wanted the world to declare her an animal, a creature of unreason, a dreamer of false dreams. She stood through two hours of testimony. She listened to friends and strangers tell the judge and jury who she was, what she had done, when and how far she had fallen. It took a while for her to grasp that she was the person under discussion. She could not find herself in their words. Not even in Elizabeth's. Poor Elizabeth, who loved Rachel but was going about it the wrong way, who was trying to fix the problem by turning things upside down, whereas Rachel wanted to turn things right side up, to get off the ceiling, to pull her claws out from the rocks.

She continued to stand as someone in the audience threw a fig at her. Someone else suggested how long it would take her to suffocate once she was hanging. Through it all she kept her eyes on Walwyn. She went home to him in her thoughts. Even as the surgeon discussed the state of putrefaction, she did not pull away. No reservation lingered in Walwyn's expression. And when Kiffin accused her of being an unnatural woman, her lover rolled his eyes with such an exaggerated motion she had to bite her lip to keep from smiling. He sustained her.

The judge sent her into Bartwain's chambers to await the jury's verdict. Two guards stationed themselves outside the door as she paced within, studying the books on the investigator's shelves, trying to sound out the titles. Someone knocked, and she assumed it was Elizabeth coming to berate her. The latch opened. Standing in the door was Walwyn. The guards stayed outside.

He moved swiftly, crushing her in his arms. He had bribed someone to get inside the investigator's chambers. He kissed her; his mouth was everywhere. Her hair, then her neck, first tentative, paternal, then harder. He pulled her to him; he would not leave her alone. His ferocity surprised both of them. This was not the time; he had not come here with that kind of thing in mind. He had come here to tell her he was sorry; instead he gave her his mouth. He was worn; he had not slept. He was whispering nonsense to her. He spun plans so idealistic and lofty only a Leveler could have concocted them. He promised to steal her away under cover of night. He would break her out of prison; he would find her a horse. They would ride together. Or they would board a ship. They would sail all the way to the colonies. Or they would travel to Clovelly along the far coast and build a cottage, just the two of them. He spoke with the frantic optimism of a man who has tasted the limits of what his life is going to allow.

She pushed him away. "Your plans are ridiculous," she said, not bothering to lower her voice. "Your plans are not going to work." They proceeded to argue.

He said, "What would you have me do?"

"I would have you be truthful about what your life is and what it is not."

"I would have you be truthful too," he said. "I have neglected everything for you. Don't you see what is happening to my life? I have become a miscreant."

"Don't you see what is happening to mine?" Rachel said.

She won that part of the argument.

They were still angry. But then she pressed her hot cheek against his and whispered: "Do you love me regardless?" And he, immediately, wrapping her in his arms: "*Regardless* is not the word."

He wanted to know why she had not said more on the stand. "My God, why didn't you speak? You are giving the jury permission to think the worst."

Rachel tried to explain. She told him that back at the trial's opening, she had planned to say she was guilty. But that was before Elizabeth saw in Rachel's eyes what she was planning to say and had leaped up from the witness box to argue her out of it, to tell Rachel not to give up. That was also before the scaffolding collapsed and they had taken her back to Newgate, where she stewed and brooded seven more days. When Walwyn asked her what she had contemplated, what she had thought about, Rachel went quiet.

To allow herself to recall that night was the first insuperable obstacle. If she could overcome that, she would remember studying the cracks along her bedroom ceiling. She would hear sounds issuing from her own body, sounds she did not recognize and could not control. She remembered smelling the stench as she lost control of her bowels and bladder. She remembered hearing someone breathing. It was her own breathing she had heard and not someone else's, although the sound seemed to have come from outside. She remembered reaching for something in the wainscot.

She remembered hearing a voice. When her mind crept toward the sound of that voice, Rachel could go no farther.

She looked at Walwyn. "I think the things they are saying about me might be true," she whispered.

"Don't you do that. Don't you say even one more word of that kind." He gripped her by the shoulders. "The prosecution is lying. The prosecution is creating a picture of you that is not true, that is sensational. If you will not trust yourself, at least believe me."

"Believe you?"

"Yes!"

She laughed. She could not believe what she was hearing. She felt old, older than he was, old behind the eyes, old inside the bones. "What is there to believe about *you*? You are you. There is no believing or disbelieving that. You are William Walwyn, the fool who loved me. That is all. That is all I can think when I think about you. Now stop hounding me!"

"You lost something. That's all. Don't make it worse. Don't turn against yourself."

"Did I? Did I lose it? Or did I push it away?"

He hesitated.

"What if the Lord gave me a gift and I refused it? What if I turned my back?"

"You wouldn't do that."

"But what if I did?" From next door, she could hear the clank of the jurors' spoons scraping the bottoms of their soup bowls.

Walwyn was saying something, but his words meant nothing at this point; his words were just sounds. He was shaking her. "Never say such things," he was crying. "Never say such things about yourself. You are wholly good."

She pushed him back. "I abandoned her."

"Why would you do that?"

She stayed quiet.

After a few seconds, he whispered, "I have ruined you then."

"No, you did not. You freed me."

"That is a lie and you know it. Any woman I know would beat me if I were to say that."

"But it is true."

By this Rachel meant: You loved me soul and eye and claw and wing, and everywhere I went, there you were. You saw and fed and watered me and now I no longer thirst. Now it does not hurt—now my life does not hurt, because I am known through and through. And you have not freed me on the outside but you did free me on the inside, and that is the side that matters; that is the one a person can do a bit about.

Walwyn asked if she remembered that night.

"Which one?"

"The night the child was conceived."

She flinched. All those nights tended to run together in her mind.

"I do," he told her. "I remember each of them separately."

"I thought I had passed the childbearing years. I thought it was impossible."

"Didn't anyone ever read you the book of Sarah," he whispered.

"You mean the book of Genesis."

"They are the same," he said, drawing her close, drawing her to him, with a smile that illumined his entire countenance.

Bartwain told White to be ready to wheel him out of the courtroom when the verdict came. He distrusted the crowd, which looked unruly.

It took thirty minutes for the jury members to finish their roast chicken and arrive at a decision. It would have taken fifteen but for juror-with-the-patch, whose opinion needed to be won over. The twelve sworn men of the neighborhood then filed back into the courtroom in a single line and announced they'd found Rachel Lockyer guilty of murder. They said she had committed a malicious assault and should die for her crime. The foreman went on to state that Elizabeth Lilburne's testimony was not credible and qualified as perjury. As she was a grieving mother, however, with two sons recently lost, they would not assign her a punishment; they advised her husband to discipline her at home. The foreman read Rachel's sentence: death by hanging. The execution would take place in a week. Then juror-with-the-patch spoke up and reminded the foreman it was Advent season. They had forgotten about that. They did not want to be responsible for hanging a woman on Christmas, or Christ-tide, as the Puritans preferred it called. The jurors huddled for another discussion. They returned to their places, their cheeks flushed from the effort of thinking on their feet. The foreman announced that the execution would take place in January, just after Twelfth Night, to avoid any conflict with the day three kings once carried gifts across a desert for a child. In the interim, Rachel would be returned to Newgate. This time she would not go to the women's ward. She would be sent to the hold for condemned prisoners, a stand-alone shack where ringbolts lined the walls like settings on a bracelet.

Standing before the court, his muscular legs planted wide, as if he were spanning the width of a rocking rowboat, Prosecutor Griffin urged Rachel Lockyer to thank the jurors for their mercifulness. They were doing her a favor, he said, letting her live through Christmas.

A cascading cry welled up and over the rafters. At first Bartwain could not place the sound. He guessed the cry belonged to Elizabeth or some other disconsolate woman. Then he realized it was coming from above. It was coming from the beams. It was the owl, the same barred owl that had sounded off on what was coming. As soon as one shriek ended, another took its place. The owl silenced the prosecutor.

Bartwain ordered White to wheel him outside. His secretary began to rock and pitch the old chair, then pushed it up the aisle, forcing a path through the pack of soldiers that now entered the courthouse, soldiers buzzing and swarming around the condemned woman like flies over a deer that has fallen.

"Get me out of here," the investigator roared over the din. He was profoundly disappointed. "Get me out before the mob starts forming. I am through with bastard cases."

Fifteen

THEN EVERYTHING STARTED unraveling.
Spectators were fleeing the fetid air, stumbling and shoving as they exited the courthouse, some abandoning food baskets in their haste. At the same time, the soldiers were dragging Rachel toward the courthouse steps, and John Lilburne was herding some of his dwindling followers forward, calling whom he could, gathering stragglers. A group was congregating at the west corner of the courthouse. John was going to practice his ideas on them, survey their reactions. Having opposed any support for Rachel while her fate remained undecided, he was now changing sides. He had no interest in providing aid to a lewd woman, but he remained more than willing to capitalize on the upcoming death of a condemned woman. The Levelers needed a good martyrdom. Rachel's trial had been a farce, a travesty of justice, he shouted. She had no legal defender. No one had allowed her to make a plea. Her conviction represented a violation of the rights of all Englishmen. As John put on his eyeglasses to take in his audience, his supporters stole sideways glances at one another in silence.

From the other side of the Sessions House, Mary du Gard looked on as John delivered his speech. She could not hear what he was saying, but she could read his countenance, which told her enough.

Mary did not consider herself a Leveler, and the members of that ragtag organization had never invited her to join their company. In her view, radicals were all alike, whether English or French, Puritan or Leveler or Huguenot. They all thought meetings and conventicles, illegal printing presses and secret societies, served a purpose. They all assumed that the busier they were, the more worthwhile their causes. And in their zeal, they invariably mistook fervency of conviction for effectiveness of tactics.

A ragged howl rose from the eastern end of the courthouse. Mary turned. The sound was coming from Walwyn. He was calling Rachel's name, straining to reach her. His countenance was unbearable. He was spitting and lunging against six Parliamentary soldiers, rank-and-files who did not know that they were beating their hero, that they were striking a man who had advocated for their own fair wage. Walwyn fought them off—he was not so old as they thought—and shouted for John to come help, but John was otherwise occupied; John was constitutionally incapable of breaking off a speech once he had started it. The soldiers rode Walwyn into the floor until he was spitting splinters. They picked him up and threw him out the side door, shouting good riddance.

Mary's eyes found her assistant near the entrance. Rachel's hair, once smooth and shining, now hung snarled and limp. A grayish pallor clung to her skin. The deterioration was not simply physical. Mary could not have pointed to one part of Rachel's anatomy and declared, "Here is the problem." It was more of an intuition, a dull uneasiness. And whatever *it* was, this thing gone wrong, it seemed to have taken up residence. As the soldiers led Rachel toward the courthouse steps, the hem of her dress snagged on something and she tripped, pitching into her captors, who began groping at her. Mary rushed forward, her hand clapped on top of her steep hat. "That is my apprentice," she cried out. "Do not lay a hand on her." The soldiers ignored her. One of them shoved the tip of his pike into Rachel's mouth until he threatened to puncture the windpipe. He withdrew as Rachel gagged. They did not stop harassing their

156

charge until Thomas Bartwain burst back into the courtroom in a rattletrap conveyance that Mary took to be a wheelbarrow, his skeletal secretary flying behind him. Bartwain's fat body, unbalanced by the sudden speed, swayed back and forth in his chair; furious, the investigator ordered the guards to stop.

Mary hurried over to Rachel and extended her hand. "Get up."

As the soldiers exchanged words with the investigator, Mary guided her assistant to her feet and down the exterior steps until the two women were standing outside the Sessions House, under a misting sky. They regarded each other warily. They had not spoken since the day Mary found the infant.

"What are you doing?" Rachel asked, bewildered.

Before Mary could say anything the soldiers were surrounding them, trotting down the steps and resuming their hold on the prisoner. They swept Rachel into their arms, wrestling her from Mary, who still had hold of her assistant's wrist irons; when Mary was forced to let go she found herself snatching Rachel's sleeve instead, holding it until she could hold no longer without tearing something. They hauled Rachel into their mule cart, which would transport her the short distance to the prison. Mary squinted through the spitting rain and watched them leaving. She could see Elizabeth hurrying toward them, bellowing, searching for Rachel. Already the mule was moving, heading across the street for the prison, its head low. Elizabeth was not going to catch them. Once Rachel had passed through the entrance, the warden would pull those iron gates shut. Elizabeth was not going to get there fast enough.

But Mary could. Mary was fast. She began running. She hitched up her skirts, sliding past the scattering crowd. She sped forward, her shoes and stockings a blur. She ran as hard and futilely as she had the day the man who would become her husband had taken her into his house, taken her with his thick fingers and his thin switch, which he used.

By the time she reached the prison entrance, the gates were shutting. Mary pulled on the bars as they closed. Rachel was not coming back. She called her assistant's name repeatedly, pounding the iron rails, apologizing for telling the truth, apologizing even though she would do it again if she had to.

Across the street, Anne Walwyn, wife of William Walwyn, waited for her husband to leave the courthouse.

She was accustomed to waiting. In her estimation it did not qualify as hardship. If anything troubled her, it was not her husband's lateness but the economics of time itself. Time appeared in Anne's thoughts as an hourglass. She would count the grains as they fell, by the hour or second, just as any woman counts something she holds dear but thinks she does not deserve. And she would fall silent when she witnessed her husband throwing time away in the manner of a profligate.

Probably she should not have attended Rachel's trial. Certainly she should not be skulking around afterward to observe her husband brawling with the soldiers and tackling Reverend Kiffin in the street, as he was doing now—seizing the good clergyman from behind and boxing his ears until Gilbert Mabbott rushed in to stop the beating, to pull the Leveler off the preacher.

Mabbott pulled Walwyn to the courthouse steps and sat beside him as their friend Richard Overton approached. Mabbott proceeded to bandage Walwyn's left knuckles while Overton bandaged his right knuckles. No one said anything. What the Levelers intended to do now, Anne had no way of knowing. She disliked both Overton and Mabbott. In her prayers she referred to one as the Seditious Leveler and the other as the Seditious Newsman; God would know whom she meant. These were the same men who over the last eight years had caused Walwyn to feel dissatisfied with his life, who had filled his mind with notions, leaving Anne with a husband who wrote page after page through the night and lit the furnace with his brilliance in the morning. Walwyn, it turned out, was her Sisyphus.

Now her husband was standing, hands wrapped in rags; Overton and Mabbott rose to stand loyally beside him. He began walking in the direction of the prison, his friends following. So did Anne, from a distance, tightening the chin strap that held her battered black hat in place. It was easier when he was in the Tower because then she did not have the option of following him. Then she knew where he was.

The men crossed over to Bailey Road, and Walwyn stopped before the gates encircling Newgate Prison. Rachel had disappeared inside. Overton placed a hand on Walwyn's back. Anne came to a standstill also. She glanced up at the prison, noticing its stark line. A windmill sat atop the roof, its great blades cutting the sky in circles. Mabbott must have heard Anne's footsteps because he turned and greeted her in a guarded tone while Overton kept his arm around Walwyn. "Wait just a minute, Mrs. Walwyn," the newsman whispered. "Give him one more minute. He is trying to collect himself." He gestured at her husband.

I understand, she mouthed.

Did she?

She supposed she did. She understood she had a husband whose thoughts had traveled far from hers. Perhaps he was imagining a sea voyage. Perhaps those blades were sails. When he had such dreams at home, Anne would wake him. She knew when he had them because she knew what the dream sounded like. She, too, had once believed the world held open longer than it does.

She would wait no longer this day.

Without another word, Anne left the men to their vigil and began the winding walk back to Moorfields. She walked by herself. She didn't mind. She was relieved, almost. She would not look back. She would not be Lot's wife.

Sixteen

⌒∾

TWO GUARDS TOOK Rachel into the hold for condemned prisoners, a small structure of limestone adjacent to the main prison. Inside, she slipped on a carpet
of excrement. One of the guards lit a torch and hooked it into the
wall. The other attached her leg irons to one of six rings bolted into
the stone. The first guard, a young fellow whose helmet seemed
too large for his head, advised Rachel to bribe the warden to move
up her execution date. "To escape the stench," he explained, gesturing apologetically at the floor as he left.

Rachel tried curling up on the end of a low wooden bench. She
could hear rain against the roof. For a while she pretended to talk
to her brother, but she could not hear him, could not imagine what
he would say.

She did not pretend to talk to the child.

She would not even think the word *child*. She would push
around it, leaving a wide berth; she would sweep all such thoughts
in the corner. She would step over anything, avoid any obstacle,
before she would think that word. Yet there it was. Every time
she tried to dodge it, misery would whisper the word for her, and
a clean whistling breath rushed through her. The emptiness hiccupped and gabbled at her, slid her crosswise. She wondered what

her mother would say to her now. Probably Martha Lockyer would tell her daughter to confess, which made sense if one had a list of things to repent. But what if a person did not know for certain? She shifted around on the bench. She would force her brother to talk to her. She would conjure him up to calm herself.

She succeeded — too well. As soon as Robert appeared, he was chastising her; he showed up midreprimand. He was saying: That's not the point. Whether you think you are guilty or not isn't the point.

It is, she replied.

No. The point is what kind of God do you have.

I don't have God, Rachel said. God has me. God has me in His cooking pot. I am being carried into the kitchen as we speak.

It was her father's God to whom she was referring.

Robert was not having any of this. He never did permit his sister an ounce of self-pity, never showed her any sympathy. When Rachel's arms used to ache from cutting hides, he would tell her to count her blessings she had arms in the first place — he had seen dying men without limbs in the army. When her head used to pound from the fumes of freshly dyed gloves, he would urge her to pray. Pray for God to ease my headache? she would say. No, Sister, he would reply. Pray for God to help you stop complaining. A woman who feels sorry for herself is a dead woman. Don't you give up. He'd delivered that last line on the morning of his execution, when Rachel had ducked into his tent a few minutes before Captain Savage and his men took him into the churchyard. Robert was too thin for the cloak they had thrown over his shoulders. He grinned when he saw his sister, kept grinning even as she threw her arms around him, even as the tent flap opened again and the light streamed in, and, following the light, the soldiers. "Don't you blame God for this," he had shouted to her as they pulled him away. "God hasn't got time to be the busybody most people make Him out to be. Don't you blame Him."

Rachel lay on her back on the bench and wrapped her shawl close. When she looked up she could see sparks from the dying torch the guards had hooked into the wall. The cold was severe that night. The cold was so sharp it threaded down her spine like a wire.

She missed Walwyn. She missed him so much she was beginning to have trouble swallowing. She rubbed her neck, the base of her chin, the same place he used to touch her. With her tongue, she tested the roof of her mouth, the back of her throat. There was nothing the matter, except she appeared to be choking on his absence.

Almost a year before, Walwyn had told her he wanted no more involvement with the Levelers. His time with them was done, he had said. When she asked why, he replied that the Levelers were becoming too much like John Lilburne. But John's cause is the People, she suggested. They were in the rented room of the travelers' inn and she was lying on top of him, her bare stomach pressed into his, her chin in her hands as she gazed soberly down at him. Walwyn shook his head. "John Lilburne's cause is John Lilburne," he said.

"I would like to read what he writes," she had replied. "I would like to see if the way he sounds in his writing is the same way he sounds in his speaking."

"And how does he sound in his speaking?"

"Puffed up."

"Then they are the same. We are all puffed up. All of us who write with him, I mean."

She frowned. "I don't like it when you disparage your gift."

"You are my gift," he said.

They used to wage battles over this. He would offer to help her learn to read and to write. "I want to learn," Rachel always said. "I want to try." And she did try, but the letters did not cooperate; the letters on the page never looked or acted the way she thought they ought. Walwyn would show her a word and say, "That is *aardvark*" or "That is *melancholy*," and she would copy it for herself, only to look up and feel betrayed; the words on her page did not resemble the words on his. She told him she was too old. "Read to me," she urged him. "It is enough if someone reads to me. That is how most people get by." No, he would reply, his face darkening; no, that is not good enough; you can do better. He did not want to be her reader, he said; she needed to work out the words for herself. He did not want to foster a dependence. This made her laugh, howl, even. They were comfortable arguing with each other; they fought thoughtfully and with vigor. To spar and joust was not a waste of time for them. They bit each day down to the gristle. At the end of these skirmishes Walwyn would produce the dreaded grammar book and slide it slyly back on her lap. Look, he would say with his slow grin. Here is a word, and another, and another, and it is easy; and here is the alphabet. See what you make of it. And she, scowling: Your alphabet does not look right. When he insisted, she would cut him off. I am too old, she would say again, pushing away his grammar book until the next time, when she would declare anew, as if they had never spoken, as if this were her first time proposing the idea: I want to read; help me to read; it is all I can think about each evening. They went round and round on this.

She missed his hands. When she thought of Walwyn's hands, Rachel covered her face with her own. She used to tell him that the Levelers liked to share all things in common, particularly womankind. He failed to see the humor in this observation. She would elbow him, saying, "Of course you have to admit it is funny." He would grow angry, blustery, say she should not disparage herself. "I wasn't," she pointed out. Once she asked him why the Levelers advocated the abolition of distinctions between classes of men. "You would have us all stand together, all on the same rung of the ladder," she marveled.

"That's right," he replied. "That's the only way it is fair."

"But there is not enough room," she argued.

He listened to her. He not only listened; he absorbed. He changed his mind because of her, because of the things she said. To Rachel this was astonishing. She had never had this effect on another person, not even Robert. Sometimes, when Walwyn was working on something, he would read a sentence or two out loud, and she could hear where her thoughts streaked across the horizon of his words, like old stars that light up the night sky as they are falling. When John and Overton read the same passages later, over foaming ale, they bemoaned Walwyn's latest pamphleteering efforts; Walwyn, they said, had stopped thinking clearly. "He is writing about love," John complained.

She missed his hands; she also missed his face. She used to grab hold of it, pulling his cheeks. She would mash and squash him this way and that, creating animal faces. He let her do it. She poked and prodded. He endured countless humiliations in the name of love. He understood she was learning to trust. He was learning to trust too, but this was hard for him as a man to admit, so he concentrated on her first. He tolerated her tortures. She plucked rogue hairs from his eyebrows. She became an eyebrow zealot. He would slap his hand to his eye and tell her she was heartless, and she would laugh until the tears streamed. Then she would slide onto his stomach, slipping her hand between his spine and the mattress; she would wander up and down, counting his vertebrae. She counted the minutes also. This was not as good a habit. She tried not to count them, but once she started it became hard to stop. She would tick them off in her head, one by one, until one of the minutes turned inexplicably heavier than the others and she would pull back, leaving Walwyn saddled with her silence, forcing him to rise and pull on whatever clothing he could remember having come in wearing two hours earlier. I do not want to go, he would tell her. Yet still you leave me, she would say.

Rachel pulled her shawl high over her neck and ears. She had discovered another prisoner, an elderly man, slumbering under a pile of discarded cloaks in a corner of the hold. Covering his mouth and nose was the hem of a cloak that levitated each time he exhaled.

"What is this," she remembered saying to Walwyn once. "What is this we are doing? Who are we? What have we become?"

"You are the one who saved me," he said.

"I never saved anybody."

"You saved me," he said again. "You are wholly good." But he stiffened when he bent down to say goodbye to her, and he moved with a sick heaviness, with a kind of sick heavy twist. She had not replied.

The guards outside the hold were quiet now. After a while she forgot where she was, and she descended into a hard and merciless sleep. The sleep was merciless because it was joyful. She waded from one green dream to another. She saw a verdant grove, a cottage sheltered under silver birches. She saw sea grass blanketing a child. Not until dawn began peeking through the narrow ventilation shaft high overhead did she open her eyes and realize how long she had been sleeping. She could hear the clatter of boots outside. The winter rain had stopped. Her stomach was growling.

Across the hold, the old white-haired man, the other prisoner, was awake and sitting on a bench of his own, the pile of cloaks strewn around him. He was barefoot, and his thin white shins poked out from the bottom of his robe. He bared his nearly toothless gums at her. "Best be waking, miss, for they take away the food if you do not set to it right away."

"Who are you?" Rachel breathed.

"No one. Just an old thief they put in the wrong place and forgot."

"They put you here by mistake?"

He nodded affably. "Don't worry," he said, reading her thoughts. "You are not the kind they forget."

Two guards stepped into the hold and delivered bowls of gruel. The young one told Rachel to stop scratching herself. "You'll take the skin right off," he worried, studying the fleabites on her arms and neck. "The more you scratch the worse it gets. You'll scratch to death."

"God does not forgive self-murderers," the other guard added as he tossed a bowl to the bench with a clatter. Reaching, the old man accidentally flipped the bowl over, splattering the floor with gruel. He used his long fingernails to scrape the spill back into his bowl. He put his fingers to his mouth and licked them. Then he returned his fingers to the grimed floors, feeling for more, his back bent over like the second half of a rainbow.

Rachel lifted her chin and looked straight at the guards. "The fleas are biting," she said. "If that is self-murder, then there is a remedy."

The young guard laughed, a hard grating gate that would not open. His teeth were black in the backs.

Seventeen

T HE MORNING AFTER the trial, Walwyn rose from his bed, raced downstairs, and got as far as the sun-filled garden behind the apothecary before Anne called him back, summoning him to her kitchen. She was disemboweling a pheasant. Fourteen was not well, she announced, her hands spotted with feathers; he seemed to be running a fever. "You can conduct your business in the city later," she said. "Right now your children need their father. You want to be a physician? Here is your chance."

So he stayed. He checked Richard every hour as his youngest tugged on his father's ears. He found no rising temperature.

The next day he tried again. This time he made it as far as the crumbling stones of Moorgate before Anne came floating behind, calling for him. Fourteen's fever was down but his cough was up, she declared. Again Walwyn returned home and sat with the boy, who was thrilled to have his father's attention. Richard did not cough; he giggled.

Mabbott stopped by with a delivery from John. Walwyn glanced at the scrawled pages the younger Leveler had sent. John wanted him to review the draft of his latest treatise, Mabbott said. He was writing it in honor of Rachel and her pending execution. He intended the pamphlet to bolster support for the Levelers.

"Why does he want me to read it?"

"He wants you to advise him as to the ending. He doesn't know if it's right."

"Tell John I am not in the business of good endings." Walwyn handed the pages back.

"He'll be disappointed."

"A little disappointment will be good for him," Walwyn said. "It will prepare him for when he is older."

Not until the end of the week did Richard's "fever" break. Anne had retired to her quarters. Walwyn sat on a pile of blankets in the next room, rereading Brooke's *Conservatory of Health* until he was certain Richard was soundly sleeping in the small bed beside him. He set down the book, crept downstairs, and escaped, passing the flower garden and heading for the street that led to Moorgate. Anne stood at her second-floor window and watched him leaving—she was not actually sleeping.

Past Moorgate, Walwyn hailed a hackney coach and told the driver to take him to Newgate. The driver balked and said it was too dangerous this time of night. "I insist," Walwyn said, and opened his purse.

By the time they arrived at the entrance, the driver was feeling responsible for him. "Don't stand too close to the gates. They'll rob you through the bars. I've seen them do it." He was not referring to the prisoners.

Walwyn brushed off this advice, saying he would be fine. Somewhere in the back of his mind he knew no one of sound mind visited Newgate after midnight, but he was not paying attention to those parts of his mind that were sound. Nor was he thinking of Anne, awake in her bedroom in Moorfields, listening to the sounds of a silent house. He reached the wrought-iron gates and pounded on them. Three guards were flipping cards in the courtyard. They waved him off; they said no one was allowed at this hour. Walwyn pounded again, bellowing Rachel's name, demanding to see her, reaching his hands through the bars to grab the closest guard by the doublet. That did it. The guards pulled the gates open, not to let Walwyn in but to let themselves out.

They proceeded to beat him, to teach the wretch a lesson. They pounded his face to a wet pulp. They punched his skin to a sticky mess like a woman punches her yeast dough, so that by the time Walwyn returned to Moorfields, past three o'clock and Anne at the second-floor window waiting, all she had to do was take one downward look at his bruised and bluish face to know what she already knew: he was not yet through with Rachel.

Eighteen

THERE ARE SEVERAL ways to make a martyr, and all of them require a printing press.

A few days before Christmas, John Lilburne shooed a blinking Elizabeth out of the bed at half past four; he needed the upstairs to himself. She stumbled down to the kitchen, too bleary to quarrel.

John crowned himself with his stocking cap and sat at his desk, which overlooked an alley. Cracking his knuckles prepared him to do his best work. He dipped his quill in the well, blotted the tip, and poised the instrument over a blank sheet of parchment, waiting for inspiration to drip.

Fifteen minutes passed. Beneath the window, a scavenger was scratching through a pile of onion peels and eggshells. The sound resembled a rat behind a wall. John reached under his desk and cracked his toes, one by one. He dipped the quill a second time and prepared to compose his concluding sentences.

John had resolved to set aside his personal opinions in the matter of Rachel Lockyer. What he thought of the woman was one thing. What he wrote about her was something else. He planned to turn her death into something edifying, to transform her into a martyr of the people, as he had done for her brother, Robert. Doing so required a clever piece of writing, given the circumstances. No one wanted to be caught defending a murdering mother. So John had focused instead on how Rachel's trial had fallen short of justice, neatly sidestepping any references to the child. Rachel Lockyer had been permitted no legal counsel, he argued. The bailiff had neglected to ask for her plea when the trial reopened. She had received no support for cross-examining witnesses or questioning the prosecution's argument. She was uneducated; she could not read; she could hardly be expected to speak in her own defense. John did not believe his treatise would change the outcome or reverse the verdict. He had no intention of pulling the woman off the scaffold. He simply hoped to put her death to good use. He would persuade his readers to forget her crime and remember the injustice. He would turn her death into something useful—into a platform. He contemplated calling the piece *The Martyred Mother*, but to refer to her as *mother* might suggest she deserved that appellation. So he eliminated the word from his heading and went with *The People's Martyr* instead.

Cracking his knuckles a second time, he returned to the final section. He scribbled along, completely engrossed, for three hours, until Elizabeth came upstairs to tell him their daughter had lost a tooth and could use comforting. From the kitchen came the singsong noises of Young Elizabeth talking to her doll, which John had whittled for her a year ago Christmas. He had put up evergreen branches and holly last year, too, in the front room. In principle, he had broken the law by doing so. Wary of the unrestrained behaviors and excesses of the Advent season, Parliament had declared Christmas a day for fasting and penance—though ordinary people still found ways to make merry. When he had given the doll to his daughter, Young Elizabeth had accepted his offering with a regal inclination of her head and said, "You forgot to give her a nose." She was exactly like her mother. This year, the Lilburnes had not put up any evergreens or holly.

"Children lose teeth all the time," John said miserably, for his wife had broken his concentration. "What do you want me to do?"

"I would like your daughter to spend some time with her father."

"Bring her up here then. Let her sit up here with me. We will look out the window together."

"You mean she will sit on the floor while you go on writing."

"She likes the floor," John protested.

A few days before, they had argued about Rachel, and John had asked what Elizabeth was thinking when she'd defended her in front of that crowded courtroom. "You looked like a fool," he told her. "You damaged your reputation." Elizabeth pointed out that John was not worried about her reputation; he was worried about his own. "They are the same," he shot back. "I want you to stay home on the day she goes to the scaffold. I don't want you traipsing around after her. I trust your performance at the Old Bailey was the end of it."

"The end of it for whom?"

"For us. The whole matter will be over before you know it. Things will turn out all right."

"Turn out all right for whom?"

"For us. For us and for the People."

"But not for Rachel?"

"For Rachel is not the point."

"Not the point for whom?"

"Not the point for us."

"But she is the People too, no less than us," Elizabeth had argued as John reached for the iron cooking pot over the hearth. It was filled with pea soup, and heavy, but he managed to ladle himself a cup.

He leaned back and crossed his legs insolently. "Your involvement with that woman is nothing more than a willful association with scandal. You lacked experience in the courtroom. You lacked the education and learning to hold your ground on the witness stand. The prosecution slaughtered you."

"This is the first time I've heard you venerate what comes out of universities. I thought you believed truth was plain and simple, John, not filled with fancy rhetoric."

"I do!" He set down his cup and grabbed her hands. "But you

did not go into that courtroom the other day to be plain and simple. To tell the truth is easy. To tell a lie requires an education."

"I received my education from you," she said.

Now she was leaning over and resting her chin on her husband's shoulder, taking in the papers strewn across his desk. Dawn would arrive in two hours. John stretched forward and tried to cover what notes he could—Elizabeth would not want him to be writing about Rachel. "Just let me finish this paragraph," he implored. "Can't our daughter wait for her father to finish his paragraph?"

Elizabeth gave up and left the bedroom. John glanced down to find that he had smeared ink across the last page of his essay. "Damnation," he muttered. He would have to rewrite that last part.

It was the concluding paragraph of the martyrology, the scene of execution, brought to life for the education and edification of the reader—a remarkable feat, considering Rachel had not yet been hanged. But John retained a capacity for invention. He planned to have his pamphlet printed in advance of the actual event, so he could distribute it on site at the scaffold. A timely martyrology was more important than an accurate one when the Levelers were losing momentum.

He rewrote the last section, quickly and with a flourish. He gave Rachel a courageous final speech in which she called for the right of all Englishmen to a fair trial and a competent defense. He dressed her in gauzy silk and let her hair tumble around her shoulders. He made her a redhead. He had her toss her fiery hair as she was speaking, to convey her spirited nature to readers. Had she tossed her mane any more, she might have been a horse. She resembled no woman John had seen on the streets of London or would find there in the future. His eyes were filling by the time he took her down from the scaffold. When the ink was dry, he curled his papers into a scroll, tied it with a string, and raced downstairs and through the kitchen, passing his gap-toothed daughter, who wept as he flew by, and his wife, who threw a loaf of bread out the door after him. He fled the rents at Southwark and hailed the first waterman he found, who took him across the river to Westminster. There John deposited his manuscript in the hands of his favorite unlicensed printer, who operated a movable-type press in an abandoned arsenal along the Thames. He ordered two hundred copies with a pickup date in the first week of January. "They must be ready then," he said, "or I cannot use them." The printer said he would do his best.

After John left the arsenal, the printer and his apprentice began setting the type for the first page, which they would ink and press in painstaking fashion, rolling off two hundred copies before peeling off the blackened letters and laying out page two. They would repeat this process for five single-spaced pages, which was how long it had taken John Lilburne to turn Rachel Lockyer, murdering mother, into Rachel Lockyer, the people's martyr. And as the pages set they would string them up on long wires that they pinned between empty kegs of gunpowder, so the words of Rachel's last speech, which were the words of John's own furious and unmet hopes, would swing there in the drafty air until they dried to the consistency of history.

Nineteen

B ARTWAIN WAS SUFFERING from a case of conscience. It was a curious sensation, almost like a low-grade fever. If he didn't dwell on it, he hardly noticed. But whenever he returned to his study to sit at his desk and finish his final report, to wrap things up, to wash his hands of Rachel, it returned.

"I'm quitting this job," he told his wife the day after Christmas. "I'm retiring." Mathilda was kneading dough in the kitchen, slapping it into submission, raising clouds of powder. Bartwain, unable to tolerate his study, had transferred his papers to the table in the kitchen. He was working on his final report. Every so often he would lift his head up and suggest ways his wife could improve her bread making. She ignored these comments.

"You can't retire," she said. "We will run out of money."

"We'll get by. I can't keep doing this. I can't keep going back to that cursed courthouse."

"Why not?" She continued kneading the dough.

Bartwain never did catch any mice but the one, the baby mouse, the son of the son of a mouse. All the others had disappeared. Maybe the fate of the one was enough to frighten the rest off. Maybe deterrence worked. But at what cost?

"Stop pestering me," he said; really, he was speaking to himself. "I have a report due. I always have a report due after a case is over."

"If you're trying to write, why haven't you written anything?"

He did not know what to say to that.

"Is this about that poor spinster?" Mathilda began pounding the dough with a shaky fist. *Pound, pound, pound.* "I will tell you something. She's the talk of the town." Yesterday, Mathilda reported, passing through St. Martin's she had heard a tallow chandler talking about the case with a salt-and-pepper grinder. "You're famous," she said.

"That's not going to help me finish my report."

"It's not supposed to," she pointed out.

The investigator had had a visit on Christmas Eve from William Walwyn, who showed up at the house without warning. Mathilda had peeked to see who it was before opening the door. The Bartwains were staunch celebrators of Advent, and they had filled their tiny house with feast-day treats and decorations of which the Puritans would not have approved—minced pies and plum porridge, rosemary, evergreen boughs, and mistletoe. There was even a small crèche upstairs. Bartwain had been in his study when Walwyn arrived. "It's some young man," Mathilda announced. Any man with fewer years than Bartwain qualified as young in her eyes.

When Walwyn entered the investigator's study, Bartwain could not resist staring. Rachel's lover was almost unrecognizable, with welts around the eyes and a broken nose from his tangle with the guards. "Now we are both falling apart," Bartwain observed, glancing down at his own wheeling chair, which he still needed.

"Take me," Walwyn said, without explanation or greeting. "Release her, Investigator, and take me."

"Mr. Walwyn." He had heard this kind of plea before.

"Let them hang me. My life for hers. Why won't they do it? What difference is it to them so long as someone is punished?"

"Your life is worth more than hers. I would be careful what you offer."

"My life is not worth one farthing more. If anything, it is worth far less!"

"Yes, yes, of course, I know about your Leveling principles. In

God's eyes the least are the greatest, the last shall be first, et cetera, et cetera. I have heard it. When I say your life is worth more, Mr. Walwyn, I mean that your life is worth more *to others*. You, sir, have a family. You have a wife and children who have earned your love and fidelity and support. You may not excuse yourself from your duties to them even if your heart has veered rashly off course. Life is not so simple, I'm afraid; Rachel Lockyer is not your only responsibility."

Walwyn had not heard him. "If in men's eyes my life is worth more, all the more reason they should trade for it. It is a fair bargain, my life for hers, in this wretched world, in this government of liars." He spat the word *government*.

"That is all very nice and blustery."

"Don't you see? I am the cause of all this. Had I never met her—"

"Do not enter the business of what-ifs, Mr. Walwyn," Bartwain said roughly. "I must strongly advise against doing that. What-ifs are a guaranteed poor investment."

Walwyn fell silent. After a few seconds Bartwain began to grow uncomfortable, so he called for Mathilda; Walwyn took the hint, saying he would impinge no more on the investigator's time. He offered to show himself out. Before he could leave, however, Mathilda appeared in the study and grasped Walwyn by the arm. No guest of the Bartwains would be permitted to show himself out; she would walk with him. Also, he was not allowed to leave without sitting down and trying her plum porridge. "It's Christmas Eve," she cheerily said, as her husband, sitting in his chair behind Walwyn, made frantic gestures in an attempt to discourage her hospitality.

"What are you making?" he asked her now.

"Biscuits." A spot of flour dusted her chin as she finished kneading. She was dear to him—she was his Mathilda. Married thirty-five years, they had no surviving children. They had outlived all of them. Now they were sixtyish and gray and almost as wide as they were tall, and so accustomed to each other's habits that whenever he sneezed, she blew her nose.

"*Cranberry* biscuits?" Bartwain ventured.

"Of course. They're your favorite."

He looked at her and softened. "I can't finish my report because I don't know why she did it," he admitted.

"Is that what's bothering you?" She dropped halved cranberries into the dough, sprinkling them across the surface.

"It's a problem," he said. "I can't stop asking why. And I have never asked that question before in these cases."

"Oh, I don't know. I think you haven't even gotten to *why* yet. I think you're still stuck on *what*. You still can't say exactly what happened to that poor little creature the night it died, can you?"

Bartwain grunted. It was a half admission.

"So you see, you have two problems, one on top of the other. You still don't know the what. And you can't stop thinking about the why. That's all right. The good Lord made us to be curious." She began cutting the dough into circles. "Don't worry. You'll figure it out. And if you don't, you'll learn to live with it." She chuckled as she placed the biscuits in a pan over the fire.

"The law doesn't leave room for curiosity," Bartwain told her. "The law doesn't allow us to ask why in cases where the loss of a child is concerned. According to the law, the fact that she concealed the child's death is enough. According to the law, her conviction is justified."

"You don't agree with that any more than I do." Mathilda cackled, wiping her hands on her apron. "If you did, you'd be sleeping nights. And last time I checked, the only one snoring in this house is me!"

When the biscuits were ready, she plucked two from the pan and awarded them to him; she also poured him a cup of buttermilk. The biscuits were not good for Bartwain's digestion, but he didn't care. He downed the milk and shoved the biscuits into his mouth, one after the other, gratefully. Mathilda planted a brusque kiss on top of his head. "Chin up, Thomas," she said. Rarely did she use his Christian name. "It will be over before you know it."

• • •

On the thirtieth of December, an unlicensed printer from Westminster successfully finished inking and printing two hundred copies of *The People's Martyr*. The copies went to John Lilburne.

The same day, Walwyn made it back inside the prison. He thought ahead this time. He was an exceedingly well-behaved visitor. He brought blankets and bread and wormwood and wine — too much for one person, too much for the time that remained, so he and Rachel shared their feast with the other prisoner, squeezing side by side on the bench as the white-haired man planted himself to Walwyn's right, his hipbone jabbing into Walwyn's. He pawed through their sacks and swigged their wormwood; he tore eager chunks from the rye loaf. While he feasted, Rachel and Walwyn talked to each other in quiet voices. They spoke only of ordinary things, such as the best way to stuff a goose, what kind of leather makes the hardiest gloves, and why the Puritans had outlawed Christmas. Walwyn left when the guards threw him out. When the old man looked up to find his new benefactor gone, he wept.

That same night, Bartwain tried again to write his final report. He was able to summarize his research, his depositions, and his reasons for ordering the indictment. Briefly he noted the outcome of the trial. When he came to the conclusion, however, the summation of law as pertaining to the case, his hand stopped. His hand set down the quill. He told his fingers to resume working, but they disregarded him. His fingers staged a revolt.

I cannot do this, he thought. I cannot say justice was served when it was not. One cannot ask *why* in a case of treason, which is the betrayal and abandonment of a country, and not permit the same question in cases of bastard murder, which is the betrayal and abandonment of a child. The law is wrong, he thought.

This realization was a kind of death for Bartwain. He stood up from his desk slowly, his breathing tight and labored.

Walwyn had been gone less than an hour when the guard with the apologetic face took pity on Rachel and released her from the leg irons. "She's not going anywhere," he said to his companion, who agreed.

When they left, Rachel rose and crept to the other side of the hold—the cloaks in the corner looked like a comfortable resting place. She asked the white-haired prisoner whose they were. He told her condemned men sometimes went to their deaths on days too warm for a cloak.

Squatting, Rachel studied the garments. She examined their thick wool, their strong seams and soft linings. She forgot about resting. An idea was presenting itself to her.

She pounded on the door of the hold until the young guard came running. When he poked his head in, she said she needed a needle and thread and some shears.

The guard refused. If she thought he was foolish enough to bring a murderer shears, he said, she had better think again. But he blushed as he looked at her, and when Rachel lowered her eyes and told him he was a good man, an excellent man, a man to make any mother or sister proud, his cheeks bloomed furiously, great splotches of self-consciousness that spread all the way down his neck.

"Why do you need them?" he asked.

"I'm going to make something," she told him.

"What will you make?"

"Gloves!"

"Gloves?"

"Yes. Wool."

"What for?"

When Rachel told him her plan, his eyes moistened. When she gave him the name of the shop where she used to work, his eyes gleamed. "Du Gard Gloves! They make the finest in town." He ducked out of the hold to hunt down a needle; he foraged through the warden's quarters and found a spool of thread. He borrowed some shears from the intake officer. Returning, he gave Rachel his hand. "Make the first pair mine," he coaxed. "Measure me first. My fingers always go numb in winter."

"I need a measuring ribbon."

"I know about you and your ribbons. I will give you none this evening. Use a chalk mark instead."

Rachel thought of her measuring ribbon, wrapped for years around her waist for ease of reach, then wrapped for a brief moment around another, more helpless circumference. She remembered counting backward from fifteen.

She swallowed and forged ahead. She marked the length of the guard's hand by chalking it on her forearm and told him to come back at first light.

When he left she got to work. She worked without a desk. She worked by candlelight. She threw herself into her mission as the white-haired prisoner cheered and clapped. She tossed the cloaks around the hold until she found two she could tolerate. Dropping to her hands and knees, she proceeded to cut and sew the cloaks into twenty pairs of woolen gloves, the warmest and fastest she'd ever made. She sewed as if her life depended on it. She made gloves for the guard who had helped her and for the old man warbling in the corner. Then she gloved the entire third-floor ward.

In the morning, a belated Christmas delivery was made to the floor for female felons. It turned out to be the wrong day for it. The temperature soared, and rain left the air sour and warm. Wool was the last thing they needed. But the women of Newgate did not notice. For the remainder of that day and well into the night, every creature and child in the place waved raven hands at one another across the smoking link light, like passengers pulling away from shore.

Twenty

MARY ENTERED THE hold on the last day of December. She did not remove her cloak. She refused to come far enough inside to sit. To Rachel, Mary's face bore the look of an unkept promise.

"I cannot stay," she told Rachel, and in the next breath she added, "You never knew what it means to be a mother. If you did, you would not have been able to abandon that child behind the market."

Rachel bristled. "*You* never knew what it means to be a mother."

They proceeded to quarrel. What counted as a mother was the subject.

Rachel spoke first. "Are you a mother if you pluck a snail from the gutters and set it high so the rains will not drown it?"

Mary scowled. "No, of course not. Don't mock me."

"Are you a mother if you raise a brother?"

"No, you are not."

"Are you a mother if you wish you were?"

"No, no! That is not enough either."

"Are you a mother if you are a daughter?"

"Now you are being ridiculous," Mary complained.

Rachel, more softly: "Are you a mother if you conceive a child?"

"Not even then," said Mary.

Rachel replied: "When, then, are you a mother?"

Mary: "You are a mother when you have lost something. When you have felt the change and cannot hold it."

Rachel, covering her face: "Then I am a mother because I, too, lost something."

Mary stepped inside the hold. "No, you did not. You cast it out."

"Still it was lost to me!"

"Only by your own sinfulness."

The young guard leaned in and interrupted to warn Rachel that the bellman would be calling for her soon.

When he withdrew, the two women went on with their discourse.

"Why William Walwyn?" Mary asked. "Why that man and not some other?"

"Because he loved me."

"So you lived how you preferred."

"I lived how I could," Rachel corrected.

In a thin voice, uncertain of itself, Mary said, "You still do not know what the love of God requires."

"Nor do you," Rachel reminded her. "None of us does."

"You never accepted my help. Why didn't you ever accept my help when I offered it?"

"You never offered."

"I did," Mary cried. "I tried. I worried so."

Rachel reddened. "Do you know what it is like to have people's concern about you always come by way of their worry and their doubt? All my life, people who say they wish to help have surrounded me. But what good has it —"

"You find fault with everyone but yourself," Mary interrupted, stepping closer and inadvertently rousing the prisoner in the corner. He sat up, blinked; he was nearly blind. He had eyes the color of spring sky over the moors. "I wish you had never met that man," Mary went on, half sobbing, flinging her words forward. "I wish you had never fallen in with William Walwyn, or Elizabeth Lilburne, or any of that Leveling faction I have learned about. They are all the same. At least if you had stayed away from them, you would have been saved from too many hopes."

"What, is it a danger for a person to have them," Rachel flung back, "like hopes are pox, or bruises?"

"A woman does not generally find herself in a pickle such as yours without having had either too many hopes or too few."

"Well, I'd rather too many!"

Mary's response went unspoken because both women already knew it: *I'd rather too few.*

In the stillness that followed Mary made her way over to the wooden bench and sat. She was younger than Rachel by almost six years. She had never had a child, never conceived a child, never once missed the monthly course of women. She cleared her throat and reached for Rachel. Grimly she gathered her assistant in her arms, though she did not look at her. There the two women sat, pity and duty passing back and forth, until Mary started as if she had forgotten something and declared she must be going. She rose and left the hold.

The word Mary had used was *abandon*. That was how she referred to Rachel's action on the night of the Smithfield market. But who abandoned whom?

What Rachel knew, what she remembered, was that it was the night of All Souls', and when she had unlocked her wainscot box it was still before midnight, still before the day turned. That much, at least, was clear. She had pried open the wainscot. She went in with her arms and came out with a child. She had worn no gloves. For once, the thought of gloves had not crossed her mind. She had wrapped her newborn in a shawl and carried it down the stairs, past Mary's closed door.

There are some things a woman wants so much she will gibber and die to get them. This by no means indicates she will have what she desires.

Rachel left the house and stumbled onto Warwick Lane. She held the bundle so close she nearly crushed it. She began running.

Screech owls flew overhead. They were chasing stars; the owls had mistaken stars for fireflies.

As she headed north to Smithfield market, Rachel told the little girl she would not miss her. One day, she explained, is not time enough to love something. Love takes years.

Besides, a woman in this situation could not miss a person, for a person requires a name, and Rachel had not named her. Yet as she pressed through the abandoned alley on the southern edge of the market, she could hear the owls hooting options. They were shrieking up and down the dung heap; they were calling the names of girls. She set down the bundle on an empty scavenger cart and shielded her ears until the names had passed. She picked it up and resumed walking.

When she reached Smithfield she threaded her way through the shuttered stalls of asparagus and orange vendors. She ducked under a low-hanging canopy, taking a shortcut toward the northern end of the market. She passed by cut flowers left overnight on a vendor's table, mostly dandelions, out of season. They were frostbitten. Whoever had tried to sell these bunches must have given up; they were lying on a table in limp rows, unprotected, necks drooping. The market was quiet.

She made her way to the northern end of the stalls, where the earth changed over to spongy grasses and thick heather brush. She continued toward the slaughterhouse, where two bony steers were standing outside the clapboard shed, unmoving, their haunches withered, their necks tethered to posts. Rachel had no idea why the manager of the slaughterhouse had left them out overnight. Surely he could have finished them off, could have completed his task on time. No creature should be left out like that for twelve more hours, tethered under the moon, waiting. It seemed to her the height of cruelty; the gift of a day can be cruel.

Beyond the slaughterhouse she waded through wooded grasses so thick and dry they nearly pulled the burden from her arms. A faint rustling followed; she did not turn around. Had she looked, she would have seen Mary trailing her, but Rachel took no notice.

All she saw was moonlight dancing on heather; the stalks were throwing their heads up to the bluish light. She pushed to the end of the grass, to the place where heather and wilderness met. London was overrun with such intersections. They would spring up where you least expected it. Here would be the city, all made up, trimmed and disciplined in the ways of reason, and then, just as you grew accustomed to it, just as you accepted your lot, out of nowhere appeared a tangle of old roots in the forest.

She entered the line of trees. The moon slipped closer through the branches. She found a plot of ground where the roots had not set in, and she dug. She crabbed her bare hands into the soil. Her hair leeched out of its bun; her skirts grew besotted with the earth. She clawed at the wilderness floor, made entreaties to it. She begged it to open, to receive her burden, to take back what God had given.

At last the earth acquiesced. It surrendered only enough to allow a shallow grave. Rachel laid the bundle into the hole and pushed the dirt back on top. She patted the earth; then she slapped the earth. She wiped her face, smearing her cheeks in the same places where Elizabeth wore her scars from the fever that had taken her boys. Unlike Elizabeth, however, Rachel was not allowed to mourn. One must not mourn a loss that comes about by one's own hand. That was the rule. You could not mourn what was your fault. If the loss came by another hand, weep all you want. If it happened by your own, you could not.

How this theory measures out with all the thousands of God's children who have flung themselves, stupid and glorious, over and over, into the best and worst of things, loving whom they should not, seizing what they must not, running where they cannot, falling when there is no one to catch them—how this serves the betterment or edification of the species is not clear; people do it regardless. People have always done it.

After Rachel buried the infant she returned to Warwick Lane without seeing where she was going. She did not make it home. She collapsed on a stoop belonging to the butcher Dalton, three houses down. She did not know it was the butcher's. She did not know it was a stoop. Dalton found her an hour later, and he and his wife stood in their doorway gaping at the fallen woman before them. Mrs. Dalton suggested fetching a doctor or a clergyman, but Butcher Dalton recognized Rachel and declared no pastor was needed. "This woman is a Leveler and a libertine," he said. So they took her back to the glove shop, where they left her for the Huguenot to deal with. When Mary, who had returned home earlier, found her assistant on the walk—on the same front walk that Rachel daily swept—she half pushed, half pulled her up the stairs, opening the door to her quarters and leaving Rachel just inside the threshold. She then returned to her chambers, where she wrestled with God all night.

Rachel spent the remaining hours before dawn on her side on the floor in the corner, the same corner where she had given birth one night before. Her breasts leaked. The milk would not stop coming. It saturated her petticoat, her dress. It soaked the floor. Everywhere it was seeking for the loved object.

When Rachel slept, she dreamed. In the dream her mother and father were shoving a blanketed bundle in her face. Above her parents' heads, the skies were raining clods of dirt, spits and spills of dried mud from the waste kennels and the scavengers. The city was raining filth. It was raining all that was lost in the war, all the soil and mud of a divided people, of a divided love, as London's children coiled and drifted down the river, the river that stank, the river of flotsam and jetsam, sea of burdens unnamed.

Twenty-one

THE BELLMAN OF St. Sepulchre was calling for Rachel Lockyer.

In 1605 a benefactor had made a bequest to the cathedral of St. Sepulchre. The gift stipulated that at midnight on the day that a Newgate prisoner was to be executed, a bellman from the cathedral would ring a hand bell outside the condemned's cell to inform him or her of the impending execution. From his priestly quarters in the basement, the bellman would creep through a secret underground tunnel, enter Newgate, and ring his chimes at midnight.

Rachel's bellman was a tired fellow, dissatisfied with his lot. He did not like moving through the underground tunnels. The lambent light from the passages made him feel like a man on the run. An hour before midnight, he reluctantly made his way through the tunnel and up into the prison, then across the courtyard and into the condemned hold, where the guards let him in. A candle in his hand, he hovered by the prisoner's sleeping head as he listened to his own heart racing. He was early. He was always early. He was not early because he was punctual. He was early because he dreaded his duty and wanted it behind him.

He waited for midnight.

When the stroke came, the bellman chimed his silver hand

bell over the condemned woman's head, twelve times over, using double strokes, a silvery *cling-cling, cling-cling, cling-cling*. Rumor had it that the sound could cause fits in bystanders who chanced to hear it.

The young guard, wearing his new gloves, heard the chimes from his card table in the courtyard and forgot the hand he was playing. "Ill luck to hear it," he muttered. This guard would not last long at Newgate.

When he finished his chimes, the bellman pulled from his cloak a tattered scroll that held a poem for the edification and preparation of the prisoner:

> *You prisoners that are within, who for wickedness and sin,*
> *After many mercies shown you,*
> *Are now appointed to die . . .*
> *I beseech you for Jesus Christ's sake to keep this night*
> *In watching and prayer for the salvation of your own souls,*
> *While there is yet time for mercy, as knowing tomorrow*
> *You must appear before the judgment seat of your Creator,*
> *There to give an account of all things.*

On the night the bells rang for Rachel Lockyer, no one but the bellman and the white-haired prisoner were with her. When the bellman finished the poem, she sat up and asked for a psalm. "I am not to say a psalm," he said nervously. "I am to say the poem for the condemned, and chime the bell; that is the procedure."

She asked again. He wavered. Something in her voice persuaded him. So, for the first time, the bellman broke with tradition. He reached for the easiest psalm he could remember, and he began to recite it. The old prisoner began saying the words too, in a whispery falsetto, across the hold.

> *I will lift mine eyes unto the mountains, from whence mine help*
> *shall come.*
> *Mine help cometh from the Lord, which hath made the heaven*
> *and the earth.*

He will not suffer thy foot to slip: for He that keepeth thee, will
*   not slumber.*
Behold, He that keepeth Israel, will neither slumber nor sleep.
The Lord is thy keeper: the Lord is thy shadow at thy right hand.
The sun shall not smite thee by day, nor the moon by night.
The Lord shall preserve thee from all evil: He shall keep thy soul.
The Lord shall preserve thy going out, and thy coming in from
henceforth and forever.

Rachel wrenched away from the blessing and she vomited. Clotted bile and brown liquid poured from her mouth and nose onto the floor. The bellman was quiet. His chin trembled. He had traveled beyond his usual level of involvement.

After a while she stopped, heaved, and wiped her mouth with her sleeve. Then Rachel let go one long cry that was also an acknowledgment. "I handed her over," she cried. "I handed her back to God." The old prisoner listened in silence.

The bellman gave Rachel an extra chorus of the bells for good measure as he was leaving. Her lungs fluttered in and out, keeping time with the chimes. When he finished the song he made the sign of the cross, which the old man promptly imitated. "God send you a good deliverance," he said.

January 1650

Twenty-two

C

THE MORNING OF Rachel's hanging, Anne Walwyn
could not find her bonnet.

She looked on top of the wardrobe, where her hats
usually sat. They were all there except the one she wanted. She
thought she might have placed it inside the wardrobe—it was not
there either. She looked beneath, in case it had fallen. She was
not sure why she wanted to wear it. It was not her everyday hat. It
was green, and recently she had begun trussing it up with a white
border. The white crosshatches against the pine-colored cloth reminded her of the boundary markers that had started going up in
Moorfields, fences circling farms that used to be fields, the slow
calcification of ownership. Secretly, Anne rejoiced to see wilderness wrestled into order. Some women had an eye for apparel or
color; Anne Walwyn had an eye for enclosure.

She found the bonnet behind the wardrobe and left the house
wearing it. Her youngest, Fourteen, toddled along behind, his
roly-poly legs straining to keep up. "It's market day," she told him
and reached for his hand, though the boy had not asked her for an
accounting. "We are going to buy vegetables." She was not going
to attend Rachel Lockyer's execution. At least, that was what she
told herself as she headed toward the stalls and shops along New-

gate Street. When Fourteen grew tired she picked him up and carried him, the boy's head bumping her shoulder.

Rounding the corner for the stalls, she came upon a teeming mass of people, three hundred strong. Anne stopped short. These people were not all here for the onions.

"Mama?" Fourteen said.

"It's all right," she replied automatically, as a mother will do. She tried to reverse her route, but it was too late. The crowd sucked them in. The press of bodies extended from the western part of Newgate Street all the way to the end of the market. This was a gallows processional.

"Mama!"

"Hold on," she commanded. Now they were wedged between a pike-bearing soldier and two itinerant preachers. All around, people were bunching together and pulling apart, bunching together and separating, forming one long undulating line of human attraction and repulsion, and at the end, the irresistible draw of a hanging. Anne saw no Leveler green, but she did see locksmiths and hemp beaters and shoemakers and weavers and gilders and tallow chandlers and butchers and glass grinders and tailors and bakers, men and women whose curiosity or boredom had tempted them away from their daily tasks and whose intransigence was gaining strength in numbers. The members of this throng were going to drink continuously, beginning at the prison gates, where the cart bearing Rachel and her coffin were just departing; the crowd would crawl toward St. Giles in the Fields and Oxford Street, eventually arriving at the scaffold at Tyburn, a lengthy journey of not less than two hours.

Once caught, Anne did not fight the crowd. Resistance was not her doctrine. She kept her hand cupped against Fourteen's head, pressing him close. She would ride the day out like the tide. She did not ask herself why her feet had turned in the direction of Newgate market rather than Smithfield or Britain's Burse or any number of equally acceptable places where she might have purchased her goods without crossing paths with Rachel Lockyer's processional. She would let the day take her.

Walwyn was waiting for the bells. He was in the courthouse, hiding. He stood as close as a man could get to St. Sepulchre's without being witnessed. Once the coffin and mule cart arrived at the cathedral, someone would hand the prisoner a flower, and the priest would ring the massive bells that pulsed through the arteries of the city. Walwyn did not venture outside. He could not do it, could not bear to see how many spectators had gathered. He felt himself to be a coward. He knew himself to be a coward. His back, which was growing older, stiffened as he moved away from the window and returned to the clerk's record of the trial, reading and rereading the same narrative, the same pack of lies, the same pack of truths, the same story without an author, the same witnesses who explained everything and nothing at once. He hunched over the pages; his joints creaked. His body had grown old without his permission. His wormwood flask slipped from his pocket. He threw the papers in a heap on the courthouse floor. He was seized with the craven, fantastically self-centered desire to see her, to enter her again, to wreck them both. Bartwain's secretary, watching, retrieved the papers, handed them back, asked if he was all right; Walwyn, nodding blindly, gathered and stuffed the papers into their leather vellum, returned the lies to their shelving. He stumbled out into the daylight, which cut his eyes like glass. The day was more self-assured than it had a right to be. It had sprung up too redolent and fertile. It was a young day, and pleased with itself; it was a day no man with regrets could tolerate.

Outside, Walwyn walked far enough to see the tail end of the processional winding past the cathedral. His hand traced a splintered groove in the outer wall of the Sessions House. Far ahead was Rachel. She was seated on top of a coffin. The coffin was in the middle of a cart. The cart was pulled by a mule. The mule was flanked by guards. The guards were riding horses. Rachel was watching those horses. She had fixed her eyes on them. She was wearing her sea green dress. The color assaulted him. They had allowed her to wash and change her clothing. Her dress shone in the bald winter sun as if someone had sewn a jeweled collar onto it, or stitched a line of stars. He fixed his attention on her face. He read her into his memory; he imprinted her onto his mind's eye. He became gripped with the fear that he too would die. He was not afraid of death for its own sake. He was afraid because if he died he would no longer be able to see her; she would disappear down the corridors of his time. It was a selfish fear, but truth was salted through it.

During the trial, Walwyn had sat behind the spectators, wearing a low hat and a high collar, and he had listened as people whispered that the defendant was "already gone." They were right, those who made that claim, but not in the way they thought. She was not trapped, or mad, or in search of Bedlam and its ship of fools. She was being released. From what, he did not ask. He did not have to ask. Though Walwyn recognized his role, he struggled to accept it.

The cart driver whipped the mule into motion. Walwyn ground his teeth and looked away, looked in another direction. He would not bless this day by bearing witness to it. He would not participate in the order of things, no, not this day. The monster of human bodies lurched forward. The bells of the old church were ringing. The bells were late. The priest was pulling the ropes hard and long to compensate. They rang like it was Epiphany; they rang like the Day of Annunciation. Walwyn sank to his knees, clapped his hands to his ears, and bowed his head against that slattern of a courthouse. He prayed.

Outside St. Sepulchre, the priest ordered the people to pray for the soul of the condemned. From where she stood in the crowd, Anne saw no evidence of their intercession. No one crossed himself, even furtively; no sermons issued from the lips of the homeless preachers. The next way station along the processional route was an alehouse, and the members of this mob looked far more eager to gather around the table at a tavern than to bow before a higher authority. Anne let herself be swept along.

It took ten minutes for the Newgate mule to trundle to a stop outside the Bird in Hand on Oxford Street. Bystanders crammed the walk. Some tried to follow the prisoner inside. Others kept their carousing on the streets, having brought their spirits with them. The gray mule was doing its best to ignore its surroundings. It nosed through its feedbag for stray oats as the guards pushed Rachel off her coffin, off the back of the cart. They were taking her under a low awning into the Bird in Hand. Once inside, the prisoner would share a ceremonial drink with her hangman. No one remembered how this tradition had come about or what it was supposed to accomplish. To Anne the plan sounded reasonable. If she were facing the gallows, she would want her executioner to come with a name and a face. She would want to meet him, to find out if he had an aunt or an uncle from Salisbury, a favorite Scripture passage, a preferred way of flavoring his mincemeat. Such knowledge could not prevent what was to happen, but it might soften the fear. And if a stop at an alehouse could not comfort the prisoner, it might offer something to the hangman instead—absolution. Anne stood high on her toes. The guards had barred the tavern entrance. Around her, the mob was swilling wine. A boy darted past the guards and entered the tavern unopposed. Seconds later he reappeared, waving his hat in circles. "They're drinking," he cried, "and more than one!" The crowd howled its pleasure. Everyone loved the camaraderie of an alehouse; everyone loved a good hanging day. The itinerant preachers prodded and jostled each other. Anne slipped on a pulpy rind and had to claw at the preachers to keep her balance, Fourteen clinging to her neck. The preachers moved in close, their rank thighs pressing, their breath stinking of gum rot. One of them gestured crudely. Anne shook her head, her hand still protecting Fourteen's head. Her arms screamed with his weight. She felt his cheek; it was flushed. He stirred; he was all fists and yawns. He asked his mother to set him down; she said not yet. But her arms would not listen; her arms set him down regardless.

The prisoner emerged from the tavern steadier on her feet than when she had entered. She almost sauntered. If she was intoxicated, it suited. The guards boosted her into the cart. One of them grazed her hips as she stepped up and clutched the cart rail. He was a showman, this guard. He had thick spider fingers. The crowd applauded. He slapped her buttocks, twice, and the cart lurched into motion though the mule had not been struck. Slowly the processional snaked through the clotted thoroughfares toward the gallows at the edge of the city. At one point Anne came so close to the cart that when it graveled to a halt past the goldsmith's, closing in on Tyburn Lane, she could see Rachel's knuckles gnawing the coffin's edge for balance. Anne glanced down at her son. Then everything stopped. The cart driver climbed from his seat and walked to the left rear wheel, going down on his hands and knees to inspect the underside. Six hundred eyes followed him. When he rose, he scanned the members of the crowd imperiously, as if they had come out solely for him, as if their one purpose in gathering was to hear a cart man make a pronouncement. "It's the axle," he announced. He could have been communicating news of a firestorm or the onset of hostilities between nations. "A stone's been lodged in it. Can't move till it's out."

A hackney man stepped forward and volunteered to help. The crowd applauded. The hackney man began his work. The crowd grew restless. It takes more time to repair a broken axle than to cause one, and the wine was running out. Someone threw a handful of gravel at the prisoner. Someone else, a tyrant, Anne thought, heaved a bleating, bleeding shoat into the bottom of the mule cart. The terrified creature scrabbled for balance, slipping in its own fluids, and ducked under Rachel's skirts, where it proceeded to die all over her, its slit throat opening and closing with its pulse. Rachel knelt down, tried to tend to it; she was visibly agitated.

That was when Anne's son declared his independence.

It took just one forceful tug for Fourteen to wriggle out of his mother's grip. He pulled her arm so hard she thought she might be caught on something. "Let me go!" he demanded. His force of will threw her off balance and propelled the boy backward; he was stronger than she had imagined. His first experience of freedom was landing hard, and bottom-first, in the carriageway. This failed to discourage him. Righting himself, he bounded away before Anne could stop him. He pushed through the forest of legs and tottered to the edge of the street, where he bent his fat little body toward the ground, Anne watching in disbelief. All God's children crossed this bridge if they were fortunate, but this little one with the weak heart had arrived early. Here he was, rebellious already, stomping his way into personhood. His black curls dusted the roadway; he was plucking something from the dirt. When he bounced up, his cheeks were blooming scarlet. His fat fingers clutched a drooping white nosegay. "Mama!" he cried, brimming with accomplishment. Without waiting for her reply, he tottered through the crowd, which parted for him. He approached the mule cart. Far ahead, in the distance, the gallows waited. He bobbled up to the cart, single-minded, bypassing the kneeling driver and the hackney man. He crawled up the back of the rail, the guards oblivious to his presence. He perched there, leaning against the outer edge of the cart, his shoes and socks catching the runoff from the shoat. His face was luminous; he really did have a fever. Rachel did not see her miniature intruder until he had leaned so far into the cart that his legs left the ground; he balanced on the cart railing with his round fulcrum of a belly and tugged at her dress with solemn insistence, confident in his own omnipotence. Richard Walwyn was one of those well-loved boys, one who takes for granted his youthful powers, who believes he will always hold this kind of sway over others.

"For beautiful lady," he burbled, and thrust the nosegay into Rachel's hand. Then William and Anne's youngest leaped off the cart and swam back to his mother, the people parting again to let him pass. Anne took his hand and she held it. She said not a word.

Someday, she thought, bold and enlightened women would laugh and cover their mouths when they read about matrons such as Anne Walwyn, when they studied the lives of the wives and mothers of the Commonwealth. These women would probably declare that their predecessors had lacked self-possession. To these accusations Anne would not have much to say, save to ask what it was love required. Love did not promise pleasures. One could hope for them, but there was no surety of attainment. She did not serve dumbly, or turn a blind eye. She served. That was enough. It had to be.

The axle repairs completed, the processional groaned back into motion, passing the stream of Mary-le-bone as the mule approached the scaffold. Anne followed a few paces behind. She kept her hand around her son's wrist. In the back of her mind dwelled the thought that she should begin using her children's Christian names.

At the scaffold they asked if Rachel had a final speech. She shook her head: no final speech. The crowd twined and hissed. William Kiffin, erstwhile officiate, arrived to join Rachel in the mule cart. He clambered up nimbly, his task being to remain beside her until the end in case she confessed or sought spiritual guidance.

Again they asked if she had any final words; she shook her head a second time: no final words. Kiffin asked if she would like him to pray. No, she said. No, I would not like you to pray. But what Rachel said no longer mattered. Kiffin would intercede for her. He would apologize to God on her behalf; he would apologize to God for a woman's shortcomings. Thomas Bartwain, observing these rituals from his wheelbarrow chair, chewed his pipe and waited; Bartwain, who was not a praying man, prayed for it to be over.

The investigator sat detached from the crowd along the western edge of Tyburn, where the fields had grown thick with burrs and the path was almost impassable. He had not accompanied the processional through the streets. Instead he had made White find him a driver and carriage, arriving only for the final moments. He could not stomach more. He could not stomach this much. He blamed his lack of fortitude on his bowels, which clutched and roiled at the slightest provocation. His secretary had refused to accompany him. Bartwain squinted through the smoke from his pipe and took in Kiffin's performance. The clergyman was perched on the mule cart. He wore a stiff doublet, a fraying jerkin, and misshapen breeches. He was bowing and blushing up there like a bridegroom. He began to call out a prayer for the forgiveness of sins. A good nonconformist, Kiffin invented his prayers on the spot; he did not believe the Holy Spirit could be found inside the Elizabethan Prayer Book.

Bartwain glanced at the sky. It was high noon. The shadows had vanished from the bottom of the gallows, that colossal triangle, that Triple Tree, as they called it, whose beams could hang more than twenty felons at once. In June, the Council of State had strung up twenty-four condemned felons simultaneously, causing the gallows to resemble a row of hanging root vegetables, each man swaying and sagging in his prescribed place like so many sacks of wintertime onions and carrots. Next to the gallows now stood the anatomy doctors. They were waiting for Rachel. They were standing in a thin line, holding their black bags. They were waiting to take the body for dissection; they were here to open a woman up for the advancement of science. Judge Blakemore had tacked this final, clinical punishment onto Rachel's sentence after the jury's verdict. If a woman could not be rendered useful in life, he had written, then let her be rendered useful in death. Give the body to science.

Kiffin was praying: "Our merciful God, who is also a God of judgment, angry and jealous, yet abundant in mercy, we thank You for calling us to seek Your face, and we ask You to turn Your kindness toward us this day, as we undertake this most difficult and necessary of punishments."

Bartwain was watching the hangman. He was an oily, seal-like fellow. Probably he should not have shared a ceremonial drink with the condemned woman. An hour with Rachel Lockyer would leave any man in a diminished state. The hangman's mouth formed an *O*, and his liquored whiskers bristled. He sneezed; his eyes were drizzling. It would take the smiting hand of duty to make this man carry out his task without faltering.

The guards put down the cart rail to slide out the wooden coffin. It landed upright, tall as they were. They lowered the box to the ground. They climbed back into the cart. They were not waiting for Kiffin to finish his prayer—they knew how long a Baptist preacher took. They wrapped the rope around Rachel's neck, although they did not tighten it. That was the hangman's job. They called to the hangman. It was his turn now. He was going to have to hitch the other end of that rope over one of the horizontal beams and lash the noose tight, so it would not come loose. The beams stood twelve feet from the ground. They were nearly as high as the Sessions House balcony from which Bartwain had fallen. The hangman began slinking toward his target. This was his moment. This was what he did. The plan was this. As soon as the noose was tight and the prayer finished, the driver would whip the mule, and the beast would lurch forward to escape the lash, causing the cart to pull away from the condemned woman, leaving her dangling. The only thing between Rachel Lockyer and God's green earth at that point would be a braided noose and seven feet. Bartwain coughed; his lungs were worsening; he wished his secretary had accompanied him. The hangman started his work. He began to tighten the rope around her neck, but the close quarters of the cart did not make his task easy. To get the noose cinched, he had to angle himself around Rachel's green dress, reaching over and securing the rope to one of the beams without losing the free end and without brushing up against her by accident. The cart groaned. The crowd began murmuring. Rachel twisted her head away from the hangman. Painstakingly, he fumbled through his ministrations. He belched. He bumbled. He fumbled some more. He apologized. Rachel kept her eyes on the horizon.

Bartwain found himself fascinated by her neck. He could not keep his eyes off it. One rarely thinks to look at a neck for a neck's sake. Rachel's was narrow, and arched, with a hollow at the base where her dress fell open. Its curve was almost reptilian; it was primed for deflection or attack. Maybe that was how she finally did it, he considered abstractly, as was his wont; maybe that was how it happened. She had turned her head. Maybe it had been as simple and livid as that. One could survive any number of impossible things by looking away during the time of the undertaking.

Not long ago the investigator had seen a strange woman balding and begging along Bailey Road. He was making his way to the courthouse when he spotted her—a featherless old bird clutching her knees and rocking along the side of the carriageway. She sat on the stoop of a lodging house that charged so little only the very poor could not afford it. This woman was very poor. Bartwain, frowning, stopped to ask her why she was doing it, why she was rocking. It was a ridiculous question, and unseemly for a man of his standing to ask, but he could not turn away; Rachel's case had rattled him. The old woman said nothing. Her eyes glinted up at him distrustfully. She was still sitting there three hours later when he checked from the window of the Sessions House. The next morning she was gone.

Kiffin was concluding his prayer: "Therefore we ask for Your mercy upon this woman, on her behalf; we ask for her repentance, even as she passes from us; we ask You, who know all things in Your infinite wisdom; You who knit her in her mother's womb and knew her fully before she was born, and determined this as her course. May it redound to Your glory, now and forevermore. Amen."

The hangman had removed the noose to adjust it for a better fit. Having encountered Rachel Lockyer's neck, he now appeared to be faltering. She reached up and caught his wrist and said something in his ear, Bartwain could not hear what. Then she helped him put on the noose, lifting up her hair like a woman being given a necklace by a suitor. When it was cinched properly, when all was ready, she turned to the crowd, searching the faces; she did not appear to find the one she was seeking. She sagged and sank against the side of the cart. Her legs betrayed her. The crowd grunted its satisfaction. If she was not going to give them a good sobbing repentance, then she would do well to grant them something else, like fainting, or madness, or a gibbering vomiting exodus. The hangman reached out to steady her. He was devoted to her now. He would not let her buckle a second time. He checked the noose; she nodded.

When Kiffin had finished his prayer and stepped down from the cart, the clergyman signaled to the hangman, who signaled to the driver, who cracked the whip, which signaled the mule. But the creature remained unpersuaded. It was not in on their little agreement. It was an old mule. It had traveled to Tyburn more times than it wished to remember. It had registered marked dissatisfaction with this morning's oats. It disliked crowds; it disliked carts; it particularly disliked broken-axled carts. The mule dug in and farted. The crowd rocked and pealed. Rachel's eyes were closed, her chest rising and falling so rapidly Bartwain wondered if she was having a seizure of the heart and might go that way, quickly. Let her go, he whispered, clenching the sides of his chair. Let God have her first. The driver cracked the whip again, cursing. The mule's flanks welted pink. Still the animal would not move; still it balked; it was possessed. It swiveled its ornery eyes, shook its head, and gave a kick. The crowd applauded. It was a sign. Everyone became transfixed with the prospect. If they could not have a good hanging, then they would have a good miracle. They were Protestants, this crowd, but beneath their Calvinist words and judgments lay a hysterical substratum of Catholic symptoms. They longed for signs and wonders.

A third time the driver flicked the whip, leaving a trail of blood speckling the mule's coat. Some blood spattered back on the driver's face. He wiped at it, smearing red across his upper lip. He struck again. At last the old recusant surrendered. The mule leaned forward, wheezing, dragging the cart behind. The wheels rolled two feet, then two and a half, then three. For a short while Rachel still clutched the rails, still kept her feet planted. But not for long: the mule was finding the pace of faith. Now she was off the cart. She dangled in the air by her neck. She hung there, suspended; she was neither of the heavens nor of the earth. She swung between worlds. The mule turned its hoary head to see what its progress had wrought. Bartwain watched also. She was kicking, spinning, rotating in circles, her arms scrabbling at the noose, trying to get a breath. She bit through her tongue; blood sauced out.

Was she thinking? He doubted it. This was the body's hour. Probably it hadn't felt anything at all since that poor bastard died, and now everything was returning; all life's sensations were being compressed into this one moment. Her body was rising up, he thought, rising up and reviving, demanding its place in the order of things.

Her hand fell open; the nosegay drifted to the earth. Bartwain lowered his head.

Mary was peering through the crowd at the scaffold. Fifteen minutes in, and her assistant was still kicking. Something was not right. The noose was not tied sufficiently tight. Mary did not blame such a mistake on God. She blamed it on the hangman, who had become the worst thing any hangman can be—ambivalent.

At the foot of the gallows, Kiffin strode back and forth, waiting for Rachel to stop breathing. Mary pushed toward the clearing. She could hear Kiffin muttering from the Beatitudes. He was not listening to the sounds above him. He was not hearing Rachel's sliding guttural spasms. But Mary heard them. Mary closed her eyes.

Her late husband used to tell her that when one became a Christian, the way in which one inhabited the world changed. For Mary, becoming a believer had meant becoming an observer. She scanned her world as a sailor surveys the shoreline—from a distance. She looked for signs of trouble; she watched for leaks. Over time this discipline had had the ancillary effect of eradicating Mary's joy altogether. The world receded each time she interrogated it.

Twenty minutes in, and Rachel stopped moving. Her head slumped to the side, arms slack, mouth open; she was no longer breathing. From the middle of the crowd, Elizabeth Lilburne began wailing, screaming Rachel's name, her round face screwing up as she pitched toward the scaffold. The soldiers formed a barricade around Rachel. This did not stop Elizabeth. She hurled herself against them, pounding their chests with her fists; she bellowed the name of her friend. In the same moment John Lilburne began making his rounds, distributing copies of his pamphlet. He was handing out his martyrology to people who could not read, who could not write, to men and women who would not know what a martyr was if one rose up from the dead and mauled them. Mary folded her arms when he offered her one.

Just then a dry wind gusted up and began plucking the loose pages out of the spectators' hands. *The People's Martyr* had been bound in haste. Its binding was not well pasted. Its pages felt no obligation to remain in order. They began blowing around of their own accord, catching an upswing of air, raining mischievously down on the old mule's head, so that it snatched a bite of parchment. The pages swirled around the scaffold. John raced in a spiraling circle, trying to collect his escaping words. The faster he ran, the more they scattered. The air was thick with sentences.

The hangman began sawing at the rope. The guards surrounded the scaffold to protect him as he worked. He pulled back as Rachel's body slid into his arms. For a minute they were face-to-face. Mary stayed on her toes to watch. Her assistant's neck was black where the rope had circled it. Her dress, soaked with sweat and urine and the blood of the shoat, gave off an acrid stench as the hangman laid her down.

Mary's hand found its way up to her own neck. She felt the veins, tendons, vocal cords. For a moment she wondered what it would be like to love life so much one could not bear to leave it. The thought of such selfishness took her breath away. She removed her hand. She reminded herself it was not Christ who had loved the world. It was God who loved the world, and Christ who died for it. The two had split the task between them. Nowhere in the Scriptures was it ever said, Christ loved the world.

The hangman was covering Rachel's body with a blanket.

Mary made her way over to the anatomy doctors and asked what they would do with the body once they had finished dissecting it. The doctors said they would not be finished for some days, and she nodded stiffly and moved away. She straightened her shoulders as her pace increased. She felt around under her chin, making sure her bonnet was fast. She was going home to the glove shop on Warwick Lane. Behind her, she could hear the doctors starting. Clicking their pincers, they circled the corpse, revolving under a cloud of pamphlets. They were black beetles hauling a carcass back to their lair.

Twenty-three

A T MIDNIGHT ON November 1, 1649, between the last stroke of All Saints' and the first stroke of All Souls', Rachel Lockyer gave birth to a girl, the fifteenth child of William Walwyn, whom she loved too much. She delivered the child by herself. Mary paused outside the door on her way to bed and muttered something—Rachel could not hear exactly what, but it sounded like *What is going on in there; what are you doing this time.* And she remembered Mary telling her that a woman who gave birth to a bastard would find no safe harbor at Du Gard Gloves. So Rachel did not open the door. She kept it locked. She did not want the first face her daughter saw in this world to be someone who condemned her.

She had a long labor. It is sometimes said bastards do not take as long to deliver and that the women in question do not have the regular pains signifying impending motherhood. Rachel had pains. The delivery did not go well. The child would not drop for two hours. Rachel was on the floor, her back against the side of the bed. When the infant finally did drop, it became caught partway; it stopped in the middle of the birth canal and would go no farther. Its head was free, but nothing else. This lasted for the longest time, until Rachel looked for something to guide the child out. She reached in the pocket of her dress for her measuring ribbon, which a glovemaker always keeps close. She bent down and tried to tie the ribbon around the child's neck, which was barely showing; its head and neck were out of the birth canal now; its shoulders were not. Its shoulders were caught. Rachel bit down on her own arm to control the shaking, and she prayed to God to help her pull out the rest. Her legs and arms were spasming like a convulsive's. She planted her right hand under her buttocks for leverage, but she slipped in her own fluids, so that her back struck the floor; in the same second her hand pulled the ribbon tight. She could not see what was happening. She did not let go of the ribbon. When she regained her balance, she tugged and pulled some more. She pulled hard on the ribbon for several seconds. Then the child did come out, all at once, with a kind of coughing sound, a kind of sick coughing twist. Rachel moved to her hands and knees and knelt before it. What she saw frightened her. Quickly she tried to unwrap the ribbon. But there was too much blood and the ribbon was too tight and the child's face was going blue.

Then Rachel heard, or thought she heard, a voice.

She stopped. She went perfectly still. She listened. She could have sworn it was God talking. She heard the voice say, *This is My daughter with whom I am well pleased.* "Who is that?" she cried. When no one answered she grew furious. She tore at the measuring ribbon, picking at it with her nails, biting at it. It would not come off. She asked her brother, Robert, to help, but that was no use; he did not answer. Her sewing shears were in the wainscot box. She reached for them, straining. She took hold of the shears and returned to the child, her hand suspended over it. She observed its struggle, its minute and infinitesimal battle. She hated it; she hated how it floundered. Its weakness, its pathetic inability to live, horrified her. She also loved it; she loved it more than she had loved or ever would love anything in this life, including Walwyn, including her brother whom she had raised almost as her own; she must get that ribbon off. She attacked the ribbon.

She pulled hard, away from the skin, and she scissored it. It fell in two pieces from the infant's neck. An angry purple ring puffed up, gasped up, where the ribbon had been, and in the same moment Rachel heard the voice again. *This is My daughter; she is Mine.* She heard it very clearly this time. It was not just her imagining things. She absolutely knew the difference. Again she stopped what she was doing. She took her hands off the child. She left the child on the floor before her, struggling silently. She did not know what to do about that voice. All Rachel's life, her mother had said, "If God speaks to you, listen." But what if God speaks and you do not understand what He is saying? So Rachel asked God to clarify Himself. And then God stopped speaking to her, which reluctantly He will do whenever any of His children insists over and over the course of years that she cannot hear Him, even as she must shout to be heard over God's sound. The voice left her alone. But Rachel did not know the voice had left her alone, and she continued waiting. She counted backward. She counted from fifteen, which was how long William Walwyn once told her it took God to welcome by name any innocent who has suffered. *Fifteen fourteen thirteen twelve eleven ten nine eight*, and again she listened—something was wrong. *Seven six five four three*—she had made a mistake. Who was she to think God spoke to one such as her? She lifted the tiny creature and put her fingers into the mouth to clear the throat of mucus and fluids. *Two one*—this child was not breathing. She had waited too long. She had waited fifteen counts. She had thought God wanted the child back, for surely He knew what its life would be. She held the infant close, the birth cord still attached. She asked the child to wake up. When the child did not, she asked God to wake up. She shook the child. Nothing. She remembered God blew into Adam once. Or was it Eve? No, God blew into Adam; God gave Adam first chance at breath. She blew into the child's mouth. She heard Elizabeth's voice, berating her: *How could you bring a child into this world?* She heard another voice, Elizabeth's as well: *How could you not?* She tried clearing the throat again. This child was no longer living. She pressed the tiny body to her breasts and closed its eyes; she covered its eyes with her fingers. Those sky blue irises were tearing into her. She said to herself: If I close her eyes then she will not exist in this world; she will exist only to me. And if she never sees me she will never suffer, for she will not know what kind of person she was born to.

She held her. She recited the verse in Matthew about the sparrows, about how if there are two in the field and one of them falls, surely our Father notices. She held her for an hour, until the child was cold. In the middle she delivered the afterbirth. When she took her hands away, her newborn daughter was curled up, one tiny hand on the measuring ribbon Rachel had used to drag her into the world, the other on her mother's breast. She was dead.

In that moment Rachel understood herself to be the worst of all possible monsters. Sounds issued from her mouth, sounds she could neither control nor articulate. The sounds continued as she cleaned the child. She cleaned her and she dried her and she pulled her into the dress she had made out of the bottom of Mary's yellow curtain. Then she wrapped her in one of the shawls she had sewn back when she still thought a person might escape one world and find another waiting. What finally happened, you see, was this. Rachel could not deliver the new world to the child, so she delivered the child to the new world. She gave her over. She gave the child her hope. Her hope became Elijah's chariot, to carry her over, to bring the child safe passage from one world to the next. Walwyn could not do this. Only Rachel could. She did not do it for him. She did it for the child. She did it, as well, for the other children, for fourteen guileless and expectant souls who did not know that their father by being human had endangered them, who had no idea their happiness even needed protecting.

She started to leave the house with her that night but could not do it. She could not move, could not walk. So she hid the child in the wainscot box. She tried to mop the floor with the bed linens but she could not do that either. She crawled over to the bed. She could not climb in. She lay on her side on the floor. She dreamed that when the child got to the new world she told the guard at the entrance not to let her in because she had glimpsed the old world she had skipped over and wanted to go back. And the guard asked the child why. It is freer here, he said; there is no one to harm you. And the child said, My mother is there; I miss my mother. And the guard dropped his head and said, You do not have a mother; that is the price of her delivering you. And then in the dream the guard turned into John Lilburne, Robert Lockyer, William Walwyn, and all the men Rachel had known. And then it was only Walwyn. As he reached out she drew back, and he said, But there was love; and a vast emptiness opened below them, and they fell together.

When Rachel woke she did not go downstairs until late in the morning; she could hardly sweep for the pains. That night she carried the child out to the woods and buried it. The following morning Mary dug it up. The beetles and the earthworms had covered it. Only its eyes were untouched. Mary shoved the bundle at her and said, "Is this yours? Is this what you have gone and done?" and when Rachel looked all she could see was blue. Her daughter's eyes were open. They had seen everything, in death and in life. She had known what it is to be a person. She had seen her mother.

Since that day Rachel had stopped trying to be Solomon; she had stopped trying to split the difference. A love that has happened and cannot go forward still holds a living purpose.

Twenty-four

WALWYN TOOK THE long way home to Moorfields. He did not go to the gallows. He left the processional after the ringing of the bell at St. Sepulchre and headed north on his own. He walked. The coarse shouts of the mob remained in his ears after he had left the city. He crossed the Roman wall west of Moorgate and arrived home before Anne did. He did not know that his wife had gone to Tyburn. The remainder of the day he spent in the apothecary, that makeshift shed behind the house. For three hours he holed up, burning through his concentration. He pulled books from the shelves, blindly flipping through remedies and anatomy charts. He passed by recipes for poultices to dry up a woman's milk after she has lost a child; he paged through the symptoms of melancholia and fainting sickness. His eyes lost their focus. For several minutes he studied the frontispiece of a handbook on midwifery, its author pseudonymous. The woodcut showed a woman draped in Grecian robes, devoid of expression, a child cradled in her arms. He set the handbook down. He retrieved his flask of wormwood, drank until his thoughts dissolved. Only then did he turn to his own work, unearthing a collection of pamphlets from the deepest drawer of the desk that examined the principles not of medicine but of liberty—these were his finest theories, his best ideas, carefully crafted treatises on the rule of law and the importance of religious toleration and the right to self-governance and the hope for a civil commonwealth. He flipped through the pages he had written and shook his head, bewildered. Who was this man who thought he could solve the world's problems with words? The arrogance!

Not until Alice, the maidservant, came in to tell him Mrs. Walwyn was ready for supper did he end his solitary confinement, close the shed, and follow the serpentine curve of the footpath back to the house. The afternoon sky was settling to dusk. He stepped inside the kitchen.

"Finally," said Anne, not to her husband but to her son.

Richard ran up and rapped on his father's legs, testing them for soundness. When Walwyn scooped him up, the boy pinched his father's nose. "You smell," he said, waving his hand. Walwyn made a face for him.

"Set him down, please," Anne said. He set the boy down.

"No," Richard shouted. Walwyn picked the boy back up.

"He's tired. He had quite the day." She paused before adding, meaningfully, "We went on a long walk."

"Where to?" When Walwyn's eyes met hers, he saw where she had been; he saw what she had seen. "My God," he said. Abruptly she looked away. She was setting out the linens.

The Walwyns generally took their evening meals as a crowd. Some nights as many as sixteen or seventeen gathered around the table, if one counted grown children and neighbors and friends and spouses. Lately, however, the youngest had flocked to tutors, and the middle children had begun apprenticing for trades. Tonight it was just the four of them, including Alice, with supper a plain and subdued affair—eel and oysters, which could be purchased inexpensively, and cucumbers roasted with thyme. Walwyn used to try to persuade Anne to rub the oysters with garlic before cooking, but she never warmed to the suggestion. They ate peaceably enough, though Walwyn could not finish anything on his plate. Neither he nor Anne could bear to look at each other, so they looked at their son instead.

Anne asked what he was working on in the apothecary. "You were out there a long time."

Walwyn invented an answer. He said he was developing a compound extraction of cloves and lemon intended to ease lung and respiratory ailments.

"Who for?"

"People who can't breathe," he said.

For reply Anne sliced her eel into five identical pieces.

When they had finished eating, she said to Alice, "Take the boy upstairs and put him to bed."

"I thought I was to clean the kitchen," the maidservant replied.

"We will clean it later. Mr. Walwyn and I must go over a household matter."

As Alice led the boy up the stairs, he called down to his father. "Read me a story," he demanded.

"Yes," Walwyn promised. "Yes, I will read you a story later."

Anne busied herself extinguishing the cooking fire. Since the first year of their marriage, she had opted to shoulder this chore by herself. Walwyn used to try to help, but she always refused. It was not a task for two people, she had said. This evening she was tamping the embers in a way that thickened the smoke into a dull blanket. Walwyn rose from the table and opened the front door, swinging it back and forth on its hinges.

"Stop that." She glanced up at him. "The rain will get inside."

"It's not raining."

"It will soon." She continued tamping until the embers whistled and sighed. Walwyn closed the door and returned to his chair. Anne wiped her hands on a cloth and eased herself into the seat across from him. From the folds of her skirt she produced a piece of needlework. While she stitched, he waited. He rested his elbows on the table. He sensed something of what was coming.

She dragged her eyes up to his. Her hands did not stop stitching. "About this morning. About the scaffold." She was stabbing at her needlework.

"Yes."

"So this will be the end of it." It was not a question.

"Yes," he said. But it was not an answer.

Anne withdrew her eyes like a general pulling back a pair of victorious soldiers. She proceeded to reinforce the white border of her needlework with a new stitch, an elegant crosshatch. First she sewed twenty white half-stitches to the right, then twenty to the left, following a boundary she had begun earlier. As soon as she finished one row she started another. It was a lovely, severe pattern, using material he had not seen in years.

"What are you making?" he asked.

She raised the needlework from her lap so he could see. She had sewn a neat white border around one of the pretty green bonnets he had given her years ago, one of those dear and useless bonnets that had sat atop their wardrobe, waiting.

"Would you hand me that spool?" she said.

Walwyn reached over and retrieved a spool of white thread from the end of the table. In his fingers the smooth end felt like a pebble, like something he might have skipped across a creek when he was young. Before he could stop himself, his wrist snapped and the spool went flying. It skipped and bounced across the floor; Anne watched close-mouthed. It skittered against the table legs. It collided with the cooking pot near the hearth. It singed itself there a minute, giving off a little puff and hiss. Then it began a long, protesting roll back to its owner as the floor's slant dictated; it advanced with glacial slowness until it came to rest at Anne's feet. She reached down and scooped it from the floor. She returned to her needlework, creating one neat white *X* after another. She angled her chair so her husband could see her progress. Walwyn watched, his face stinging from the leftover smoke. She was sewing a fence.

Twenty-five

IT WAS CLOSE to sundown before Bartwain made it home. First he had to return to the courthouse, where his secretary did not appear to be speaking to him. He had piled into his satchel all the notes and papers he could manage; he was clearing out his desk, though he did not want to admit it. "I need to complete my final report," he said defensively to White, who had not asked a question. Bartwain told the driver to give him and White a ride home, but the horse began limping so badly Bartwain wound up ordering the fellow to stop and let them out; he did not want the beast to go lame on his account. He made his secretary wheel him the rest of the way home. White obeyed in silence. Bartwain admonished him to mind the kennels; he did not want to be tipped into a sewage creek. Carefully his secretary picked his way through the alleys and carriageways of Westminster, though several times the chair wobbled and nearly toppled. When they turned toward the investigator's house, the chair thudded into a muddy rut left by a carriage wheel, causing Bartwain's head to whip backward. He had to pray White would not let go of the handles. He recalled the physician at the courthouse telling him it was a good thing he went through life swaddled in as much fat as he did; his girth cushioned his bones.

When he made it to his house he sent White on his way before climbing gingerly out of his chair, hobbling for the stairs. He did not stop for a snack in the kitchen. He was too tired to eat. He could not even endure a biscuit. Upstairs, Mathilda was folding blankets.

"You made it," she said. "How did you do?" She was wearing her scalloped nightcap.

Bartwain undressed, put on his nightclothes, and collapsed into bed. His lower back was tightening, his broken wrist throbbing. "I'm not getting paid enough," he said to his pillow.

"I agree," she replied.

He crashed into a dull and motionless sleep that lasted approximately three-quarters of an hour. Then Mathilda was patting him.

"Wake up," she was saying, lively as ever.

"What is it?" He was furious. "What do you want? Can't you see I'm spent? Can't you see what this day has done to me?"

"Of course I can," she assured him. "But that's not my fault. Besides, it's your secretary. He's back. He's at the door, asking for you."

Bartwain fumbled for the ties on his robe and moved downstairs to the kitchen. Looming in the doorway was White, a specter of unrest, his eyes rheumy and yellow.

"What's wrong?" Bartwain immediately said. "What happened?" A cold dread wrapped itself around his abdomen.

"It's that woman." The faintest hint of satisfaction flickered across White's face. "That what's-her-name, as you once called her."

"Rachel Lockyer?"

"Yes." White leaned in to say more, but when he saw Bartwain's wife he drew back. Jerking his head at the wheeling chair, he motioned to the investigator. "You'd better come with me."

Walwyn did not find out about it until hours after Bartwain did. Bartwain lived closer—he lived three streets away. When the doctors realized what was happening, they called for the investigator. They wanted his advice about the possible legal ramifications.

Bartwain and White reached the house where the doctors were working and found Elizabeth Lilburne waiting for them in the door; she pulled them inside with some impatience. The investigator dragged his failing body up from the chair, entered the front room, and turned to where Elizabeth was pointing. He saw Rachel's unclothed body laid out on a long table, surrounded by trays of instruments, one basin on the left for organs, a second on the right for bloodletting. One of the anatomy doctors was poking and prodding her shoulder. Another was rubbing her feet, which had swelled with pooled blood; he was dictating notes to a clerk. A third doctor was circling the table, muttering.

Then Bartwain saw it. She was moving. More specifically, her chest was moving. Her lungs were taking air in and pushing air out. Her chest was rising and falling. There was no sign of life anywhere else, but those lungs were something. Bartwain staggered backward.

"This woman is not dead yet," the circling doctor paused to tell him. "Either it is a miracle or the hangman failed to do his job."

Elizabeth had heard the news an hour earlier. She'd learned about it from John, who had followed the doctors to the Westminster house—he wanted to see what they did with the body, in case he could write about it later. John became the first witness. When he saw Rachel's chest rising, he shouted at the doctors not to cut into her. The doctors were more surprised than John was. One of them jumped, stabbing Rachel in the shoulder with his surgical blade. As the doctors rushed to stanch the bleeding, John found an errand runner to fetch his wife, who he knew would not want to miss this. Elizabeth, hearing the message, left her daughter with the neighbor, begging his pardon for the inconvenience as she raced to the river. Crossing the crowded London Bridge by foot would have taken over an hour, so she hailed a waterman, who rowed her in half the time. When she arrived at the house in Westminster she shoved past the doctors, took one look at the body draped over the table, and said, in an offended voice, "But she is not wearing any clothing." The chief doctor replied no, she was not, because until very recently they had not thought the woman would mind one way or the other. He then explained to Elizabeth that while Rachel was not quite dead, she was not quite living either. She is in the balance, he said. "Well, what are you doing to change that?" Elizabeth shouted. She began pushing the doctors into place, herding them, moving them through their paces. She threw her cape over Rachel's exposed skin as a covering.

Walwyn did not hear of these events until the following day. His friends forgot to tell him. Or maybe they did not want to tell him. Or maybe they were not his friends. Bartwain was the only one who thought of him. Bartwain, who never liked William Walwyn, remembered him in this moment.

The Leveler was home, chopping wood behind the house, silver hair falling into his face, not thinking anything, urgently thinking nothing at all, when up came old Bartwain, shuffling along the footpath, scowling.

Bartwain told Walwyn that though he did not half believe it himself, there was news, it seemed; there was news from the autopsy house. She appears not to have expired, he told him. Or, if she did expire, she appears to have returned. She is fighting for breath as we speak. The doctors have put aside their dissection and are tending to her. As the investigator spoke, he saw out of the corner of his eye a woman in the back window of Walwyn's house, a woman concentrating as though pushing something, as though rolling a boulder up a slope, a woman with watery eyes and a bun pulled so tight it looked like punishment.

"It could well be that she does not survive the—" But Bartwain could not get any of his cautions and caveats out. Walwyn dropped the log he was not chopping. He dropped the ax. He dropped his unallowed thoughts. He dropped his duty, his principle, and his religion, such as it was. He walked down the path, in full view of his wife, who was watching. He neither saw nor heard a thing save a lone jaybird mocking him from the poplars. It was a gray and dreary January morning and the mist clung so thick that to walk outside was to be pricked by a thousand needles of rain. Over his shoulder he thanked Bartwain for his kindness. I am off to the city, he said. His voice held joy. He ran. He sprinted. He passed

Moorgate, passed the dog skinner's house in the distance, did not stop, did not listen, did not hear anything from that direction. Not today. Today was not for sorrow. Today was for Rachel.

He passed into the northern edge of the city. A crowd slowed him down outside the courthouse, as around the Sessions House milled a hundred shivering souls, huddled under heavy cloaks and wide-brimmed hats, gossiping, whispering. Already news was spreading. News from the next life, they were saying, marveling, asking each other if what they had heard was possible, if God still interceded in the lives of humans. For a few seconds Walwyn hung back, listening. He saw several faces he recognized but none he knew well, and when two apprentices from the Whalebone began pointing through the fog in his direction, calling his name, he left and began jogging south. He headed toward Westminster, toward the house where the anatomy doctors worked. His jog became a run. He encountered more delays, including one that held him more than thirty minutes—it was a carriage accident. An old man had stepped into a busy thoroughfare without looking. A passing coach had rattled too close and its driver swerved too late, landing half of his vehicle in the ditch and the other half on the old man, pinning him beneath. Now the driver was off the front seat, cursing, and the elderly fellow was under the carriage; they needed help pulling him out. Walwyn was not going to stop, but then he saw who it was. It was an old man, a very old man with hair so white as to be translucent, a man with two twigs for shins that poked out from his prison garb. He brightened with recognition as Walwyn bent down in the road to him; he looked up at Walwyn and said, spitting bits of tooth, that he had forgotten how fast the world moved; he had forgotten how fast horses and their riders traveled. The world goes by so fast, he said, marveling; the world goes by so fast. So Walwyn stayed. He slogged through the mud alongside three burly Scots to haul the carriage off the man, to heave the wheel high enough to slide the fellow out, one limb at a time and most of them broken, the freed prisoner beaming wildly the whole time, not minding the pain, not begrudging this final bodily insult. Through failing eyes he gazed up at the sky as it mixed with the smoke from the tallow chandler's and with the steam coming off the horses as they stood to one side, pawing and whinnying and waiting and looking longingly at the vendors trundling by with their shiny apples on carts; and he declared old London beautiful. You are my angel, he said to Walwyn. All this took some time. When it was over and the carriage righted and the old man off to the side of the road with someone tending him, Walwyn resumed his race, his legs shaking from the effort to heave aside the coach, his boots sopping with mud and manure. He did not notice. He splashed past a Parliamentary carriage built so high whoever rode in it must have thought he belonged to God. As he ran, his mind lurched back and forth, skittering across the surface of his thoughts; his thoughts that morning were intolerable. He rounded the cathedral, the clapboard frames of the doctors' house appearing through the mist, until an unexpected sight brought him up short. He clattered to a halt so fast he fell. He tripped over his own life.

Gliding toward Walwyn, an apparition in the rain, was his wife of more than twenty years, and seven of his children walking in lockstep behind her. They were coming to retrieve their wandering mongrel. Anne had overheard Bartwain's words while Walwyn was outside woodchopping. Fast as she could, she had borrowed the neighbor's carriage. She had gathered all the offspring she could find to come with her, to head her husband off. If she did not head him off here, at the pass, at the very start of the pass, he would be gone. She knew it; he knew it. His eyes told her. Her eyes told him. His eyes said: Let me go; I must do this. Her eyes said: You will come home to Moorfields.

Walwyn tried to stand. The rain was in his face. He looked down and mud was everywhere; mud was spackling him. He rose to his feet and raised a hand to shield his eyes—the mist was coming in at an angle. Anne mistook his movement for a wave of greeting and she turned and said something to her children, who began fanning out and trotting toward their father all at once, the doctors' house thirty yards behind them. He could see his children, and behind his children he could see the house. He could not look at one without taking in the other. Anne kept her gaze on him over the heads of her children, who cornered him, braying and barking; they plied Walwyn with tickles. Richard flung both arms around his father's knees. "Come home!" he demanded. Anne stood back, appraising. Only when Walwyn was thoroughly treed did she approach, flanked by the twin sentries of caution and deliberation, which on another day he might have mistaken for patience.

"Papa!" declared Richard again. He rapped on Walwyn's knees. Walwyn picked him up and the boy threw his arms around his father. Walwyn buried his face in his son's neck.

"We came to bring you home," Anne said. "I thought you had errands in the city, and since the rain is so heavy I wondered if you might want a ride." The clouds over her head were starting to part.

"You are so dear" was all he could say. "How dear it is of you to come fetch your old Walwyn." He could see and feel the doctors' house, a living breathing thing, behind her. He could see silhouetted men pacing back and forth in the window, doctors with their black bags, conferring, doctors with their instruments.

"Where were you heading in such a hurry? I hope we are not interrupting." She glanced at his muddy boots. Richard pulled on his father's ears.

"No, of course not," Walwyn whispered. "I was just so eager to finish up these errands and get home."

"Well, we will be there soon enough."

"Let me down!" Richard wailed. Walwyn set him down, though the boy kept a tight grip on his father's fingers.

"I'm sure there is something we've forgotten," Anne went on over her shoulder. "Did you find potatoes for tomorrow's roast?" She was halfway in the carriage before she turned around. "Aren't you coming?"

"Yes," he said. But his boots would not move. He checked to see if they were mired in mud; they were not. The black house was straight ahead, yawning, howling at him.

"Aren't you at all glad to see us?" Anne asked, her voice wobbling for a brief second.

"Terribly," he replied. And he was. How could he not be? He loved them. He loved them and it was necessary.

Wordlessly he lifted young Richard high, swinging him up against the slowly lightening sky, enthroning the boy on his shoulder. From this vantage point Richard could tug Walwyn's beard, which had not seen a blade in days. "You need to groom," the boy commanded. Together father and son followed Anne and the rest of her brood into a carriage drawn by two gray geldings. Walwyn was last to step inside.

Twenty-six

Report of the Investigation, Trial, Execution, and Miraculous Recovery of Rachel Lockyer, who being executed at Tyburn Tree, did after revive, and is now recovering.

Submitted to the Council of State in completion of the chief investigator's requirements by Thomas Bartwain, Criminal Investigator.

There has happened in the City of London a remarkable event, which has caused so much talk that false accounts are already being printed. To show what has happened, and for the correction of errors, the facts of the case are here collected and presented to the reader, that he might know the course of events as they unfolded, and determine for himself how it has come to pass that a woman who was condemned and executed has been returned to the company of the living.

There lived of late on Warwick Lane a tradeswoman named Rachel Lockyer, a glover's apprentice. Having laid eyes on a certain man, she refused to be parted from him, though she was not his wife. At length she found herself with child. She hid her condition from those who knew her and delivered the infant, independent of aid, in her sleeping quarters. A newborn child was found two days later buried in the Smithfield market, an event that did cause the matrons and preacher to report to the coroner, who commenced an inquiry to see if it could be murder; for the suspicion was that she being the mother had murdered it, and buried both it and her shame in secret. Shortly thereafter the Council of State did take me on as Investigator. The facts did not lean in this woman's favor. Upon completion of interviews with witnesses I composed and signed an order of indictment for the crime of murder as defined according to the 1624 Act to Prevent the Destroying and Murdering of Bastard Children. The woman's trial was set for one week following. Though the testimonies heard on that day were many and varied, almost all who spoke conceded in some manner that this woman was guilty, if not of the murder, than at least of the child's concealment, which the law takes to be the same; the jurymen agreed with this opinion. When the day arrived for her execution she went to Tyburn gallows and they hung her from it straightaway. She hung on the rope some twenty minutes, until the hangman sawed her down, thinking her dispatched to the next life, she being clearly observed by all present, including myself, to have stopped breathing. The body being lowered to the ground, the hangman covered it with his cloak.

Hereupon the curious nature of events began to unfold: The body was lifted by the anatomy doctors into the coffin and transported to a private house owned by one of the surgeons, Mr. Lilburne following the doctors. On reaching the house, they laid the corpse on the dissection table, where Mr. Lilburne, standing by the head, suddenly observed Rachel Lockyer to show some small sign of life by appearing to take a breath; and in breathing (the passage of her throat being straightened) obscurely to rattle. Having noticed this, he gave a loud outcry, so that the physician holding the dissection knife started and stuck the corpse's shoulder by accident. The anatomy professor visiting from London College also observed her to take a breath, and swiftly ordered a stop to the proceedings, all the physicians and faculty in the house crowding around the body. Perceiving that some life might yet remain in her limbs, they discussed with one another what to do next, it violating their profession not to undertake everything within their means to act in the direction of her recovery; yet it disappointing their scientific curiosity to forgo an opportunity of dissection.

After some lengthy discourse the proponents of her recovery won out. The doctors sat the body upright on the table and pried apart the teeth, which remained gripped together in a death's embrace. After opening the jaw with pincers, they poured down the throat some hot liquids, first a scalding wormwood, then scurvy-grass ale, and these caused her to rattle still more. They then turned to the extremities, and placed hot compresses on the arms and legs, rubbing and chafing vigorously, and calling Mrs. Lilburne to rub the chest and stomach, she having arrived an hour earlier. They then poured more spirits, until some hours later Rachel Lockyer briefly opened her eyes, causing Mr. Lilburne to fall into a near faint, saying he could not believe someone whom they were prepared to cut open was alive and blinking. The anatomy professor replied that she was not out of the woods yet.

This was the course of their ministrations over the next four days: as soon as the patient would show some sign of life, or give off some warmth in the extremities, they would let her blood. I observed this firsthand, being called to the house that night and returning for several days following. The first time they tried, no sooner was her arm tied, but she suddenly twisted away, as if suffering a seizing convulsion; the vein being opened, she immediately bled out seven ounces, so fast the physicians could not stop it swiftly. They bound her arm and placed her in a heated bed, where they pressed warm oils into her extremities and chest, and poured lye soap and water over the wound where the rope on her neck had been knotted. Meanwhile crowds began arriving. Reverend Kiffin from Devonshire Square, unable to believe what he was hearing, traveled to the house in Westminster to see for himself, saying repeatedly he had seen Rachel Lockyer expire on the gallows. When he departed they called for Mrs. Lilburne and told her again to rub the patient's limbs. Within three hours Rachel Lockyer opened out into a tremendous sweat. Her face also began to swell, as her feet had done, and her throat went waxy and red where the rope had knotted it. Mrs. Lilburne questioned the anatomy professor, asking why they were troubling to save this woman if she was to be sent back to Tyburn as soon as she recovered; surely they would not send back to the gallows someone whose recovery was so clearly an act of providence. The anatomy professor said he did not believe in signs and wonders, for such events had ceased after the Primitive Church, and God now spoke to Christians using only Reason, and Nature, and the Scriptures. Mrs. Lilburne, not in agreement, traveled to the home of Mr. William Walwyn to seek his help and support. Receiving her request, he straightaway composed a formal plea for a stay of execution, soliciting the justices of the peace for the obtaining of a reprieve, that in case she should be recovered to life, she might not be taken back again to execution. Whereupon those worthy gentlemen, considering what had happened, and weighing all circumstances, readily apprehended the hand of God in her preservation, and being willing rather to cooperate with divine providence in saving her, then to overstrain justice by condemning her to double shame and sufferings, they were pleased to grant her a reprieve until such time as her pardon might be completely obtained. But some of the clergymen argued there would be no use granting a reprieve simply for a person failing to die when she should; an error of the hangman had allowed her to live (said they), but it should not be allowed to keep her from dying; a hangman's mistake did not alter the original verdict. For some hours a group of religious and learned men debated these questions, until having his fill of them, Mr. Walwyn ordered them all to leave, and most agreed (as they were filing out) that in the end it was better to pardon her.

This being decided, the physicians once again and several times nearly lost her, the woman's internal wounds being so severe, some said she would not survive the week. But by and by she gave indications she could hear, by opening an eye when they spoke to her, this being the case when they mentioned gloves; and when they said the name *Robert* she opened both, and looked straight at them a minute. The physicians, fearful lest the swelling of her neck increase, applied a poultice, and took from her left arm seven ounces more blood. They prepared a drink of steaming posset, and sent Mrs. Lilburne again to minister to her. The next day they found her much improved and able to speak. Around noon they ordered another clyster, and a cataplasm, which is a plaster compounded of certain ointments to prevent a contusion. By six o'clock she was sitting up of her own strength, and conversing with her visitors in good humor, saying she was quite certain God had made a mistake, and His interventions were intended for another prisoner. She had a good color, and some who visited that day (myself among them) agreed she looked stronger than she had during the trial. When the faculty of the physicians' school inspected her, they asked what she recalled of her ordeal. She replied that she remembered nothing past the night in the Newgate hold where the bellman had prayed the 121st Psalm over her. She had no knowledge of anything that took place after, neither of being carried on the cart that took her to Tyburn, nor of being observed by the crowds that lined the street; nor did she recall the gallows. She was like a clock whose weights have been lifted for a while and then put back into place, not recording that a lapse in time has happened.

That night she complained of terrible pains in her side, and upon examination it was revealed she had a new contusion. The physicians having departed for the evening, only Mrs. Lilburne and myself were left to dress it. The next morning we sent again for the physicians, as she was complaining of numbness in her tongue, to which it was explained that she had bitten through a part of it when she was hanging. The day after that her pulse returned to normal. By degrees the blackness that had been spreading around her neck turned to blue and then yellow. Over the course of the next five days it vanished. She stayed under the care of the physicians several days more, until they said the best recovery was to get her home to her family. Mr. Lilburne replied that she was one of those women who did not have any, but Mrs. Lilburne said what she had was good enough, namely, friends. After some discourse the Lilburnes agreed to let her return to their rented lodgings near Winchester House, so they could provide for her care; and Mr. Walwyn paid a sum to support her upkeep and recovery. This is the same place where she has continued to reside since, it now being more than three weeks since her day of execution. Being able to eat, walk, drink, and sleep without disruption, she has said to the physicians that she does not wish to keep the coffin wherein she laid, even though they offered to give it to her for a keepsake. So many visitors have sought her out that John Lilburne has asked those who can afford it to pay for the privilege of seeing her. So every visitor has given as he is able, and the Levelers have collected the profits. This is said to have caused William Walwyn to spill over with rage, for, says he, before long pilgrims will be coming from all corners of the world to touch the hem of her cloak, a practice that disregards the precept that all men and women come into this world equal. But she has stayed on at the Lilburnes', quietly and without complaint, and visitors from all corners are coming to see her, to marvel at the same woman whom they previously condemned, and to say how God has blessed Rachel Lockyer.

Having done now with the medical aspects of this case, it is fitting for me to conclude with a word about the larger investigation, for after all, she was thought to have been meted a just punishment. I have spoken with this woman in the days following her execution. I have concluded that while she transgressed the law by concealing the death of her infant, the law as it stands is inadequate. There exists immaterial as well as material evidence in cases such as these, as in a case of treason. Both kinds are of value, material evidence being such facts as the state of the bedclothes, or the lungs of the infant, or the report of the coroner; but immaterial evidence being the intention and state of the soul. This matters as much as any other evidentiary claim, and indeed at times will surpass the latter. Herein the law falls short. It is possible this glovemaker's delivery might have gone differently had she not attempted to give birth alone or to bury her sorrow by herself. Why she insisted on such a solitary course I shall never know for certain, but her fear and shame were likely great, or if not that, her stubbornness.

Some might also think I should now relate some tale about what she saw during her brief sojourn to the next world; for surely she was gone from this life some minutes, so perhaps (some say) she saw demons if she was guilty, or the communion of saints if she was not. Others say she must have brought back with her some special knowledge of the end times for which the saints of our day are waiting. From such speculations the reader must come away unsatisfied, since this woman was so far from knowing anything while she was dead that she remembered not even what had happened while she was still alive. It is not so different from a man who has had too much strong drink in an effort to quell his grief, who upon waking remembers the cause of his grief but not what was done to quell it. So also for this woman, who has been given what most of us will not receive, that is, a second chance. The good philosopher Hobbes has said, "A friend is he that loves, and he that is beloved," and if this be not a true course, I know not what is.

Thomas Bartwain, Investigator

Twenty-seven

R ACHEL AWOKE.
She opened her eyes, and the ceiling wavered into focus.
She blinked and in came the walls. She was lying on a
low mattress in a room that had a sheet suspended from the ceiling as a partition. Papers and pamphlets covered the floor. A stack
of pamphlets, four feet high, was pushed against the wall beside
her. She was lying on her back and when she looked up to see
where the stack stopped, the pamphlets seemed to form a tower.
She was in the bedroom of John Lilburne's rented house in Southwark.

Her eyes drifted over the papers and books and pamphlets.
Slowly, over the course of several minutes, she realized she was
reading the frontispieces. She was reading the titles. She was reading the spines, for those of John's works that had them.

She rolled the titles around in her mouth. At first she did not
realize what she was doing. If you have never read before, the first
words slithering toward you declare neither their identity nor their
intentions. They decline to tell you who they are or what they will
require. You are not sure what is happening; you cannot see the
gift coming; you see only words, sliding forward, ragged and misshapen, living.

Rachel, the words were saying. *Wake up.*

She could read. She was awake. Which came first? She swallowed. The back of her throat was riddled with sores. She touched her neck, felt the puffed and swollen skin. She removed her hand. She reached for the closest of the pamphlets.

It was a copy of Freeborn John's latest work, *The People's Martyr.* Rachel thumbed through it, at first uncomprehending. Then she read it straight through. She read it in one sitting. It was a page-turner. When it was over she pressed her thumb and forefinger against the lids of her eyes and lay flat against the mattress. She stayed that way some time. She did not think about all the lies John had told so much as the words he had summoned and recruited to the page. The words were beautiful. They swam toward her; they slid up onto the bank. The words became flesh and then the flesh took on wings and then the wings made a picture; she could see things in her mind as she was going along. The words tapped at her, a woodpecker drilling a trunk. Then the tapping became new words and the new words grew, and what was grown was love.

She opened her eyes. She sat up, blinked again. She slid to the edge of the cot and put one foot down on the floor, then the other. She stood up. She stood up and took hold of what remained her life.

Three weeks after the anatomy doctors had sent Rachel to the Lilburnes' to finish her recovery, Elizabeth decided her friend was well enough to go home. But where was that? She broached the subject with Rachel over breakfast. "I think it's time," she said.

In the past few days Rachel had rediscovered her appetite. Presently she was devouring pudding studded with stewed raisins. She had slept through most of January, including through the announcement that the Council of State had issued her a formal pardon. She had almost missed the one-year anniversary of the death of the king, which was coming up shortly.

"Time for what?" she asked, her mouth full.

"To decide what comes next."

Rachel conceded that she hadn't decided what came next.

"Well, what have you been doing with yourself all this time?" Elizabeth's voice contained a hint of frustration.

"Sleeping," Rachel reminded her.

"Oh. *Well.* I suppose I can allow for that." Elizabeth reached out, snatched a raisin from the pudding, and popped it in her own mouth. Then she said, "I'm going to miss you."

Rachel pushed aside the bowl, took hold of Elizabeth's hands, and promised to make her a pair of gloves before she left. "The finest calfskin," she pledged. "I'm going to make you the kind you could never afford."

"You speak as if you're already gone. Where will you go?"

Both women understood one thing, if nothing else. Rachel had been restored to life. But she had not been restored to the same life.

Since her spectacular recovery from the gallows, the overwhelming consensus, from the justices of the peace to the criers and peddlers on the street, had been that Rachel Lockyer could not have murdered her bastard or God would not have resurrected her. Sermons had been preached, broadsides published, ballads composed and sung, all in honor of this humble tradeswoman whose miraculous revival had temporarily restored the people's belief in providence. No one was saying much at all anymore about the infant. Such talk had become unnecessary, maybe a little depressing. The child was gone, after all.

Elizabeth expressed her concerns about her friend's future to her husband after supper. She was standing by the third-floor window, looking out; John was at his desk, whittling. She said Rachel was almost well enough to leave, but the problem was where to send her.

"Why does she need to go?" John appealed to his wife's reflection in the window. "I'm in no hurry to see her leave. She needs us."

"No," Elizabeth corrected. "You need her."

He was whittling a wooden fox for Young Elizabeth, whose

birthday would come next week. He had not written anything since *The People's Martyr*, which had not sold well in the stalls. It turned out no one wanted to read the last dying speech of a woman who had given no last speech and who had not, in fact, died.

"She's ready," Elizabeth repeated. "We can't hold her here." She had sent a message to Walwyn the day before, letting him know Rachel was preparing to leave.

"Maybe she wants to stay."

"No. She's nervous, that's all. Being nervous about what's next isn't the same thing as wanting to stay." Steady rain was washing the window, forming rivulets down the thick, uneven panes. As the rain came harder, husband and wife dissolved and reappeared in the glass, dissolved and then reconstituted. John had wedged his wooden fox between his knees. Elizabeth pointed out that its ears were not right. John grunted and pulled a splinter from the left ear. He pulled some more and the ear ripped off. The fox took on a lopsided, accusatory air.

"Now look," he complained. John was an impatient creator.

In the weeks since Mary had made her discovery behind the Smithfield slaughterhouse, none of the Levelers had asked one another if Rachel was guilty, although some had wondered about it privately. At a certain level, they already understood. The Levelers were failed revolutionaries. They knew what it was like to create and lose something for which one is then held responsible.

Elizabeth was rubbing her puffed sleeve in a circle against the window. "Rachel has done well staying with us. But you have also benefited. I've never seen so many visitors in one month." She peered out at the street below.

"Yes," John said, wistfully. He set the wooden fox on the desktop, where it toppled.

The night before, after they finished supper and scattered sand across the floors to ward off pests, Elizabeth and John had left Rachel and Young Elizabeth resting on blankets in front of the hearth; John had taken his wife's hand and guided her upstairs. He laid her on the mattress. He undressed her before a single quavering candle. He was insistent and therefore pitiable. He went after her like an alms beggar, with thrusts so urgent his yard softened. He hiccupped and coughed; he slipped out by accident. Elizabeth waited. His eyes were sagging into hers. His eyes held some thought she did not recognize. "John," she said. He lowered himself again. He pressed his index finger inside her, wedging her open, then inserted himself behind. It was an old trick that generally left Elizabeth with bruises from his knuckles and not much else. Wax from the candle began dripping on the pamphlets. "John," she said again.

He shook his head, lips pursed. "Don't." His thighs were trembling as he reentered her.

"John," she declared a third time.

It was too late. When he withdrew, unspent, neither of them could speak. He rolled onto his back. Together, husband and wife looked up at the rafters.

"I have become a soap maker," he whispered.

"What harm is there in that," Elizabeth whispered back, placing a cool hand on his stomach. "It is an honest living."

For reply, he had pinched the candle out.

"John?" she was saying now, still at the window, still looking out. "Our lives are not the same as they used to be."

"I don't so much mind if things change—" He stopped. A scuffle had broken out below, near the bishop's old brothels. The worst of the stews were no longer in business; that was what Southwark officials said. But the officials did not venture near Clink Street in the evenings, where the Lilburnes lived; they did not hear the hard sound of poverty each night beneath the window, as the Lilburnes did.

"Then what? What do you mind?" she said.

He rose from the desk to stand beside her. Together they looked down at the city below the Thames, peering through the streaked panes, which had been poured into their settings unevenly. "I don't know how to say it." His head lingered close enough that his breath warmed her neck. His scent was sweet there, and unexpected.

"Yes, you do," she whispered. "You say things finer than anyone."

"I fear I have lost God's favor." John's voice caught on something when he said it. No one else would have noticed it, but Elizabeth did. She could hear it. She could see it in his reflection. She could watch it blinking like a firefly, all the way out the window, out to the scavenger piles. The People were gone from his voice. From here on out they were not coming back. John would have to go back to the Tower and even there he would not find them. His days as Freeborn John, as the torchbearer, were over.

Late that evening, well past midnight, Elizabeth dreamed of her two boys. She heard them yowling at her; she watched Tower and his infant brother banging on the table for beets. She awoke and sat up in the dark, gasping, a sad wind whistling up and down her pipes. She climbed out of the bed. She crept downstairs to Young Elizabeth, who was lying on a blanket before the hearth. She picked up the girl and carried her up two flights of stairs to her own bed. For the remainder of the night she slept curled around the little girl, arms fastened tight.

Twenty-eight

WHEN WALWYN RECEIVED word that Rachel was preparing to leave, he went to Anne and stood before her as she scraped watery gruel from a cooking pot. He said, offering neither introduction nor excuse, "I must go to Southwark." He did not equivocate. He did not race out of the house this time. He simply said: I must. In his hand was the note he had received from Elizabeth. Anne glanced at it for several seconds before pushing it away, before pushing his hand away. She returned to scraping. She reached for a ladle and began slopping the gruel into bowls.

"We could give them eggs, you know," he suggested as he watched her. "The children might like eggs for breakfast. It would be a treat."

"Eggs for breakfast are not in the budget," she said.

"They are in the budget if we say they are in the budget," he offered. "We could put eggs in the budget ahead of time, a year in advance if you wanted. We could have eggs every week, if you wanted."

She did not say anything to this. All she said was: "You will come back?" She would not look at him.

"Yes," he said. "Yes, I will come back."

He borrowed a neighbor's horse, a two-year-old colt that was not pleased to find a bit in its mouth. He talked to the colt as he rode, to calm it. They passed through the city center, headed south; they passed the old fish wharf with its barnacled posts. When they crossed the London Bridge, with its shops and three-story buildings cramming the deck, neither he nor the colt could look at the water. The colt settled down by the time they reached the Southwark gatehouse. It trotted past Winchester House toward Elizabeth and John's residence. Arriving, Walwyn tethered the colt to an iron railing the neighbors had erected in an effort to separate the paying renters from the brothels.

Elizabeth opened the door, and Walwyn threw his arms around her, leaving her temporarily without words. He wore the twin scents of sleeplessness and tobacco. "I wonder if I might see her," he said.

It was January 30, the one-year anniversary of the execution of Charles I. Throughout the taverns and into the streets, people who had despised their king and wanted his divine rights stripped were now raising their cups to his memory, putting their arms around one another, singing ballads that called him martyr.

"I hear you're still trying your hand at physic," Elizabeth said as she showed Walwyn to the third floor.

"It passes the time," he said. They reached the third-floor landing. Elizabeth fumbled in the dark for the latch as he asked how Rachel's recovery was proceeding.

"Better." She pressed the latch; it stuck. "You know, no one could believe God would intervene like that on behalf of a murderer. But they also can't believe a woman who gave birth out of wedlock could deserve a second chance. For, clearly, the child was hers." She jiggled the latch. "So the pardon might have saved her from Tyburn, but it has not saved her from the rest."

"The rest of what?"

"Why, the rest of her life."

"What does she say about all this?"

"Ask her yourself." She opened the door to Rachel.

• • •

She was seated in a wooden rocker, clutching a book, her old three-legged dog curled around her feet. Whoever wrote the book must have had a great deal to say, for the volume was such a size that Rachel was forced to keep a tight grip on the edges so it would not slide off her lap. When she saw Walwyn she stood up. She did not let go of the book. "There you are," she breathed. "I was waiting so long for you."

"You can read," he marveled.

"Yes," she said. "Yes, and you were not even here to pester me." Her dog, delivered by Thom the messenger on Mary's orders, sacrificed its warm patch to rise and nose Walwyn's fingers.

"You helped obtain my pardon," she added.

He nodded. The effort to talk, to throw words around the last year, required more skill than he currently possessed. All his concentration centered now on not touching her. He yearned to touch her, but something in her countenance prohibited it. When you have died before as many people as Rachel did, there is not much left you can call yours. You have reached the bottom, and everyone has seen you could not climb up. No woman wants to own such things, to concede she might bleed, or be impregnated, or love foolishly, or that her body might ache, roiled with uses, or that she might not even remember all it has gone through. He asked if she would forgive him. But the question would not come out as a question, only as a name. *Rachel.* His mouth folded around the word and refused to leave its side. The cloth in the window stirred, restless.

"I cannot imagine a day without you," he confessed.

"And yet you have made it this far . . ." She was smiling, standing there, taking him in, telling herself to keep breathing, watching the hair falling into his eyes, studying his arms with those sleeves pushed up like they were the first time she met him, that night at the Whalebone, when he was this lone figure at the end of the table who glanced up from his writing, from his solitary thought, and saw her, who forgot his name when she entered his field of vision. He had responded with his whole body to her that night, and she with hers. She had not been afraid. She was not afraid now either. She should memorize how he looked, how he carried himself, so she would not forget. She studied him. And the closer she studied him the more she saw, and the more she saw the more she understood, until right then, right there on John Lilburne's carpet of pamphlets, a tide of bright smacking hope rose up in her. It was a wave appearing out of nowhere. It did not belong to her. She knew that much. Hope did not belong to this day, not to this house, not to this year. She had not earned it, had not inherited it, had no money to purchase it. Hope was not her property. Yet here it was. Now she was moving toward him, putting her mouth on him. She was holding him as tight as a woman holds anything that was never truly hers. And she was asking, Do you love me; because for her this was the same thing as saying, I know I love you. And he was saying that he wanted her to tell him everything that happened, everything that had taken place during the months they were apart; start from the beginning, he murmured, do not leave anything out; do not leave me out. He kept talking, even as she kissed him quiet. His hand was on the small of her back. He was saying: What will we do now? What will happen to us now? And she was guiding him, comforting him; she was now the philosopher; every woman becomes the philosopher at some point; it is only a matter of time. And she said: We will not lose hope.

Elizabeth, who had been standing guard on the other side of the partition, leaned her head around the cloth and interrupted. Her eyes bored through both of them as she proclaimed, "You've been given back your hope but now you have to live with it."

For Rachel that also meant: Now you have to live past it.

She had to live with it. With what she did. With what she failed to do.

She also had to live past it. Which meant: She had to live past Walwyn.

This, then, was the battle of Rachel Lockyer. She battled two gods at once, her mother's and her father's. The two now spoke as one, having consolidated forces.

She said to the gods: But I do not want to go. And the gods said: Yes, you do.

She said to the gods: But I do not know how. And the gods said: You are learning.

She said to the gods: But I have not the strength. And the gods said: Strength is breathing. You need only take one breath at a time. Anyone living is doing it.

She said to the gods: But he was my whole heart. And the gods said: And you are his.

Some hundred years later Elizabeth disappeared down the stairs, and Rachel flung her arms back around Walwyn. She ran her fingers along his jaw, along the lines circling his neck. She kissed his chin, his earlobes. She returned her arms to his waist, held him strong and hard and tight. In her eyes was the answer to the question he never asked.

He asked it now. Did you give her a name? he said.

Not one that can be considered as such, she told him. She pressed her fingers into her eyelids as she spoke. But she had thought of the sparrows in Matthew, the ones that fall to the ground, and how God picks them up.

Walwyn put his head in his hands.

She opened her eyes, kissed the top of his head. Stand up, she whispered, though he was on his feet. Stand up. Go now. Go now; hurry. Do it fast. Don't delay. Don't stay here any longer. Don't drag this out. I cannot tolerate it when you are slow. You know that. I always told you that. I cannot bear it. It is your worst feature. Go now, leave now, or I will never be able to do this.

Swallowing hard, he said he would look in on her from time to time. You are very fair, he whispered. In his mind's eye, every time he laid eyes on her was the first.

I am fair enough, she said, and smiled.

You are the finest glovemaker the city has ever seen, he told her. You are a master.

The next week, the glovemaker, the artist, inscriber of his soul, would pack her bag and leave Southwark. Then she would leave the city of London for good. She would not return to tell him in which direction her life was opening.

Twenty-nine

NOT UNTIL HER recovery was nearly complete did Rachel receive a visit from her mother. It was not a long visit. Martha Lockyer was not a woman who felt at home in other people's lodgings, so she was in and out with some efficiency. Neither Elizabeth nor John had met her, so when the thin-lipped Mrs. Lockyer, reserved and wary but with the same lilting stride as her daughter, showed up on their doorstep on the first day of February, Elizabeth had no idea who she was and tried to send her away with a farthing—she took her for a beggar. Then the woman gave her name and Elizabeth stopped short.

Martha Lockyer was nondescript in character as well as appearance. She was not old, but she was not young either. She did not frown, but smiling failed to brighten her. She asked if this was the house that held the woman who had been raised from the dead. Elizabeth, speechless, showed her to the third floor. Mrs. Lockyer flew to her daughter, who was packing her belongings. She went down on her creaking knees, where she began praying her way around the Roman calendar of saints, teeth chattering with pride. Elizabeth had to hurry away two other visitors in case a pair of Protestant ears should overhear the sounds issuing from the bedroom.

After Martha Lockyer took her leave, Rachel made her way

downstairs to the kitchen. She sat at the table, picked up a cloth, and helped Elizabeth wipe plates. While she worked, she told her friend what had happened.

She said her mother had prayed for a quarter of an hour, thanking the Virgin for Her mercies. Rachel tried to speak, to say something, but her mother shushed her with the martyr's prayer of St. Ignatius: *I will praise Thy Name continually, and I will sing praise with thanksgiving. My prayer was heard, for Thou didst rescue me from an evil plight.* It was the same prayer Martha Lockyer had recited more than twenty years before, on the day her husband passed. Rachel reached out, extending both arms. She said, "But Mother, I am here. I am here. Look at me. I am your child, your flesh."

"You are not my child." Her mother shook her head. "You are a miracle."

Then Elizabeth realized Rachel's mother had made a pilgrimage of twenty years and twenty miles not to see her daughter but to touch a living relic. She had come to Southwark not to ask how Rachel was recovering, not to extend concern or dispense advice or even to pronounce judgment. She had come to see if God still intervened in the world of temporals. And once Martha Lockyer had confirmed that He did, she asked if she could take a lock of her daughter's hair with her when she left. Rachel let her. It was what she had.

Epilogue

MARY WAS A member of the Huguenot Church of the Refuge on Threadneedle Street, a clapboard sanctuary that leaked when it rained and groaned when it was dry. Each week for five years she had attended Sabbath services, and each week for five years she had listened as the clergyman repeated the same sermon: God loves strangers in a foreign land, he said; God loves the persecuted. Beyond the church, at the end of Threadneedle Street, lay a wooded hill where members of the Huguenot congregation could bury their families and neighbors. Not long ago, Mary had purchased a plot.

She made her way to the church on a Friday in early February. She had not gone to visit Rachel, though she had heard the accounts coming out of Southwark. She had sent the dog instead—she suspected Rachel preferred its company. Besides, she had too many customers to take time away. She swept the floors herself now.

Mary knocked on the front door of the sanctuary. The exterior façade had been blackened by countless small fires that had burned during the war, although the top floor had survived unscathed, two round windows intact. When no one answered, she made her way around the back. She would find the place on her own.

As she walked, Mary pressed through the veil of what was said, what was not said, what was written, and what was not written, in the weeks since she had found the infant; and she realized she was no longer certain what it meant to say, as Christ did, that something was finished. For Christ came back. She wondered if any of His disciples, on hearing that news, had felt a slow despair rising. The Scripture told only of their surprise and disbelief. It did not say if any of them was ruined by it. What if there had been one disciple, just one, who needed the Lord to let him be, who had started to make his way in the world, who had just begun to learn there was more to being a pilgrim than following? And then there Christ was, resurrected, back in the thick of things.

Halfway up the hill, she passed through a patch of thistle and honeysuckle. The path steepened. She gritted her teeth. Under her breath she cursed all those prodigal sons and daughters who wandered, joyful and licentious, through the best years of their lives, only to turn penitent and prizewinning after the journey flogged itself out. When would it be the eldest son's turn to be blessed, and kissed, and welcomed back into the squall of faith? Cresting the hill, she came upon a patchwork of stone ruins. She chose the smoothest of the stones and rested for a moment. She could not breathe, it seemed. Her comings and goings were not as they used to be. From here she could see far ahead, as far as Moorfields. A pillar of smoke curled up from the dog skinner's fire. The dog skinner, too, was probably an elder son.

She rose from the stone seat and stepped toward the far edge of the hill, which gave way to an encroaching thicket of rosebushes before beginning the long downward slide into wilderness. Legally this was still part of the Church of the Refuge's property, but the pastor had abandoned this patch, had given up maintaining it. This was the place. Mary had purchased the burial plot with her own earnings. She moved forward, lifting her skirts to avoid tripping over field maple roots gnarled like old knuckles in the grasses. The mist hung heavier here than at the crest of the hill, and the trees shut out the light. She pushed through the bushes.

Briars clung to her stockings. Behind the roses waited a secluded grove, guarded from the elements. It was a quiet plot, a mound of earth no larger than a confessional.

Then Mary did what she came there to do. She did what any elder brother finally will do when he learns his curse is not to bear the consequences of breaking the law but to endure the long loneliness of upholding it. She pulled from her hip pocket a single white flower, tied around the stem with a sea green scarf. It was the same color scarf Leveler women had knotted in their hair as they streamed through the streets of London for the funeral of Rachel's brother, for the army's martyr. She left the colors beside the little girl, and then she stood there for a moment, and prayed safe passage.

Afterword:
Secret Births in Early Modern England

The infant-murder trials of early modern England can be compared to the witch hunts of colonial North America, and some historians have identified common roots. Each reflected a shared Puritan concern with the damaging consequences of sin and the concealment of sin—the attempt to hide a trespass. Each also suggested a distrust of persons, especially women, who stood on the margins of the local community, and each attempted to control and regulate these women in ways that reduced whatever imagined threat they posed to the identity, cohesion, and moral order of the community.

Infant-murder trials in early modern England—*infanticide* was not a word commonly used during this period—typically targeted the poor and the unmarried, usually women and girls of humble descent. Determining if an infant had been stillborn, had died of natural causes during or shortly after birth, or had died from neglect or an act of violence was notoriously difficult. The draconian law of 1624 attempted to resolve the prosecutorial problem of insufficient evidence by capitalizing on the defendant's reluctance to speak; the law turned the act of concealment into proof of guilt. Put differently, the law stripped these women of the one defense upon which they might have relied in other circumstances—their silence. By conflating the concealment of the death of an illegitimate child with murder, the 1624 statute left little room for mercy, for pleas of accidental death, or for a defense that took into account the reasons prompting the mother's behavior, whatever that action (or inaction) might have been. Although Rachel's story and the contents of her trial are fictional, the dialogue in her trial is modeled loosely on transcripts from the Sessions House in Old Bailey covering infanticide trials in the late seventeenth century. These trials rarely asked about motive and focused instead on the material evidence—what could be seen, touched, and quantified, such as the condition of the child's body, the state of the bedclothes, and the verification of the pregnancy. Defendants did not often speak at these trials; those who did usually did not speak at length. Historian Allison May has noted that this behavior can be understood in light of larger social conditions. During a pregnancy and after a traumatic delivery, an unmarried woman's survival depended in no small part on her ability to keep silent, to deny what was happening. It is not so strange that she might struggle to speak in front of a courtroom; she had spent much of the previous year doing exactly the opposite—trying to remain silent.

When a case such as Rachel's was brought to trial, the judge and jurors and prosecutor could ask questions of the witness in whatever order they wanted—I suspect that chaos sometimes prevailed. I am not a legal scholar, and my depiction of Rachel's trial relies far more on historical imagination than on any formal training in legal history. I was not able to verify whether or not witnesses during the specific time period of 1649 to 1650 were allowed to volunteer their testimony over a prosecutor's objections, as I chose to imagine Elizabeth doing. But the transcripts of court cases from later decades and into the early eighteenth century suggested that friends and family members sometimes took it upon themselves to vouch for the character of the defendant without awaiting an invitation from judge or prosecutor.

In the eighteenth century, public opinion in England gradually began to sway toward leniency as more people began to sympa-thize with the plight of the unwed mother, and as the law's as-sumption that concealing an infant's death was tantamount to murder began to come under increasing question. With the rise of modern judicial practices and new theories of the self as a com-plicated and competing array of instincts, drives, longings, prin-ciples, and impulses, infanticide trials began to incorporate ac-counts of motive into defendants' cases. The motive most often pleaded was temporary insanity—which, one might argue, is not so much a motive as an attempt to prove a motive's absence. The insanity plea marked a different kind of appeal than the mid-sev-enteenth-century argument from ignorance—the claim made by some women that they did not learn they were pregnant until they went to the outhouse (or house of office) to relieve themselves and there suffered a sudden miscarriage or stillbirth. Over the span of two centuries, then, our thinking about women in these situations has traveled a curious course, from actions made out of ignorance to actions undertaken by reason of insanity. One could argue that this is not a significant improvement.

Some seventeenth-century Englishwomen attempted to resolve their plights by ending their pregnancies prematurely, either alone or with the help of a midwife. Their methods included bloodlet-tings from the foot and the ingesting of steel filings and herbal abortifacients. The women who undertook these actions did not see themselves as ending pregnancy so much as restoring or bring-ing back the menstrual cycle. To us this might sound like a mental sleight of hand. But in the seventeenth century, pregnancy was a more contested and negotiable state than it is considered today. In early modern England, it was indeed possible to be "a little bit pregnant."

I am indebted to, among many other excellent resources, Laura Gowing's "Secret Births and Infanticide in England," in *Past and Present* 156 (August 1997), pages 87–115, which explores the "col-lective trauma" of illegitimate childbirth during the early modern period, particularly the effect of these births on relations among women, on the telling and keeping of secrets, and on societal ideas about maternal shame, allegiance, and remorse. Any errors in historical research or misjudgments in creative interpretation are wholly mine, of course, and should not be attributed to my sources.

Author's Note

Accidents of Providence is a work of fiction that borrows from history. The story takes place during the first year of the English interregnum, the tumultuous republican period that began with the 1649 execution of Charles I and the establishment of the English Commonwealth, continued with the Protectorate under Oliver Cromwell and later Richard Cromwell (1653–1659), and ended with the restoration of the Stuart monarchy in 1660, when Charles II (son of Charles I) was returned to the English throne after an overseas exile.

I drew some of my descriptions, characters, and events directly from historical artifacts and sources. Others are composites based on historical artifacts and sources but reinvented or recrafted for this story. I also invented descriptions for characters, places, and situations about which the historical record remains silent or unclear or where the story itself seemed to prompt it. For example, while we know that after the Great Fire of 1666, there was a windmill on top of Newgate Prison to provide ventilation, I could find no verifiable record of the windmill's existence in the decades prior, so I simply chose to imagine it being there as early as the 1640s. To take another example, the collapsing of the scaffold at the Sessions House at the beginning of Rachel's trial is an imaginary event with a verifiable historical precedent: before the start of

John Lilburne's treason trial at Guildhall, the scaffolding inside the courthouse collapsed, delaying the proceedings.

Historians have written a great deal about the English Levelers, and there are wide-ranging opinions about their influence, their ideas, their organization, their views on women, their activities, their household practices, their religious beliefs, and their members. Revisionist scholarship questions their existence as a coherent or unified group, claiming that accounts of the Levelers and their influence are exaggerated. At the other end of the spectrum are those traditionalists who see the Levelers as the principal forerunners of the American Revolution and the Declaration of Independence. I have permitted myself to sidestep these scholarly disagreements in favor of imagining the Levelers' inner circle as it might have looked in the final months of 1649, the waning days of their influence.

Some of the characters in this book are based on real people who lived in London during the seventeenth century. I have combined verifiable information about their life histories with my own ideas about their personalities and with my own story line. John Lilburne was a writer, lieutenant colonel in the Parliamentary army, and well-known leader of the English Levelers. Although it is debated how organized the Leveler movement was after 1649, we know that Elizabeth Lilburne, John's wife, led a march or two on her husband's behalf in an attempt to obtain his release from prison. Elizabeth also seems to have been involved with several "petitions of women" that sought the Levelers' release. We know that Elizabeth gave birth to one of her children in Newgate and seems to have named one of her sons Tower in honor of the prison her husband frequented. She fell ill with smallpox in 1649, and though she survived, she lost her two boys to the disease. John was released from the Tower in time to say goodbye to them. He returned soon after.

Katherine Chidley was a haberdasher and Independent preacher who published several theological treatises and was known for despising Presbyterian conformity. She founded a church with her son. William Kiffin was a prosperous merchant and Particular Baptist minister. At one point he enjoyed a close collaboration with the Levelers, as did many of the independent churches, but in a period of shifting political and religious alliances, this bond did not last. Kiffin was rumored to be behind some of the personal attacks on William Walwyn's character in the late 1640s. Gilbert Mabbott was a newsman and writer who edited the *Moderate* for a time before being removed by opponents who accused him of sympathizing with the Levelers.

William Walwyn, husband of Anne and father of "almost 20 children," as he later phrased it, was a leading intellectual force behind the Leveler program in the 1640s, though he dropped out of active participation after 1649. There is no historical evidence that he was involved in any kind of clandestine relationship, although his enemies in the Baptist and Congregational churches liked to accuse him of sexual improprieties. Walwyn was known in the seventeenth century as a "Seeker"—someone who eschews one particular theology or doctrine in favor of thinking broadly about the nature of faith, posing Socratic questions about the meaning of belief, duty, love, and the divine nature. Walwyn, Lilburne, Overton, and Prince resided together in the Tower of London for nine months in 1649 under suspicion of treason against the new Commonwealth government, although only John was brought to trial. Bonfires burned in the streets of London after John's acquittal. Walwyn was imprisoned again briefly in 1652, but scholars are uncertain about the reason why or how he obtained his release.

Robert Lockyer was a private in the New Model Army (the remodeled Parliamentary army under radical and disciplined Puritan oversight) and was court-martialed and executed at the age of twenty-three for his involvement in a mutiny within Captain Savage's company. The cause of the standoff was the refusal of Lockyer's commanding officers to pay past-due wages to their soldiers. Little is known about Robert's family, though some reports indicate that his mother and sisters walked beside the coffin at his funeral. In *The Army's Martyr*, a Leveler martyrology published in

1649, the author—probably John Lilburne—described Robert's funeral as a spectacular procession that swept through the city of London, with recorders estimating that four thousand mourners attended. Many donned the sea green color of the Levelers. Women brought up the rear of the processional, wearing scarves of the same color.

Mary du Gard is a fictional character. The idea for Mary came to me when I read a reference in a work of English social history to a twenty-seven-year-old "singlewoman" who paid a fee to earn the freedom (a merchant's license) to be a glover—a rare accomplishment in those days. Women in early modern England could work and participate in business, but their involvement usually came about through the name or oversight of a husband, brother, or father. It was rare for a woman to become a business owner or proprietor on her own.

Rachel Lockyer is also a fictional character. The idea for her came to me when I read several 1651 pamphlets detailing the execution, trial, and "miraculous" recovery of a young unmarried woman from Steeple-Barton who was hanged after being convicted of killing her infant. This young woman, Anne Green, claimed she had not known she was pregnant before delivering the infant stillborn in the privy. The jury did not believe her. She survived her hanging, most likely because the noose was not sufficiently tight. The final report by Thomas Bartwain—also a fictional character—is modeled after the 1651 accounts of Anne Green's remarkable story. Green was alternately revered and reviled in print after her recovery. Several sentences and turns of phrase in Bartwain's treatise are taken directly from a 1651 report of Green's hanging and its aftermath.

When Thomas Bartwain warned William Walwyn about an anticipated act against adultery, he was making an accurate prediction—though he misunderstood whom the act would target. Adultery briefly became a capital offense in England in 1650, but the statute proved difficult if not impossible to enforce. The statute made the adultery of a married woman punishable by death, but not the adultery of a married man. That is, while both a man and a woman could be put to death under the 1650 act against adultery, the punishment was only applicable in cases where a married woman had strayed. Historian Keith Thomas has suggested that this double standard reflected the Puritan assumption that a woman's sexuality was not hers to govern as she chose.

In the 1650s, William Walwyn left the world of Leveler politics and became a lay physician, dispensing medicines from his apothecary in Moorfields. He outlived most of his companions, dying in his eighties.

John Lilburne continued to pursue his calling as a voice for the oppressed, undergoing several more trials for seditious writings and being banished from England for a brief time. He finally renounced political life altogether and became a Quaker. His wife, Elizabeth, remained the most enterprising and resourceful of the group. She had more children with John after they lost their two sons. During his period of banishment, John left her under the protection of a powerful clergyman, since he was unable to ensure her welfare in person. That clergyman was William Kiffin. Elizabeth outlived her husband.

Acknowledgments

I am grateful to Brooks Holifield, David Pacini, and Bobby Paul for challenging me to become a better reader and so a better writer; to Kat Carrico, Carol Flowers, Elizabeth Gallu, Claire Meyer, Claire Sterk, Donna Troka, Aubre Wells, Jennifer Wheelock, and Melissa Wiginton for their support and encouragement; to S. Alex Alexander for the outstanding research assistance; to my editor, Jenna Johnson, and my copy editor, Tracy Roe, for their incisive and helpful comments; to Mary Campbell, Beth Burleigh Fuller, John Scott Randall, Yishai Seidman, and Johnathan Wilber for their contributions at various stages of the publication process. I am grateful to my parents, Gordon and Marion Brown; to my sister, Candace; and to my many aunts and uncles for cheering me on from afar. Thanks also go to the members of my indefatigable book group: Shawn, Cathy, Matt, Gerhard, Anna, and David. Finally, I'd like to express my gratitude to Henry Dunow, perspicuous reader and generous spirit, who discerned in my writing the prospect of a book.